It So Happens

It So Happens

Patricia Ferguson

LARGE PRINT
Oxford

First published in Great Britain 2004
by
Solidus Press

Published in Large Print 2006 by ISIS Publishing Ltd.,
7 Centremead, Osney Mead, Oxford OX2 0ES
by arrangement with
Solidus Press

British Library Cataloguing in Publication Data
Ferguson, Patricia
   It so happens. – Large print ed.
   1. Old age homes – Fiction
   2. Large type books
   I. Title
   823.9'14 [F]

ISBN 0–7531–7668–8 (hb)
ISBN 0–7531–7669–6 (pb)

Printed and bound in Great Britain by
T. J. International Ltd., Padstow, Cornwall

In memory of Freda Bromhead,
writer and poet, 1903–1995

Prologue

A dark night, blacked out: a night for murder.

Even inside the house, behind the curtains and closed shutters, there is little light. The man coming slowly downstairs holds the banister for guidance, and at the bottom gropes one-handed along the passage, turns, and passes down another flight of stairs.

He checks halfway, waiting. There have been movements, a squirming beneath his other arm. The banister pauses beneath his hand, the stairs below him hold their breath.

Seconds pass. No further movements reveal themselves. The man continues, awarding each tread in turn, coming at last to the door at the bottom of the stairs.

Opening it the light dazzles him. He screws up his eyes as he enters the kitchen, where an oil lamp glows above the table. There is a secondary glow, of red, from the range.

The man lifts his head, listening. Light demonstrates his facial bones, the sheen of his forehead, and the stubble along his starveling jaw. He crosses the kitchen to the range, and slowly kneels before it, resting his free hand for balance on a kitchen chair.

1

He listens again, but still God sends him no word. Leaning forward he places the bundle he carries down on the floor, where warmth will placate it while he undertakes the next task.

Beside the back door, on a hook, the key awaits his hand. Outside the air strikes chill, he must hold in the cough, and for a moment he stands still, steadying himself. He is in a small flagged area. Several items stand here, exposed to sun and rain, purposely untended: a delicate chair, swollen with rain, its striped seat mould-blackened; a dining room table, its buckled veneer almost hidden beneath piles of rotting material, a brownish tweed greatcoat, curtains of once plum-coloured velvet, and, in one corner carefully arranged in pairs at attention, shoes: stiffened purulent brogues, swollen black oxfords, high heels of slack mouldering leather lined with the peeling slime that had once been kid.

All these things are being punished. They are to rot, to disintegrate helplessly at the man's will and by his hand and in his sight. He feels their essences, emanations of despair, of pleading, as he passes, but pretends to notice nothing, so that the dying items will feel yet more fully his power and their own abjection. Opening the outhouse door he takes up the shovel waiting inside. It is a good shovel, it will do as he wishes, he can feel its assurances in its smooth handle.

A faint moonlight illuminates the garden. The man stands for a moment, the willing shovel in his hand, peering through the waving darkness of trees for a glimpse of the river beyond. Then he makes his way slowly down the flagged path, past the little square of grass, past the two apple trees, through the vegetable patch, past the quiet henhouse, and right up to the fence. Here he can hear the water, quietly going about its business. This will be the place.

He digs quickly, with the expertise of practice. Every so often he has to stop, to calm his own breathing, and to drag his sleeve over his brow, mopping at the water that streams into his eyes and down his cheeks like tears. The hole is soon deep enough, wide enough. He stands by it for several minutes, until his breathing slows down and he can walk again.

In the kitchen the creature is awake. He observes its hairless reptilian languor. As he picks it up it flexes, its back arching vigorously, but he does not let go. He carries it in front of him, holding it firmly. There is still a chance it will reveal itself, perhaps take on its truest form, in order to engulf him.

Outside it at once raises its voice. The man is alarmed at how much like a real baby it sounds, but he is not fooled, not for an instant.

The place he has made is fitting. It fits. He places the creature into it.

For a moment, then, memory informs his fingers, like an electric shock. His hands remember tucking a child into a cosy bed, and rise up in perplexity at the cold crumbly soil, rise of their own volition to his head, to grasp and pull in panic at his hair.

But the moment quickly passes. This is his duty. He has no choice. He covers the creature's face with blanket, and steadily lays the earth, cleansing, bountiful, upon it. Finished, he does not firm the soil with his boot, as he would after planting anything else. Instead he addresses the quietened being beneath its earthy covering, and speaks aloud:

"There was no light," he tells it, and then turns, and goes back to the house.

CHAPTER
ONE

Alethea Troy's old flat had been on the top floor two streets back from the sea front, with a sea view if you stood on a chair in the kitchen. Over the years Miss Troy had grown used to this near miss but never quite resigned. When she felt low for other reasons nearly being able to see the sea, but not quite, summed up her life all too neatly, she thought. Certainly she had hardly expected a change for the better at this stage.

Yet the view from her second-floor bedsit at Cabotin Court was surely the very finest in the house. The great beech tree outside almost filled her window, complex, vigorously mobile, as moody and responsive to the weather as the sea could ever be and jolly nearly as absorbing, thought Miss Troy, to sit and look at.

And sitting by the windowsill you could also look down past the narrow strip of garden and the railings to the generally busy pavement, and a zebra crossing, and best of all a bus stop, where all day long a procession of strangers unconsciously displayed themselves. Miss Troy, with her book or a half-written letter, would sit down to work by her window and find that an hour had suddenly gone by without a word read or written, so entertaining was the bus queue.

In the early mornings there were regulars to look out for and speculate upon, possible cleaners, domestics, nurses: the Knitting Woman; Mrs Cottage Loaf, named for her hairstyle; Miss Librarian, poor thing, in her anorak, and the trio of half-grown schoolboys, sedately commuting; later still, two elderly men in neat padded jackets and flat caps, one of whom read furtively from something he kept folded into one hand.

And then the constant flow of women, old ones with shopping bags and young ones with babies, young women with one baby in a sling-arrangement over their bosoms or crammed into a tiny folding pushchair, and grasping by the hand a large obstreperous toddler intent on taking its coat off in the gutter; how such young women, usually further encumbered with handbags, shoulder bags, plastic bags of baby necessities, and later still, shopping, managed so much as a two-minute bus stop wait without, so far as Miss Troy could see, ever coming to blows or tears was, Miss Troy thought, remarkable, admirable.

Sitting at her window she began a poem about them, and had satisfactorily finished with it before realising quite what it meant to be writing it at all.

"I feel at home," she wrote to her goddaughter Fredericka, "which is certainly not what I expected, or at any rate not so soon. I hardly miss the flat at all, and if I do I merely have to remember all those stairs."

For Cabotin Court, of course, had a lift, and all irregularities requiring a step up here or two down there had been carefully covered with ramps made non-slip with rubber matting. All the corridors had handrails. All the bedsits had alarm-buttons, and a long red alarm-pull dangled over each bath.

"Which gives one morbid ideas," wrote Miss Troy. "I find myself trying to picture the circumstances in which I would feel ill enough to pull it but well enough to decide I ought to. Of course this is an absurd thing to worry about. But it is all I have been able to come up with so far."

This was hardly true, but Miss Troy despised complaint. In any case she would never have complained to Fredericka, who admired her, she knew, for her cheerful courage under all circumstances. And if sometimes dear Freddie made it a little too plain that she regarded her godmother as indomitable, if now and there seemed a hint of expectancy in her eyes, as if she were waiting for Miss Troy to say something gloriously in character, well, that was perhaps tiresome but it was still a great deal more congenial than the behaviour very-old-lady hood so often seemed to provoke in even the most sensible.

"Just before we begin," the man on the local radio station had said, introducing her on the (also local) publication of some of her verse, "I'm sure you won't object, Miss Troy, if I tell our listeners that you are nearly eighty-seven!" It wasn't merely that he had made no mention of this sort of thing on the list of questions he had supplied earlier; it was his tone, so warm, so indulgent, and the fact that he had not assumed it during any private preliminary conversation. Its use now informed Miss Troy that she was here live on air with him not because of her poetry, but because of her age. All this came to her instantly, even as he spoke, but she paused quite a long time, deadpan for several seconds, for him to sweat through, before she said clearly,

"Not at all, age is fascinating, isn't it, how old are you?" The look in his eyes, just for an instant before the charm won through again, had been a pleasant enough revenge to look back on even now, several years later.

Meanwhile certain other difficulties need trouble no one but herself. Clearly something, or rather something else, was going wrong with her eyesight; in bright sunlight, for instance, she could hardly see across the road. Recently, one sultry afternoon, she had sat by her window watching a very young woman trailing over the zebra crossing in the highest of slim high heels, and with a baby in a pushchair.

"Oh dear!" Miss Troy had murmured aloud. What did the poor girl think she looked like? Such a wincing, such a parody of glamour! Walking about in shoes meant for hopping out of taxis straight into parties, shoes for a cocktail hour at the least; no doubt she is blaming herself for the pain as well, thought Miss Troy, and imagining everyone else can manage four-inch heels all day. Girls in magazines seem to, so real feet get no mercy.

At this Miss Troy experienced a delightful small thrill, a quickening inside, which presaged the possibility of a new poem.

The Little Mermaid walked on knives for love, thought Miss Troy, and look what it did for her. No

8

man will see you anyway, not behind that pushchair. You're invisible, all but your feet.

But as Miss Troy took up her biro the sun came fully out, and glare suddenly filled her window with a garish brilliance. The beech tree's little leaves coalesced into flicker, the bus stop shimmered, the road heaved and dissolved. Gasping Miss Troy had turned away, covering her blinded eyes with her hands.

Of course it hadn't lasted long, just a few minutes really. With the curtains drawn and the sudden inspiration of a pair of dark glasses sight had gradually returned. She'd gone off the high heels poem though. And it had struck her, as she sat in the gloom, that perhaps the poor silly girl simply hadn't had enough money to be sensible. What would I have bought at her age, thought Miss Troy, if I'd only had the money for one pair of shoes?

Which was not only depressing in itself, so boringly reasonable, but suspect, in that Miss Troy, since coming to Cabotin, could no longer be quite sure whether any liberal sentiment was purely her own or whether she was taking it up in order to avoid any possibility of appearing to agree with Mrs Derry.

Mrs Derry lived across the corridor, and was known for her goodness of heart.

"Do anything for you," said Rosemary Sholto, the Deputy Warden, when Miss Troy had first moved in, and this was true; though at a price, exacted in conversation. During the week unwritten law required that Miss Troy sit next to Mrs Derry at lunch, and it was really impossible to ignore her completely, even though she seemed to require no replies, not even murmured interjections.

Mrs Derry specialised in illness. Not her own, but other people's; not only those of her own immediate friends and relations but the illnesses of old friends she had just heard from after a gap of many years, and those of her children's friends' parents, and of her dead husband's business associates and their friends; and Mrs Derry liked to get all these connections quite straight in her mind, aloud, before embarking on the patient's latest symptoms.

When, as occasionally happened, Mrs Derry had no ailment news, she tended to be equally unstoppable with items culled from the *Daily Mail*, delivered in tones cosily assuming agreement. Though it was possible, Miss Troy at length discovered, to divert her with Lucy. A little hint as they sat down could get Mrs Derry onto Lucy-reminiscences through most of the main course.

"Such a gentle, loving soul!"

And Miss Troy's mental picture of Lucy, pop-eyed, wheezing, barrel-bodied and bandy, was as fine and cruel a caricature of Mrs Derry herself as anyone could possibly hope to come by.

"People just don't understand how loving a Pekinese can be!"

CHAPTER
TWO

Lunch was the only meal provided at Cabotin Court. The place had begun as Cabotin Almshouse, where twelve indigent but virtuous old females had lived rent-free, under certain strict conditions including twice-daily church services and the wearing of purple broadcloth. A great deal of building work and other change had gone on since then, and the present warden, a Miss Betty Potts, presided over nearly thirty, with men admitted since 1962 and couples in the three larger flatlets since 1979.

Betty Potts was the fourth warden of Cabotin Court, or, if you counted from the Almshouse's foundation, when the warden had been known as the First Sister, the nineteenth.

Miss Potts sometimes playfully referred to herself as First Sister in her occasional pre-Sunday lunch speeches, unaware perhaps that this might lend force to the suggestion that as well as regretting the old title she would also have enjoyed the First Sister's powers of summary eviction and on-the-spot fines; that she was in fact restrained from doing so only by the force of modern law.

There was a certain amount of mild grumbling about Betty Potts amongst the Cabotin inmates, a consensus, Miss Troy had discovered, that she was inclined to the authoritarian. She was certainly very strict on smoking, even cigars at Christmas; and had refused all attempts at the keeping of budgerigars.

"Of course it's a lot like being back at boarding school," wrote Miss Troy to Fredericka. "So perhaps resenting the Headmistress is only natural. Though actually I think I prefer her to the deputy, a Mrs Sholto, who wants me to like her, which of course is always rather suspicious. If obvious, I mean. She has already privately intimated that if it were up to her I should keep as many budgerigars as I chose. I told her I was allergic to feathers. Which is a lie. You see I am already completely institutionalised."

During the week lunches were cooked and served by kitchen staff. The cook was a very fat young local woman with a moustache. Her name was Susan, and occasionally her great round face could be glimpsed through the serving hatch, while plates were taken round and collected by two rather silent black women, Mary and Fidelis. Mary's smile revealed two gold teeth; Fidelis never smiled at all.

Miss Troy, who was curious by nature, longed to question all three of them. Were Mary and Fidelis originally from the same country? How old were they? What sort of home-life had Susan, so young and so unpromising? Miss Troy pictured her at home, filling an armchair in front of the television, while her parents,

12

twinned hugenesses, sat jammed together in a three-seater sofa. She would never have had a boyfriend, and sometimes her father would jeer at her for it.

Whereas Mary's gold teeth seemed to hint at domestic felicity, a half-grown family of children laughing and arguing and doing their homework; while perhaps Fidelis sat alone upstairs in the rented back bedroom, and what was she doing? Writing letters home, perhaps, to a small child left far away, or to her mother, reserved, beautiful Fidelis. Once Miss Troy had seen her waiting for the bus, a stranger in a dark blue raincoat, looking, thought Miss Troy, even more subdued and submissive than lone women usually did at the bus stop, which was saying a great deal.

On Saturdays, lunch was usually some kind of salad, prepared by Susan the evening before. But on Sundays Mrs Sholto was in charge.

Rosemary Sholto had been deputy warden at Cabotin Court for nearly five years. For nearly five years, Sunday had been her favourite day. Rosemary was plump and brisk and fiftyish, with a big square face and large imposing arms and legs. Within, however, she knew herself to be rather a delicate creature, easily bored, prone to depression, a poor sleeper: sensitive, in a word.

It was astonishing to Rosemary, the way people went on failing to spot her sensitivity. Sometimes, out of exasperation, she felt like pinching them, or tripping them up. Rosemary had been an expert pincher in childhood, always managing to leave two half-moons of bruise.

On Sundays, though, Rosemary awoke humming with anticipated pleasure. For she was a natural cook. She rarely used recipes, but remembered every one she had ever read, and used them as if unconsciously. Her pastry melted delicately in the mouth, her gravies were rich with jellied stock, her stews bubbled with moist tiny dumplings aromatic with herbs.

Her greatest artistry, however, was reserved for puddings. She loved reading about them, making them, and eating them, but most of all she loved giving them to others. To see other people's faces lit up with happy greed was for Rosemary one of life's deepest pleasures, and one which, until coming to work at Cabotin, she had not fully experienced before.

Her husband, while generally a hearty, appreciative eater, had tended towards tomato ketchup, and not been much of a pudding man at all. While young Maureen had complained so bitterly and so often about her mother's cooking that Rosemary herself had almost come to believe that she had some hidden malign intent towards her only child's developing figure. For several years she had grimly put together undressed salads and plain brown rice for Maureen to pick at while the poor girl tried to starve into submission a genetic inheritance of big square face and imposing arms and legs, which were, of course, just as much Rosemary's fault as her high-calorie cooking, as far as Maureen was concerned.

With her husband dead, and Maureen at university, Rosemary had looked around for what she called "a little job," without much hope of finding one, or any of enjoying herself if she did. She had taken up her duties at Cabotin Court most anxiously, and on her first Saturday, with thirty-odd next day to cook for, had lain awake nearly all night mentally weighing up vegetables and imagining disasters, setting the kitchen on fire, scalding Mrs Haws (spry inmate drafted in as assistant), killing off the lot of them with a virulent strain of salmonella, or merely not pleasing, collecting plates barely touched, with no one wanting seconds except Mr Fortune, whose greed everyone knew to be almost uncontrollably indiscriminate.

As it turned out, the meal had been a triumph, the first of a continuing series, and Rosemary had come to realise that with thirty or so to cook for, thirty or so of an age and frailty almost guaranteeing a strong interest in food (so many other pleasures now denied them), thirty or so on the whole non-dieters, and of a generation brought up to believe double cream soothing to the nerves; that with such people to cook for, Rosemary could really let herself go.

Particularly with puddings. To begin with, following Miss Potts's rather austere instructions, Rosemary had confined herself to the familiar, to the sort of puddings everyone knew and so often disliked, fruit pies and crumbles, rice puddings, stewed fruit, and custard. But she cooked these school dinner horrors with butter, glazed them with beaten egg, enriched them with cream and flavoured them with vanilla sugar and cinnamon sticks. The apple pies steamed with freshly grated nutmeg, the custard was proper crème anglais, and the roly-poly, while hardly, to Rosemary's mind, a challenge worth meeting, was as light and yielding as a suet roly-poly could possibly be, oozing jam from every moist clinging slice. Mr Fortune had positively shed tears at the sight of it.

Rosemary had noticed. She began to branch out a little, and if the budget was too much of a constraint dipped into her own purse.

"Because their faces, Maureen, when they tasted the butterscotch apples!"

A choice, that was Rosemary's present aim. An old one, and a new one, spotted dick or crème brulée; lattice jam tart or mango sorbet; maids-of-honour or hot chocolate soufflé.

"But it's always the old favourites that go first," said Rosemary. "Brings it all back I expect, bless 'em."

Today, a fine Sunday in May, Rosemary had lined up: a smooth mushroom soup, made properly with chicken stock; a melting pot-au-feu, in the oven since eight that morning with the potatoes slowly crisping their jackets alongside, and green beans whipped from the steam at the perfect moment of just-done squeakiness; and desserts fit for the Queen, should Her Majesty suddenly decide to honour Cabotin with her presence (a recurring fantasy of Rosemary's, and her usual benchmark). Would Her Majesty choose the fabulously light toffee pudding, or the creamy vanilla shape, served with damson cheese?

Rosemary would have had no qualms offering Her either of them, though privately her money would have been on the shape, for over the years she had noticed it to have a similar effect on elderly members of the higher social classes as suet roly-poly had had on Alfie Fortune, gone now to join his starveling ancestors, poor old soul, but how he had enjoyed his last few years of Sunday lunches!

The only slight fly in today's ointment was Rosemary's assistant, not the still-spry Mary Haws this week but one of her occasional replacements, Annie Cameron.

"All set, Annie?"

Annie Cameron, of course, gave no reply. Rosemary tapped her rather hard on her shoulder, making her jump.

"Hello!" Rosemary shouted, her voice booming round the kitchen, which was part of the old Great Hall and thus very high-ceilinged. "I said, are we all set?"

It was Annie's blank face that most annoyed Rosemary. What was she always turning her hearing-aid off for, anyway? Saving her batteries, no doubt, the old skinflint. It was maddening. You'd go up to her and say something and get this blank look while slowly, so slowly, Annie would reach inside her cardigan and start fiddling with the little box at her waist, and there'd be a series of nasty wailing squawks for you to wait about during and her to look pained at, and after all that you still had to shout.

"Where have you put the spuds?"

Here Annie, still twiddling at the hidden dial, at last registered being asked something, and made her habitual interrogative sound in reply. While the meaning of this ("What's that again?") was clear enough, its verbal composition remained a mystery.

"What is she actually saying?" Rosemary had asked Mary Haws one evening. Mary hadn't known either.

"She says 'bib-bib'," said Mary, after a pause. "D'you think it might be Gaelic?"

"Bib-bib?" said Rosemary, in Annie's voice, and they had both giggled ashamedly.

"I said, where have you put the spuds?"

"Bib-bib?"

"Oh, for Pete's sake," said Rosemary and, rather showily acting someone not putting up with any nonsense, she heaved aside the steel doors of the big heated trolley until she found what she was looking for.

The sight of the potatoes, the smell of the pot-au-feu, calmed her instantly.

"Smells nice, doesn't it?" she yelled over her shoulder at Annie Cameron. Annie smiled back. She had a shy pretty smile and it made Rosemary feel quite flustered again, though she was not aware of this, or of why.

But once she had come across Annie sitting alone in the lounge, laughing at something in a book she was reading. Rosemary herself was not much of a one for reading. Annie's laughter, echoing all round the lounge all by itself, had obscurely bothered Rosemary. It did not seem to tie in with the blank face bib-bibbing, or the dopey fumbles with the hearing-aid. It had sounded to Rosemary like the arrogant private laughter of a woman who exaggerated her infirmity for her own ends, who kept her hearing-aid turned off the better to enjoy a stand-offish isolation; who stayed deaf in order to render everyone else dumb.

Though Rosemary had not gone so far as to think all this out, she had concluded, from these largely subterranean arguments, that turning off your hearing-aid in company was simply a monstrous piece of cheek. "She's got a nerve," she would tell herself, watching Annie Cameron settle into an armchair with a sigh, and unfold her spectacles.

So the shy engaging smile didn't fit in at all, and made Rosemary feel flustered. She knew this uncomfortable sensation, however, to be Annie Cameron's fault.

"We'll dish up, then, ok?" she cried, impatiently.

"Bib-bib?"

Oh bloody hell, thought Rosemary, unplugging the trolley herself and pushing open the double doors into the Hall. She stood for a moment in the doorway, surveying the inmates. In for another treat today.

"Good afternoon, everyone!" she called, and the Cabotin old folk began setting down their newspapers, or turning back from the window, where the cherry trees were making a very fine show, or breaking off their several murmurs of conversation or, in Violet Dobbs' case, hastily chewing up the blackcurrant bon-bon with which she had been trying to stem her furious lunch-time abdominal rumblings.

Mrs Dobbs was dreadfully bothered by wind. It had started when she was carrying her first child. She had not been married very long, and had gone to enormous lengths to conceal her difficulties from her husband, who had thought her so dainty, and often said so. There had been one terrible night at the pictures, so long ago that it was a silent film they were watching, with Greta Garbo and John Gilbert; a weepie, luckily for Mrs Dobbs, who had been dreadfully restless sitting there trying to keep on top of things, or more exactly to contain things, and who had thus been able to pretend that her gulpings and swayings were the result of holding back tears rather than anything else.

The relief, still vivid after all these years, of diving into the Ladies after the Anthem! And the embarrassment of there being two girls already in there, hanging about in front of the mirror, combing their hair and chatting, and then clearly averting their scarlet faces and trying not to laugh when, after giving vent to a series of the most uncoilingly elongated and violent farts possibly ever to be emitted by a human being, Mrs Dobbs had had to unbolt the cubicle door and walk out again right past them, since Joe so hated to be kept waiting!

CHAPTER
THREE

From her chair Miss Betty Potts, the fourth warden or nineteenth First Sister of Cabotin, looked about her, meeting eyes here and there until everyone fell silent. There was a moment's pause. Rosemary, fretting a little beside the trolley, for the beans, she felt, would dwindle into mere ordinary edibility if they had to wait much longer, closed her eyes in case she looked at Mary Haws and had to laugh.

For now and then Miss Potts felt called upon to recite a Grace composed by a clerical son of the Almshouse's founder, which, after thanking the Almighty, in a rather perfunctory manner, for the inmates' daily bread, dwelt in what might almost be thought lip-smacking detail on the multitudinous sins of the present company; it was more like a charge-sheet than a prayer, Rosemary had told Mary Haws, and ever since they had both had trouble controlling themselves whenever Betty put her bony hands together and began.

"O most merciful Lord consider now we beg these thy poorest servants that here resteth . . ." But today the warden was evidently not in the mood, and merely asked to be made truly grateful for all that she was about to receive, so Rosemary could relax.

"Amen," said Annie Cameron beside her, noticing folded hands here and there. The clatter of spoons and serving dishes, and a soft flattened roar of conversation, just reached her. It was still too much. She reached inside her cardigan and switched off the battery, awarding the room silence.

Without sound the room clarified, composed itself, and became a scene. "Cabotin Great Hall: Sunday Lunch," thought Annie. A picture someone ought to paint. The bright sun barred the long oak tables with gold, and standing this far back, by the kitchen door, you could take it all in at once: the long bars of golden light, the high arching beams of the ceiling, the meek rows of heads below and in between, the great quantity of silence, suspended there without effort, like smoke on a still day. A picture of peace on a day like this, thought Annie.

But what exactly made it so? Was it a question of enclosing sufficient space? Or light? Or was it merely a prejudice of her own — and a common one, given the hordes all tramping round those National Trust places — that ancient must mean tranquil?

Because so often it just does, thought Annie. Was that a by-product of the ancientness, though, or a conscious design? Take the floor, for instance; a stone-flagged floor had a meaning, nowadays. It had implications. Surely it cannot have had them when it was new? What would it have looked like in those days anyway? Smoother, probably. Replacing what, hardened dirt? Rushes? A hygienic advance, that's what it must have been: a floor you could sweep.

No, thought Annie, suddenly struck. A floor you *had* to sweep. That was the trouble with easy-clean floors, you had to keep on cleaning them.

Had seventeenth century females stood muttering on the threshold then?

"Oh, give me the old rushes any day, clear 'em out once a year, what's wrong with that, look at this, freezing cold, shows everything, you're on your knees day and night, scrub scrub scrub, Annie, are you with us?"

Puzzled for a moment, Annie, aware of these words without, as far as she knew, having thought them herself, thought them over now, decided that they were indeed someone else's, and presently noticed Rosemary smirking not a foot away.

"Are you with us, dear?"

"Bib-bib?"

Rosemary took Annie rather firmly by the arm, and drew her to her place.

"Bon appetit!"

Wants to slap me, thought Annie, without resentment, as she took up her knife and fork, but here she was wrong, it was a good pinch Rosemary longed to deliver, to the soft pliable stuff of the inner upper arm, slack beneath the cardigan, and serve her right, thought Rosemary, as she spread out her own napkin.

"Delicious," said Violet Dobbs to her right. Mrs Dobbs was a little afraid of Rosemary Sholto, but then Mrs Dobbs was a little afraid of almost everyone, and could not volunteer the mildest remark without a quaking sense of risk.

"Really nice," she added, in case delicious hadn't been enough all by itself or had sounded a bit snobby or something, really it was a snobby sort of word, whatever can have made me say it?

Sometimes Mrs Dobbs' anxieties in such matters showed on her face and bothered people, but Rosemary didn't notice. She heard only the praise, instantly felt much better, and nodded her thanks. She had too a very nice mental picture of herself doing it, graciously. The mental picture she generally employed was about thirty years of age and much lighter about the jaw-line than the actual Rosemary, lighter all over in fact. Rosemary liked the mental picture very much and often summoned her up, frequently putting her through the same paces over and over again for the pleasure of watching her perform.

Look at that tilt of the head then! Queenly, that's what that was.

Alethea Troy, seizing her Sunday chance to get away from Mrs Derry, was sitting beside Miss Potts, and already wondering whether to bother another time, since so far the warden was turning out to be almost equally as hard-going as Mrs Derry, in her way.

"Such a beautiful afternoon!"

Miss Troy agreed.

"Anything planned?" Miss Potts was not really, thought Miss Troy, that much younger than some of her charges. Surely into her sixties? Though from one's own absurdly antique vantage point, remembered Miss Troy, it was increasingly hard to guess. But surely she's old enough, at any rate, to know better than to use that bright talking-carefully-to-a-dotty-old-lady tone with me.

She touched her mouth with her napkin. That afternoon there was, in fact, a meeting of the small literary society to which she belonged, and afterwards she and the Pughs and Lorna were going to the pub; they would perhaps be able to sit outside beneath the beautiful perry pear tree in the garden. Need Betty Potts know any of this?

"Just a nap, I'm afraid," she said firmly.

"Oh. I thought it was your book club today. Isn't it? Third Sunday?"

"Perhaps you are right," said Miss Troy after a tiny pause. "How clever of you to remember. Thank you."

Betty Potts looked down at the table, with a complacent smile. She was a thinnish woman, with hunched rounded shoulders and a tight aquiline face, noticeably powdered and painted; wears nail varnish, Miss Troy betted to herself, before allowing herself a quick look. Ha! Scarlet talons. And what a grisly name, thought Miss Troy, with a connoisseur's appreciation. The inversion sprang so readily to mind; no doubt Potty Betty's schoolfellows had made early ruthless use of it.

"Have you been Warden here for long?" she asked politely, refreshed by these thoughts.

"Three years. Since December '82."

"Ah, so you were in charge of the refurbishments?"

Betty Potts breathed in rather loudly through her nose. "Oh dear me no," she said sharply, dropping the warm bright talking-to-an-inmate voice. "I claim no responsibility for those."

"You mean — as in, blame?

Betty smirked. "The changes are not all to my taste, shall we say."

"Oh? In what way?"

Miss Potts inhaled once more through flaring nostrils; really slightly menacing, thought Miss Troy pleasurably.

"One hardly knows where to begin," said Miss Potts. "Of course the whole thing was on a very tight budget. But I think that need not have shown quite so much."

Miss Troy, who had thought her surroundings perfectly adequate, even rather smart as institutions went, was surprised, though at the same time impressed. Well, passion is always rather impressive, I suppose, she thought. But really, what could the woman be on about? Before she could frame a politer version of this, Rosemary interrupted.

"Ladies. Can I tempt you?" Suggestively, she waggled her large serving spoon.

Mrs Sholto resplendent, thought Miss Troy, looking up at her; Mrs Sholto rampant.

"Toffee pudding. Or vanilla shape. Or a bit of tinned fruit from yesterday. Decisions, decisions!"

Miss Troy was silent, transported as she was across more than eighty years to the nursery up on the fifth floor of her grandmother's tall London house, where darling Maisie, her nanny, had read aloud adventure stories so that the daily steamed fish and cabbage thought so suitable for delicate children in those days had slipped down almost without effort, and they could move on to the pure glistening beautiful mysterious shape, generally a quivering milk-white jelly rabbit, which Maisie, to spare it any suffering, would instantly behead with a tablespoon.

"Shape, I haven't heard that word for years, oh, yes, just a little, mmm, yes please . . ."

"And?" Rosemary raised her eyebrows at the warden. She thought it was a bit much that Miss Potts was somehow still Miss Potts after all this time, and got round it by trying not to call her anything at all, in public.

Betty stared at the trolley, considering. Sometimes she snubbed Mrs Sholto by choosing Saturday's leftovers, for it was clear to her that Rosemary was not simply doing her job and producing a wholesome and economical meal, but showing off; getting carried away, Betty called it to herself. There was no need to go to such lengths.

Without ever having thought about it Betty thoroughly disapproved of the idea of enjoying one's work. Quite often she thought about sacking her deputy, whom she found vaguely annoying even during the week. But today there was an afternoon meeting of the Friends of Cabotin, a small but well-heeled group of local ladies, one of them even an actual real Lady, and the prospect of this meeting, from which Rosemary was excluded, put Betty into a rather forgiving frame of mind.

"Bit of both?"

Certainly the tinned fruit looked very chilly. Whereas the toffee pudding was gently steaming, crisp and golden on top, clearly moist and melting within, oozing here and there small trickles of light caramel. For a moment Betty hesitated, as she felt herself to be above interest in such things. Besides, to enjoy one of Rosemary's confections would somehow, she felt, involve loss of face, even if she took it and ate it without comment. She chose the shape ("Just a very little, please"), and as it was placed before her enjoyed a small sense of triumph as smooth and cold as the shape itself.

"The gates, for example," she said, when Rosemary had moved on. She stared into her untouched plate. "I would have replaced the gates."

"Sorry?" It looked the same, Miss Troy was thinking, and quivered as it should, but what on earth was it flavoured with? So delicious, and familiar, but still slightly wrong somehow. Could it be —

"Rosewater," said Miss Troy suddenly. "It's perfumed with rosewater. D'you think?"

"I've no idea," said Betty, to whom the toffee pudding was still faintly calling; there was still some of it left, she could see. Enough for seconds. "You must have noticed the gates. They were put up in 1962. They would be perfectly suitable for a house built in 1962. I have nothing against them as gates. But as the frontispiece to a formal early seventeenth century building they are pure vandalism."

"Really?"

"The original gates were removed in 1940 as part of the War effort. Now there are at least three different eighteenth and nineteenth century prints that I know of, that could have been used as reference points when any replacements were under consideration. Failing this elementary step, there are the gas brackets. Obviously the gas brackets on the gateposts are not original. But whoever designed and installed them wanted them to look as if they were. One can see from the later print that the curves of the gas brackets echo those of the original gates. Surely anyone replacing antique gates for a building of aesthetic as well as historical importance could have noticed this clue, and made the gates to suit the brackets!"

"Um, yes," said Miss Troy, who was still trying and failing to remember what the 1962 lot looked like. Weren't they always kept open, anyway, to allow cars in and out of the forecourt?

"The originals," said Betty, lowering her voice, "were almost certainly gilded, with the Cabotin Arms worked into the centre, and probably enamelled."

"Well, if it was 1940 there would have been —"

"Oh, I don't for one moment question the original sacrifice. Of course the War effort was paramount. But I would rather the gates had not been replaced at all, I would rather the gap had been left as a memorial to that sacrifice, than that those suburban housing estate abominations should have been hung in their stead."

There was a pause, while Miss Troy finished her shape. She was uncomfortable, for she felt that Miss Potts had betrayed too much of her emotional life to a stranger, and so must be a little crazy. Potty Betty indeed. Besides she was bothered by a memory of her own: of the cocktail party chatter, soon after her arrival in town, that the wartime council, panicking beneath an uncontrollable landslide of old mangles, bedsteads, miles of sawn-off railings, and lorry loads of battered cast iron frying pans, all patriotically given up to be melted into Spitfires, had desperately arranged for the whole lot to be scooped up by night, towed out to sea, and secretly dumped in the deep water outside the harbour. Not for me, perhaps, decided Miss Troy, to let poor Potty know of this surely apocryphal story. Instead she said:

"Perhaps you could replace them, now that you are in charge?"

"I am merely in charge of day-to-day running," said Miss Potts, "and in fact the fabric of the building is the responsibility of the local authority, which will, at a pinch, maintain the drains but of course would never even consider putting money into such a project."

"No . . ."

"Hello, ladies, seconds anyone? Bit more shape, Miss . . . Troy, isn't it?"

"Yes, that's right, but no, thank you, it was delicious but I simply couldn't."

"Anyone? Any more for any more?"

"You should'a seen their faces," said Rosemary later that afternoon to her daughter Maureen, who had dropped by on one of her occasional visits. "Eyes all lit up! Mrs Burke-Hope had thirds! Poor old thing."

Maureen, who was Molly to her friends, in fact to everyone she knew except her mother, fidgeted in her chair. She was fond of Rosemary and old enough to feel that she had been a pretty good mother on the whole, but all this evident joy in giving still came as something of a surprise.

"Thought I might do them a peach tart next week, what d'you think?"

Molly might sigh, and re-cross her legs, puzzled, and a little guilty at feeling so; she could never guess at her mother's rich reward. Behind the pudding trolley Rosemary as usual had felt that collective hum of pleasure, that thirty-fold surge of attention, that intoxicating sense of being at last the most admired woman in the room.

And if this delightful sensation had in fact been brought about by a fabulously light toffee pudding, and not by Rosemary's own personal charms, that was of small account, for the follow-up mental picture had taken care of all that anyway, pushing the toffee pudding slightly to one side, nudging onto centre stage the younger slimmer mental-picture Rosemary, gracefully dishing out happiness to others.

Who could guess at such obscure delights? Certainly not Molly. Nor, as it happened, could Rosemary, whose delights they were. Rosemary thought she was only thinking of others.

"Or one of my honey granitas. What d'you think, Maureen?"

CHAPTER
FOUR

Miss Troy, who had carefully set her alarm for three, fell asleep the moment she lay down, and dreamt that she was swinging on the gate of her grandmother's tall London house.

"Come on lovey," said Maisie tenderly, "you get down off there, you know you're not supposed to."

It was so lovely to see Maisie again that Miss Troy woke up sighing with happiness, and was able to hang on to Maisie's smiling image despite the alarm. Even when she was fully awake again, waiting for the kettle to boil, she could summon up that round cheerful face, the long unrestrainedly curling dark hair. And the image was somehow new; nothing to do with the ancient stock of Maisie-memories which in any case Miss Troy had hardly looked over for years. It was as if the dream had magically given her a photograph to look at. A new memory, after so long. Miss Troy felt quite emotional. Whatever brought that on, she wondered, as she took her tea over to the view.

Darling Maisie. And I haven't thought of her for years.

Annie Cameron was trying to write to her son Michael, who lived in Canada, and who had recently left his wife. Annie had thought herself rather fond of her daughter-in-law, that strapping freckled long-legged foreigner who wrote and telephoned just as often as David, and sent frequent videos of the grandchildren, and called Annie Mom.

And I was wrong, thought Annie, wondering at herself. I am not rather fond of her. I love her. I love her children, and I love her.

But of course her son was paramount in her heart. The difficulties of writing to this man, whose behaviour she could not begin to justify, so oppressed her that before long concentration lapsed, and leaning back in her chair she uncomfortably dozed off. Sleeping sitting up was something Annie usually avoided. Today her unconscious, playfully prone to metaphor, set her daughter-in-law in a narrow canoe, adrift on foaming rapids.

"Mom, mom, help me!" screamed Annie's beloved daughter-in-law, while Annie stood encased in terror on the bank, watching as the canoe, spinning and lurching in the spray, hurled itself towards the massive jagged rocks ahead.

Just before the canoe struck the dream changed. The Technicolor screaming vanished; now Annie was back in her armchair, but the armchair was no longer in the corner of her little bedsit at Cabotin Court, but outside in the open. For a moment Annie sat still in the darkness, smelling the unfamiliarity of the space all about her.

She had a sense of nearby walls, and of a further moving darkness behind her. Then she saw, close beside her, within touching distance, a wooden table. The sight of this table filled her with dread. She made a jerky move, trying to push herself further away, and then realised that on the table, all by themselves in the middle and lit as if by a spotlight, was a pair of shoes, standing almost akimbo heel to heel.

They were women's shoes, with fairly high squared heels, and blunt toes decorated with tiny draggled bows, and very old, wrinkled and battered from within, widened to someone's broad bulbous feet. And as soon as Annie saw them they began at once to move. Slowly, very slowly, the battered toes shifted, their soles gritting a little on the table, swinging towards each other until the shoes lay facing her side by side, as if drawn to eyeless attention.

Unable to move, clutching the arms of her chair, Annie watched as they began to inch their way towards her, one by one, in tiny slithering steps, nearer and nearer, now she could see the scuffing on their toes, the forlorn stretching of their seams, they were going to reach her, they held a message, she saw, of some desolate pleading, that if it touched her would instantly kill her with pity and fear.

With a snapping gasp Annie awoke.

Several minutes passed.

How many times, she at last told herself scoldingly, how many times have I told you never to sleep sitting up. You know what happens! Presently she remembered the on-the-rocks nightmare about her daughter-in-law, and was so taken by its transparency that she soon forgot the shoes altogether.

Violet Dobbs was dreaming too, but she was not asleep at all. The solace of her life was romance, and this afternoon, her eyes closed, a copy of the *Radio Times* still held loosely over her quiescent post-lunch stomach, she was organising a love scene.

Mrs Dobbs was not fussy about form. She was just as ready to throw herself into filmed romance as into novels, and currently she was entirely engrossed in the televised fortunes of a fictional American policeman called Jerry. Jerry had a nice gentle face and large lustrous Italianate eyes, and Mrs Dobbs, idly channel-hopping one evening a few months ago, had noticed him straight away, though he had then been a very minor character, prone to unexplained absences and crowd scenes.

Over the last few episodes, however, he seemed to have become steadily more important. He had been brought repeatedly into the Chief's office and told off for bending the rules; he had been discovered in a bar, bitterly drinking beer straight out of the bottle; and his partner, a little chap with a pointed beard, had been shot dead by some baddie or another, but Jerry blamed himself for it, and got hauled into the chief's office for another telling-off, during which he had thrown his badge onto the chief's desk and shouted a great deal, though he had finally picked the badge up again and gone away looking very fed up. It had all been fairly hard to follow but in last week's episode he had been assigned a new work-partner, and it had turned out to be a pretty young woman, with whom he had instantly got on very badly.

Watching this Mrs Dobbs had scarcely dared breathe for excitement. As a Romantic veteran it was obvious to her that Jerry and Paula were going to fall in love. Heroes and heroines nearly always started off disliking one another, a convention Mrs Dobbs had no argument with. She herself had always found sexual attraction too disturbing to manage, remembering it chiefly as a type of paralytic seizure. Given that heroes and heroines would also be struck by some less clumsy version of this affliction (though, not being Violet Dobbs, they would be better at hiding their difficulties without blushing, choking, tripping over their own feet, or being completely unable to think of anything to say), suppressed awareness would surely tend to make a heroine temperamental and snappish, or a hero brusque and off-hand. It was all quite plausible, to Mrs Dobbs.

So when Paula had sneered at Jerry and hoarsely told him to "Get real," Mrs Dobbs' heart had begun to race. All week she had thought of them again and again, and as soon as the new *Radio Times* had come out had the relevant paragraph, disappointing though it was, off by heart:

"*10.00 City Pride. Rosalind squares up to Earnest K. Delamar and Frankie's ex-wife is called to the stand. Meanwhile Jerry is staking out the harbour . . .*"

36

It was a little worrying that Paula was not mentioned by name. Television series had disappointed Mrs Dobbs before. More than once they had come up with a lovely hero and suitable heroine, involved them week after week in desperate adventures, and still not allowed anything to happen, "anything" being Mrs Dobbs' private term for the initial stages of sexual involvement.

Years ago "Police Woman," for example, had kept Mrs Dobbs hooked for months. Joe had still been alive then and had watched it with her happily enough, never suspecting for a moment how his wife had lain awake beside him for hours at a time picturing all kinds of pleasantly conducive scenes in which Police Woman finally got off with her Police Man.

But on screen the pair of them went on week after week working undercover together and escaping death by inches together and occasionally exchanging tender glances that made Mrs Dobbs hold her breath; but still never coming to grips.

Eventually she had begun to wonder whether all this will-they-won't-they might be just another crafty weekly ingredient, like car-chases and villains suddenly pulling out hidden guns. It was an uncomfortable suspicion. It meant that someone knew what she was feeling. It meant that someone was doing it on purpose. It meant that someone understood.

Mrs Dobbs, who did not understand herself nor want to, immediately lost all further interest in Police Woman, and went back to novels. Their authors understood too, of course, but the whole thing was so much more private somehow. Besides books didn't tease. They didn't notice you enjoying them and stretch themselves out indefinitely in order to stop you from reaching the final chapter. Time passed in them, events occurred in order. Whereas Police Woman's adventure this week might have happened last week or next month for all the difference it had ever made to her or Police Man.

But all that was long ago now and since Joe had died Mrs Dobbs had watched television more and more. Sometimes she could pretend things were still normal, if it was a repeat of something that had been on when Joe was alive, and that he had enjoyed, "Dad's Army," say, or "Birds of a Feather"; even here, at Cabotin, where Joe had never set foot.

Mrs Dobbs had brought both their armchairs with her and often glanced over at Joe's as if she were exchanging looks with him the way they often had at home. This was painful but not acutely so. Sometimes Mrs Dobbs spoke to the armchair as well; it was standing in for Joe, that was all.

"That was a good one, wasn't it," she might say, as the "Dad's Army" credits rolled. "Shall I make some tea now, yes, think I will," so that it was as if Joe was with her still for a moment.

Staking out the harbour, thought Mrs Dobbs now, and she put Jerry into a small van with one-way windows and lots of bleeping electronic equipment, and then sat Paula beside him. Clearly the situation had possibilities. They would be alone together, and enclosed.

So she made the van smaller still, and made time pass without anything very much happening outside, so that they would have nothing to do but talk to each other. She didn't bother with what they actually said, but if they'd been stuck in a tiny van all day it was bound to get personal sooner or later.

Of course it was really too soon to start anything; they had only just met, and everything would be so much more thrilling if there was a gradual build-up over several weeks. Besides, a secondary romantic convention often demanded, especially in American television series, that sudden love affairs ended as quickly as they had started, frequently because the newer character had been shot dead. Really it would be safer all round if Paula was hardly in this week's episode at all.

All the same Mrs Dobbs thought no harm in making Paula notice Jerry noticing the long graceful curve of Paula's neck; she made uneasy silences; she made them both start talking at once, to break off in similar confusion, and she made them catch one another's eyes, to look away in sudden thrilling shyness. In short she made the dark cramped van pullulate with longing, and was there herself, being both Jerry and Paula and neither of them, being the tingling air between them, seeing, sensate.

"Jerry?" Her hoarse intimate voice. "Hey look at this."

"Yup. That's our guy . . ." (taking photographs probably, click whirr click whirr click whirr).

"So. What now?"

His wry smile, his shrug. She answers herself: "We go on waiting, right?"

"And waiting and waiting," he says, and turns to find himself closer to her than he had realised, pause, they both stop smiling. She is looking at his mouth. They lean closer, slowly, very slowly.

"And waiting," she whispers, almost against his lips, her eyes closing . . . *Bleep bleep bleep bleep*

Yes, that would do very nicely for now. In the scramble to deal with whichever bit of electronic equipment had gone off all that melting longing would vanish, leaving them suspicious and uneasy and more snappish than ever, and that was all to the good because of course they would have to have at least one major row before things could get going properly.

Still it had all gone very well. Mrs Dobbs turned over comfortably, and presently showed herself the whole scene all over again, right from the beginning.

Annie had given up on the letter to Michael, and gone rather groggily for a lie down. As she sat down on her narrow divan to unbutton her cardigan, she was struck again, as she often was in the quiet of the afternoons, by the age of the room in which she was preparing to sleep. This was in the oldest part of the complex. What had it been like, in the days when flagstones were new and easy-clean?

Numerous trips to the library, and applications to local history groups, had yielded little information. Once there had been record and account books dating from the days of the first First Sister, but these, Annie learnt, had been stored for safe-keeping during the War in the vaults of a local bank, and the bank, together with the entire street it stood in, had been obliterated in an air-raid.

One cloth-bound late Victorian notebook, apparently someone's rough copy, had evidently not been thought worth saving, and was kept now in a locked cupboard in Miss Potts' office. Applied to, Betty had clearly regretted telling Annie about it in the first place, and not been at all happy about letting her have a look at it.

But, it seemed, she had not been able to come up with any convincing reason why Annie should not do so, not off-the-cuff, anyway, and had reluctantly handed it over one afternoon on condition that it did not leave the office.

(As if, thought Annie, I might give way and deface it, left to myself. Well, this is the nearest she can get to refusing me altogether, I suppose. And her impulse is always to refuse things, because that is her nature.) "Oh, thank you!" said Annie aloud.

Merely touching the notebook had given her a delightful thrill of pleasure. She had turned it over in her hands. It had not looked old, or even used, just a little faded, as if someone had left it out in the sun for an afternoon. The corners were still sharp. A faded, newish little book, but inside the passage of more than a hundred years had turned black ink to sepia.

The handwriting was large and childish, with lots of loops, setting out a list of present inmates and their previous occupations. And every one, Annie noticed in some surprise, had had an occupation; not one spinster or widow or wife. Then she had realised that wives and mothers would not have applied. These had been women with jobs, who had grown too old to work. Washerwomen, seamstresses, milliners' assistants, a waist-coat maker. A mangler. That one gave Annie pause.

("And what do you do?"

"Oh, this and that. Bit of mangling. Mainly mangling, actually.")

And what could have been the matter with Mary Jane Rawlings, whose entry read "calls herself a lady's maid?" It seemed a small enough claim. Though clearly a cut above mangling. Perhaps Mary Jane had given herself airs.

There had been little else to go on. On page six someone had been refused permission to plant a window box. (The Betty Pottses had been more peremptory in those days, thought Annie). The following page, the last one, read "Feb 14. Mrs Strudling passed away peacefully at six o'clock. Sinks all in order."

Annie had looked up then to see Betty saying something, but as her desk was in front of the window, so that she had her back to the light, Annie had not been able to understand her. Annie could see her expression clearly enough though, the usual faint not-quite-suppressed irritation.

"They always take it personally," a deaf friend had once told Annie many years before. "Remember, it's not their fault you can't hear them. It's all yours."

42

"Sorry," said Annie automatically, as she handed the book back. "Thank you very much."

"— much in it, was —" said Betty, amongst other things, as her face momentarily turned to the window while she reopened the half-glazed cupboard door. A lifetime's practice enabled Annie to fill in the blanks.

"No, but it was very interesting all the same," she said.

Pushing off her shoes one by one Annie lay down now and closed her eyes.

Pity no one knew any more when the residents had stopped being presented with a length of purple broadcloth. In the seventeenth century, according to the secretary of the local history society, the gift had been renewed every three years; though in the course of the next hundred the cloth trade had so fallen off that the charity had nearly foundered altogether, and new inmates granted a room had been required to take on the previous occupant's old frock as well.

But surely all that had died out too, by the 1880s. Annie sat up briefly to pull her soft velour dressing gown over her legs.

Mary Jane Rawlings, self-professed lady's maid, would surely have hated wearing some dead woman's nasty old purple. Perhaps she had laid herself down in this very room, and wondered into the night where she had gone wrong, how she could have ended up here with a bunch of indigent ex-manglers. Or perhaps Mrs Willis had sighed here for her window-box, or Mrs Strudling peacefully passed away.

Good many deathbed scenes, thought Annie. Any amount of those. Right here. This bed probably. This very room. Hope I won't flash on any. That wouldn't be very nice.

She turned comfortably onto her side, and fell asleep.

CHAPTER
FIVE

Though officially off-duty, Betty Potts was at the desk in her office, putting the half-hour before the Friends of Cabotin arrived to good use. Asked, she would have said that she was catching up with her paperwork. This would not, strictly speaking, have been true, for Betty had caught up with her paperwork long ago, had drawn ahead and positively lapped it, in fact. Paperwork had no chance, against Betty Potts.

This afternoon, for example, all official business had already been sorted, noted, answered, and filed. Accounts, up-dated to the previous hour, had been checked on the office computer, with running totals transferred in ink to the old-fashioned Warden's logbook. Sunday there was already over, fully documented, with one line left blank to record the deliberations of the Friends and two at the bottom, in case of emergency, as usual.

In fact it was a private letter Betty was working on. In her youth she had been taught to answer all letters by return of post, and now prided herself upon doing so. She wrote quickly, in a firm hand, detailing the small doings at Cabotin, recent visitors, a new resident expected, an exotic postcard received. Posted this evening, the letter would go off first thing and arrive by second post or early on Tuesday morning.

As she wrote Betty pictured, with a small and isolated piece of her mind, the letter's recipient, an elderly cousin of Betty's own mother. She saw the cousin bending down in her dressing gown to pick up the letter, straightening on the doormat with a sigh, with an outright groan, at being once more so smartly trumped.

For Betty was at least partly aware that to answer letters by return of post had lately become something of an aggressive act: a rebuke, at the very least. All her friends and relations always owed her a letter, or felt that they did. No matter how long they themselves had taken to get round to writing to Betty as oldest friend, cousin, niece, aunt or recently great-aunt Betty, given the vagaries of the modern Post Office, would have her answers on everyone's doormat within two working days at most.

She suspected, with that same small isolated piece of her mind, that writing to her, Betty, gave her various friends and relations a nice warm glow of virtue. This, if it were so, was an insult. Reply by return ensured that the glow, should it exist, be wiped out almost before it had begun, which served everybody right, from Betty's point of view: if it took you weeks, months, or even years to perform a simple duty of politeness like writing a few lines to a relative, you certainly did not deserve to feel pleased with yourself when your sluggish conscience had finally prodded you into action.

Rather you deserved an instant swiping volley, whack! the ball smoking back in your court before you'd had time to turn round.

Thump went Betty's small fist on the stamp of the envelope; a psychic blow to the heart of the elderly cousin, who indeed would recognise the handwriting with mingled boredom and dread.

The blow struck there was really nothing more to be done until three-thirty, when the Friends should arrive, all discreet silks, navy blue, gold and large hard handbags. Sometimes Betty quite liked the Friends and felt that she herself was one of them, but she could never relax in their presence and occasionally suspected them of talking about her slightingly before they arrived. Once one of them had been quite badly trodden on by a horse and Betty, hearing of this, had privately laughed a great deal.

If only there was a decent room to receive visitors in! Everything would be different then. As it was Betty could hardly blame the Friends for looking down on her. Who could respect anyone whose office had a false ceiling stuck with polystyrene tiling? Or who worked all day at a cheap mass-produced pine-veneer desk with spindly metal legs, set upon carpet grotesquely patterned in swirling snowflakes of muddy green, orangey-brown, and black!

Though none of these things, not even the neon lighting, bothered Betty so much as the gap in the wall beside the corner. It was quite a large hole, papered inside, like all the office walls, with woodchip wallpaper painted cream. Betty's immediate predecessor, a Mrs

Chatman, had explained that the gap had probably once been some sort of fireplace, that the workmen had uncovered it when taking out the old gas fire during the refurbishments, and that she had intended to have the gap fitted with useful shelving but never quite got round to it.

But Mrs Chatman had also, it turned out, never got round to reading the Cabotin logbooks. Though it was true no one would ever be able to flick through the ancient books of the Almshouse's earlier years, since every one of them had been exploded into dust, those covering the immediate post-War years were sound enough. And Betty, a few weeks after taking up her duties, the computer system installed, inmates investigated and formatted, official paperwork caught up with, private correspondents all firmly back in debit, had without much interest idly taken up the earliest, 1945–51, and found herself hooked.

For simply in itself the book spoke to her of decline; not just Cabotin's, but all England's, even the world's. It was part of a clearly pre-War set, bound in bottle-green leather, with smooth heavy pages, and the Cabotin arms stamped onto the front covers, though only this earliest also had its dates stamped onto its spine in letters of gold. A little label had been gummed into the marbled endpapers, stating the name of the manufacturer (Est. 1807) and an address in Glasgow, and in italics:

This book can at any time be replaced by giving the number . . . .

On the dots a pre-War someone had carefully inked "1177" into each volume.

Whereas the latest logbook, the one Betty herself had inherited from Mrs Chatman, was a blue plastic ring binder, with a biro'd label ("Jan '82") Sellotaped onto its spine, and on its front a picture of a cat with pop-eyes and a blue satin bow, apparently cut with pinking shears from a birthday card.

(She had made short work of pussy, and sent off an instant imperative to the firm of stationers in Glasgow, giving the number, just in case, but of course the letter had eventually been returned to her, since there was now not only no such firm but no such address either. Scornfully unsurprised Betty had bought a real book as similar as possible, which meant not very, to the pre-War set, and using her own money, since the blue plastic ring binder had been perfectly adequate to its purpose, she felt, should you happen to be a person with absolutely no sense of tradition, style, nor respect due to an ancient institution.)

Within, the old logbooks had varied a great deal.

1945–51's First Sister, Miss Berkely, seemed to have found her charges tremendously entertaining, and had frequently gone to the trouble of recording their rural simplicities in phonetic form, and at some length. She had also complained a great deal about the cold, recorded breakages, and given small tea-parties, detailing the ration-era ingredients she had gathered together and, like some minor domestic Baron Frankenstein, ruthlessly manhandled into a frightful semblance of cakes and biscuits — the eggless,

49

sugar-free sponge cake, the petit-fours made of bread dipped in condensed milk and browned beneath the grill — all of which had surely, no matter to what fraught galvanic processes she had subjected them, lain irremediably lifeless on the table.

Her successor, the terse Miss Wynn, 1951–59, wrote lists. She had listed the inmates, weekly; their complaints, daily; her own complaints, daily; and their departures, as required. Her residents, Betty noted, passed over. Mrs Berkely's had breathed their last, and sometimes gone to meet their Maker; whereas Miss Jakes, 1959-64, quickly began to lose people.

"Today we lost Eliza Fanshaw," she had written in December, 1959.

Go and look for her then, Betty had sneered to herself on reading this; for Miss Jakes, after a slow start heavily freighted with Miss Wynn-style lists, had very quickly shown what manner of woman she was, or rather, exactly who she was: Nemesis, as far as Betty was concerned.

Within weeks she had stopped signing "F. Jakes, First Sister" and started writing "F. Jakes, Warden" instead, casually secured the Board's agreement at the next Governors' Meeting, ordered herself some new stationary and had all the signboards repainted.

"So much more in tune with modern thought!"

Nor had she stopped at her title. Miss Jakes had been a relentless moderniser. In the spring of 1962 she had had gas-fires installed in every room, and later in that year laid new hardboard and linoleum floors and refurbished the Hall kitchens; and in the following year turned her attention to the old First Sister's Sitting Room.

Betty had read of all this with the most anguished attention. For days, while she worked her way through the volume, she had thought of nothing else, rushing official duties, taking 1951–64 to bed with her despite its size and weight, once even smuggling it out of Cabotin altogether for a long train journey. She had hardly been able to put Miss Jakes down.

This was at least partly due to the details Miss Jakes left out. The installation of the gas fires necessitated the removal of all the old fireplaces. Miss Jakes described the new but not the old, and Betty had instantly pictured early Victorian grates, the sort with flat sides to put kettles on, and so vividly that she had quickly forgotten that she had made them up. So when she later read that Miss Jakes had sold the lot of them to a scrap metal dealer for £2 10s. she could scarcely breathe for rage.

"Oak, I think," wrote Miss Jakes blithely of the floorboards, as her workmen nailed lino all over them; and Betty saw broad seventeenth century boards, burnished with three hundred years of humble care, and groaned aloud.

"What monsters!" wrote Miss Jakes cheerfully of the two kitchen dressers. "The kitchen is masses bigger without them. It seemed rather a shame really as they were evidently made for Cabotin and have the Arms carved on their cupboards, and a date, 1648, but really, poor old things, they just had to go."

51

"Vandal!" said Betty fiercely, aloud, so that everybody near her on the crowded train looked carefully out of the window. But there was worse to come.

"Paid Mr Caldicott 10s. to take the range. I must say I'm absolutely thrilled to see the back of the beastly thing!"

For there could be no doubt where the range had come from. Springing up from her desk where she was reading this further maddening instalment Betty had crouched down to inspect the awkward gaping hole that Mr Caldicott had left behind. Yes: definitely; it was, of course, range-shaped.

In imagining the range Betty really let herself go. The dear little doors, for hot and slow ovens! The comforting solidity! The cosy rack for warming plates, the brass tap to the urn which one might lovingly polish! Above all the cheerful glow and flicker of the coals in its stout barred grate! For of course on cold days she would have lit the fire, and she and the Friends would have taken tea before it, with the pot kept warm on the hob, and the room would have had that special dignified reality that only old rooms can have, and so, by mysterious extension, would she, Betty Potts.

That the repellent Jakes had actually paid to have such riches torn out and lost forever was, perhaps, really more than Betty could bear. It preyed on her mind. For weeks she could not open the door of her office without helplessly picturing what it had surely been like when it was the First Sister's Sitting Room, ante-Miss Jakes: flag-floored, with one rather upright armchair in front of the range (where a kettle was always singing), a rag-rug, perhaps a little spotless white lace on the mantle . . .

It was perhaps just as well for Betty's state of mind, and blood pressure, that Miss Jakes had missed out all references to the Sitting Room cupboards, which had lined the room since the seventeenth century: from floor to ceiling, an intricate system of cupboards, shelves, and tiny locking drawers had held supplies of soap, spices, sugar, tea, sealing wax, string, woollen blankets, linen, cutlery, pewter, china, glass and anything else a First Sister felt should be kept safely under her personal supervision. Miss Jakes had had them all removed, in pieces, and had made a bonfire of them out in the back garden behind the compost heap.

"Ripped out the old oak cupboards from the Sitting Room today, and golly the place looks so much bigger!" is the sort of thing Miss Jakes might well have written. But she did not, and so Betty was spared picturing the panelled gloss of ancient polished woodwork, and thus quite likely an apoplectic fit as well.

But on the whole there were a great many things Miss Jakes did not bother to mention, as they were simply too obvious. The residents' rooms' old fireplaces, for instance, had been installed in the 1840's with a view to the strictest economy, and had held barely a shovelful of coal, fires Bob Cratchit might have sniffed at; besides most of them smoked so furiously that the inmates could warm themselves only in a persistent choking haze, unless they opened a window, which of course let in the freezing cold.

And in the exceptional winter of 1961-2, two inmates had almost certainly died of cold, one of them rather a favourite of Miss Jakes's, a gentle old maidservant, who had carried great bucketfuls of coal to countless roaring well-to-do firesides in her prime, only to freeze her own blood in her eighties, for want of a decent fire. So Miss Jakes had reasoned, touching that worn icy hand, in the early January of 1962.

But in the logbook she had only written, "Today I lost Janey Pearson, a dear friend," and more than twenty years later Betty, not noticing the personal pronoun, and with no other clues to go on, could only once more sneer "Go and look for her then!" instead of realising that here lay the key to almost everything, the gas fires, the lino, even the kitchen dressers, which had in truth funded the lino, though Miss Jakes, feeling herself to be, aesthetically speaking, on thin ice there, had concealed this fact from her account book, the logbook and, presently, her own conscience.

What did kitchen dressers matter anyway, if another Janey Pearson was not to die of cold in her own miserable institutional bed?

Besides the dressers had been very crudely made, and were heavily infested with woodworm and built on a scale which rendered them almost unsellable, or so the dealer had claimed. (But he had been wrong. He had not sold them at all. They had sat slowly decaying first in his showroom and then in the old barn he used for storage until some ten years after his own death, when his son had finally sold them, to a London firm of interior decorators, in 1981. Certainly the dealer's son had made a reasonable amount of money out of them, but as by then he had no record of how little his father had given for them in the first place, he only reckoned up the decades' worth of storage space the wormy old monsters had taken up, and felt himself quite hard done by.)

And the lino the dressers had paid for had really kept out the worst of the howling Arctic draughts that had whistled through the gaps in the floorboards, which were not, as it happened, oak at all, but pitch pine late-Victorian replacements and rather unevenly laid. Miss Jakes had been carelessly mistaken, but Betty could not know that.

Nor, since they had been so commonplace to Miss Jakes, was there any mention in the logbook of mice, mould, cockroaches or the rat that had one evening burst through the rotten plaster behind the left-hand kitchen dresser, and lain dazedly on the shelving while the cook screamed and made hysterical passes at it with a fish-slice. Miss Jakes had been ashamed to be in charge of such a house, so though she had called in the rat-man she had censored the rat.

Whereas it had simply not occurred to her to write about the range. It happened that Miss Jakes had been brought up in a house equipped with a range. The thing held no charm for her. She saw no point in recording her struggles with it.

For no matter how cosseted with attention and the finest (and most expensive) coal, the range balefully refused to produce anything like radiant heat, its myriad viciously protuberant knobs and handles seemed designed to bark the shins and smear with greasy black anyone approaching it with less than the utmost circumspection, and the fumes it emitted when coaxed at last to burn a little were sickeningly redolent of oven cleaner, burnt cheese, and bleach. There was no getting round lousy workmanship, and Miss Jakes, who soon doubted the thing had ever worked properly even when it was new, quickly gave up trying to use it and, if she had to work in the Sitting Room, kept her hat and coat on.

All this Miss Jakes had not bothered to record. Nor had she, for different reasons, made any official record of her suspicions concerning her own immediate predecessor, the list-compiling Miss Wynn, who had made such unusual use of the First Sister's Sitting Room storage space. Where could the wretched woman have got her supplies from, on such a scale? If it was home-brew, why had she not returned the empty bottles, instead of stacking them reeking behind every warped and buckling cupboard door? And why, when she was so clearly neglectful and incompetent, had no one thought to remove her from her post?

These and other similar mysteries Miss Jakes had sometimes mentioned, carefully, at Governor's meetings, and found them to have a curious effect on the members of the Board; one or two of them, jolly and loquacious beforehand, would go rather quiet afterwards, and reflective, and inclined to agree without fuss to whatever modernisation proposals Miss Jakes presently had in mind.

All these things, her suspicions, the mice, the cockroaches, needing to wear a coat in her own Sitting Room and blowing on her fingers as she wrote, all these things were, Miss Jakes felt, unbecoming to an official record, and best forgotten. Perhaps she had no idea how comprehensively they would be so. Certainly she did not imagine for a moment, and why should she? that her logbook, so selective, omitting so much, was still a picture of life and times, patchy, misleading, open to all sorts of conflicting interpretations: in short, a history.

If she had put in the rat and how it had frightened her, if she had described the sodden plaster in the kitchen or the range's irremediable smell, or the touch of Janey Pearson's icy dead hand, how differently Betty might have seen her, and how Betty's peace of mind and blood pressure might have benefited!

CHAPTER
SIX

Annie Cameron awoke again, suddenly, and lay still for a moment, her heart pounding, considering it. Had it been a flash, or not?

In the dream she had been standing in a garden, in the dark, watching someone digging. An old man steadily digging; but she had watched in such a transport of despair that even now, fully awake, she trembled.

A disturbing dream, but with nothing else to go on Annie dismissed it as nothing more and sat up, swinging her legs sideways in the manner recommended by the Health Visitor to minimise dizziness on rising. She counted to ten as prescribed and stood, slowly, counting to five again just in case, before risking a glance down for her slippers.

As she bent to put them on the dream seemed suddenly to appear again, as if someone had suddenly thrust a postcard of it under her nose, and this time she knew that the man's jacket and shirtfront were stiff with drying blood.

"*There was no light,*" said a voice in Annie's head.

Annie knew this voice well. It was the soundless, laconic and generally inscrutable voice of clairvoyance. She had heard it, now and then, all her life.

"But mammy, we don't need to run, the train's going to be late!" A small milestone in Annie's life: the last time she had so incautiously communicated any of the voice's pronouncements to anyone else; for the look her mother had turned on her, when they arrived a full five minutes late at the platform and found it still crowded, had been full of suspicion and distaste. She had hated any suggestion of the freakish. Even at five years old Annie had realised how lucky she had been not to have divulged exactly how late the train was going to be: a precise seven minutes would have been much harder to pass off as coincidence.

So after that she had kept quiet, which had been easy enough given the nature of the voice's most usual announcements:

Mavis has a new blue hair ribbon.
The bus will come after two cars have passed.
That man has a pork pie in his pocket.
Her dog is called Blackie.

Every so often, every couple of weeks, Annie would quite clearly hear a generally useless piece of information, usually on the most trivial of matters. Those that could be checked:

Robert got the strap in class today
Leek pudding for tea

were invariably correct, but had no application. They might be puzzling;

He is wearing silk drawers

or even entertaining;

It is a wig;

but as she grew up, and read what little she could find to read on the subject, it was clear to Annie that if she indeed had the gift of second sight it was of a particularly pointless cut-price variety, a Woolworth's nothing-over-sixpence sort of gift.

The loss of her real hearing, which occurred gradually from her eighth year, had no effect on the inner voice, but with the menarche came visual flashes, fast postcard-type views of other people's lives. These too were of no practical use. Her boss's breakfast table, where his wife was reading the paper; Aunt Agnes picking up a chicken; her own mother peeling potatoes. Were these essentially uninteresting pictures of the past, the present, or the future? It was the sort of thing that at least mattered, in most cases of second sight. But not in mine, thought Annie, with resignation and, as she grew older, some amusement.

For many years after they were married Annie did not tell her husband of her inner voice or the flashing pictures that sometimes accompanied them. They had practical difficulties enough, without adding pointless mysticism; besides she had not forgotten her mother's response, which in retrospect looked more like disgust than anything else.

But when she fell pregnant for the first time the flashes grew more insistent. One or two were nightmarish; a row of houses suddenly exploding into flame, the dead body of a woman falling from the sky, but usually they were quite ordinary, someone cutting sandwiches, or peering under the bonnet of a car.

Though often there was something subtly disturbing about them, as if after all there was some point in the scene not immediately apparent to anyone just watching it, or as if the point lay in what had happened next. Annie put a lot of effort into not wondering, but constantly appearing cheerful, and not at all mad, not at all someone subject to inexplicably worrying pictures of a woman buttering bread, was something of a strain. The flashes of foreboding stopped when she miscarried, and began again with her second pregnancy, which also ended in miscarriage.

"It's nature's way," said Annie's mother, for she was of the opinion, which she was perfectly ready to voice, that defectives should not marry, and certainly not marry other defectives. She was ashamed of her daughter's deafness and blamed her own husband for it, since, as again she quite often remarked, there was no history in her family of anything subnormal.

"Except for her heart," Edward had once signed at Annie behind her mother's back.

"You're not going to let it happen again, are you?"

"We want a family, mother."

"Well, I think you should be ashamed of yourselves. Why d'you think you've missed twice? You're not meant to have children. It's not right. Bringing another afflicted child into the world. What sort of chance is it going to have, of being normal? The pair of you. It's not right."

"How did this vile hag get to have you for a daughter?" signed Edward to Annie, but with a polite smile as he motioned at her mother.

"What's he say?"

"He said, did you want some more tea, mother. Do you?"

"Monkey tricks," sniffed her mother, passing her cup.

"She must have done something right," signed Edward cheerfully. "You're a wee smasher, did I ever tell you that?"

"Now what's he grinning at?"

"Nothing, mother."

But the third pregnancy had ended like the others, and the fourth in a stillborn daughter. Annie's mother had had a heart attack by this time, and seemed a little less certain about things. She had inspected the slender waxen little corpse with pursed lips, but pronounced her grandchild bonny enough.

The following year, whilst sweeping out the back yard, Annie had a flash-with-voice of herself sitting on a park bench in the sunshine. In the flash she seemed to be sitting next to herself, admiring the plump blond child on her dream-self's lap.

It is your son

said the familiar inner voice, and Annie found herself standing in her backyard shedding tears of happiness; and at the same time astonished, for never before had the voice told her anything important, or about herself.

It was during her next pregnancy that she was forced to tell Edward about her oddities, for one day as she lay on the settee with her feet up, her ankles all swollen, she had a clear waking flash of a road accident, with fatalities. She saw dead men lie bloodied on a grassy roadside.

It is your husband, said the voice, uninflected as ever. Edward was to go down to Yorkshire by car, with two colleagues, to visit a potential new supplier for the textile factory they all worked for; the trip had been arranged for the following day. All afternoon Annie wrung her hands. There was no one to consult. She felt dizzy, and lights flicked on and off in her head, which ached fiercely. She made the decision: she would tell him, when he came home.

But by then they had been married nearly eighteen years, and had known one another far longer. She had kept the pointless informative voice from him; detailing its trivia now would hardly convince.

"Don't you see? It *was* leek pudding!" No, that would never work. If only she had spoken of it earlier, if only she had told him exactly when the bus would come, or exactly where he had left his hairbrush, that she had known where to look!

And how much could she rely, anyway, on the flashes-with-voice? Nearly all of them seemed to have been bits of other people's lives, and impossible to check on. They might well be proof of nothing more than that she was slightly unhinged.

What would he think of her also, for claiming such a secret over so many years? Even if he believed her he would be upset, if nothing worse, to think she had kept something so important from him.

"But it wasn't important, it was just my silly wee voice!"

So why take any notice of it then? What was he supposed to tell his boss? "Sorry, I can't come, my wife's silly wee voice says I should stay at home all day!"

Picturing such unhappy scenes kept Annie busy until she heard Edward's key in the lock, at which she rushed into the dark passageway, screamed at him that he must not go on the trip tomorrow or he would die, and fell at his feet twitching in the first of a series of convulsions to do, Edward gathered later at the hospital, with the baby somehow poisoning her blood.

The doctor operated later that night, and Edward, for the first time missing a day's work while his wife's life hung in the balance, missed also the trip to Yorkshire, and the car crash in which both his friends died. The baby, though it weighed hardly more than four pounds, lived and thrived. Annie had had no worries about him, once she had seen the thin blond fuzz on his fragile little head.

"So was the voice wrong, then?" asked Edward, many months later.

"How d'you mean?"

"Well, I wasn't killed, was I? It wasn't me."

"No. I don't know. Sometimes I think — oh, it's silly . . ."

"No, tell me."

"Well, I wonder if sometimes I hear things that are really meant for other people. The car crash one. It was Marion's or Connie's, wasn't it, and I heard it for them. I don't like thinking that. But the others, the daft ones: perhaps some of them would be important, I mean if they were getting to the right person. But they stop at me, and I don't know what to make of them. Sometimes when I have dreams I wonder if they're really someone else's, got loose somehow. And I pick them up. And they're no use to me."

"Dreams too?"

"Oh, not very often. But every now and then they're just too particular, d'you know what I mean? I dreamt about that woman making sandwiches the other night, d'you remember her? That woman's nothing to do with me." Annie laughed, for the sun was warm and the baby pleasantly heavy on her lap, and the park was full of happy-looking people strolling by in their summer Sunday-best, strolling, it so happened, to music from the band in the bandstand, that neither Annie nor Edward could hear.

It is your son, she remembered: not her flash at all really, but Edward's.

There was no light, thought Annie now, considering. She crossed over to the kitchen side of her bedsit and filled the kettle.

An old man gardening, blood on him somewhere. No light. Had it been dark, in the flash? Annie closed her eyes, trying to picture it. Perhaps. More interesting than usual, certainly. Had he been burying something, perhaps? He had hardly seemed urgent, he had not looked guilty. His movements had been methodical, practiced. Had he been burying treasure, for safekeeping? Though that would not of course explain the blood. Or her own reaction, of course.

Annie sighed. There was, of course, nothing to be done about the vision except wait and see if it came back, as it probably would, once or twice. She made herself a very small pot of tea, and as a concession to Sunday, awarded herself two chocolate gingers.

Betty Potts, nineteenth First Sister, at that moment preparing tea for the Friends with her own hands, was brooding again about the Cabotin gates. She could see them broadside on from the kitchen and they were as bad for her health as the range. All down to Jakes, of course.

"Alice M. says the old gates were taller," Miss Jakes had written, "but there's simply no way of knowing for sure. I, for one, think they look smashing. Mr Greenway kindly installed them in person, and a man from the *Advertiser* took some photographs. I declare these gates open, I said, opening them, and everyone laughed and applauded!"

"Um, did you want the cake?"

"Uh?" Betty was startled, for she had been watching Miss Jakes twittering at the impassive tradesman, and at the same time given her frizzy hair, splayed front teeth and a big coarse bum in a sagging knit frock.

66

"It's only one of my banana cakes," said Rosemary, falsely apologetic. "I didn't have the time for anything really special, but it should be, you know, all right."

"I'm sure it will be delicious," said Betty coolly. "It's kind of you to go to so much trouble." Especially when you're not invited, was the plain but unspoken end of this sentence.

"I'll do you a Swiss roll next time," said Rosemary, apparently oblivious. "That's Lady Habgood's favourite, you know."

"Yes." Betty checked her trolley. Teapot, hot water, six cups and saucers, six plates, six knives; strawberry jam, whipped cream, and scones, all from Marks and Spencer and perfectly adequate on their own, and then Rosemary's beastly cake, which everyone would coo over and stuff their smarmy faces with, but she is not coming, she is not coming in if I have to bolt and bar the door, thought Betty grimly.

Heaven knew there was little enough real responsibility and status in the job without making out that what there was had to be shared with someone as fat and insignificant as Rosemary Sholto.

"I'll give you a hand with the trolley, shall I?"

"No, no, thank you, I can manage." With some difficulty Betty manoeuvred the trolley to the side door and drew it out into the passage, but Rosemary would not be shaken off, accompanying her superior all the way along it to the very door of the office, jingling her bunch of house keys and remarking on the weather, so fresh and lovely, and how well the hotels along the front were doing, even this early in the season, until Betty's heart began to beat faster at the prospect of outright unpleasantness.

Thank you, Rosemary was all that needing saying, in the right insultingly bland yet dismissive tones, but as Betty drew breath to attempt this Rosemary looked at her wristwatch and got in first:

"Oh my goodness look at the time, I must be off out. Tell Lady Habgood won't you, Swiss roll next time and that's a promise! Byeee!"

And she was away, bouncing along the corridor on her chunky little heels. Betty pretended to herself that she believed in Rosemary's afternoon engagement, because not doing so would mean recognising that Rosemary had been bravely and rather pathetically pretending, in order to hide her disappointment, and full knowledge of this might have given Betty a twinge of the conscience.

Probably with the daughter, thought Betty stoutly to herself, until she noticed she had forgotten the milk jug and the danger was passed. Leaving the office door open she trekked back to the kitchen, searched through almost every cupboard before remembering the fridge, and got back to the office nearly five minutes late. The Friends were already there, standing by the window in a little perfumed circle.

"Ah hello, we were just wondering where you'd got to, Betty, look, we've got a new girl!"

Melanie Habgood, as ever elegantly coiffed and dressed (but there was nothing, Betty always gratefully remembered, that she could do about those ankles) led

68

forward a stranger who smiled pleasantly at Betty and said,

"Good afternoon, I'm, oh dear, are you all right, oh heavens, oh!"

For Betty, still clutching the milk jug, had turned up her eyes and fallen in a dead faint on the swirling orangey-brown snowflakes of the office floor.

CHAPTER
SEVEN

Rosemary felt so cross at being excluded from the Friends' meeting yet again, that she walked all the way into the centre of town without really noticing, though normally she caught the bus. Her feet were aching quite badly as she reached the quiet Edwardian squares that lay just in from the sea front. Walking more slowly she crossed over to the prom and found an empty bench facing out to sea.

Though it was only May the sun was bright and the narrow strip of beach quite crowded with people trudging noisily about on the shingle. Rosemary eased her feet out of her shoes, just at the back, and flexed her poor feet. She felt unappreciated. She pictured that woman's office and made Lady Habgood say, "What a pity Rosemary isn't here," in a very meaningful voice, and made Audrey Hopper add "You must make sure she can come next time, Betty!" and the one with the funny eyes said, "Absolutely delicious cake!"

"She's so talented!"

"A born chef!"

"You should take more care of her, Betty!"

And none of them touched her shop-bought scones and old Potty went positively black with rage.

Didn't really want to go anyway, thought Rosemary, and then felt seriously miserable, for it suddenly seemed to her that there was actually nothing in the world that she really wanted, and that everything she had wasn't up to much. A daughter she hardly saw, whose visits lasted half an hour at most. A job of ill-paid drudgery. Night storage heating in the bungalow, and winter coming on. Nothing to look forward to. A widow.

Rosemary's eyes filled with tears. All those people on the beach, all the couples strolling, arm-in-arm in the late summer sunshine! She pictured herself from behind, a small figure huddled alone, or no, why should she, not huddled then but sitting upright with a touch of heroism, bravely all alone and looking out to sea, a widow amidst the happy crowd, and if she could see me now she'd feel rotten and serve her right.

Or not, knowing her. Rosemary's shoulders sagged again. She closed her eyes and raised her big square face to the sun.

"Excuse me. D'you mind if I sit down?"

Rosemary opened her eyes. She could scarcely see in the glare, could just make out his hat, a trilby, and a possible moustache. He had one hand up, touching the front of the hat.

"Not at all," cried Rosemary, thinking how long it had been since she had seen a man touch his hat like that, so charming in the best sense of the word.

He sat; the bars beneath Rosemary's own bottom correspondingly shifted a little, intimately, and Rosemary suddenly felt cheerful again. She wondered if

71

he would speak to her, and decided that if he did not, she would; she would remark on the weather or something and they might have a nice little chat, and her heart began to beat fast at the thought. She looked steadily at the horizon, where the two differing bright blues of sea and sky so pleasingly mingled. She could just see his trousers out of the corner of her eye, and his sleeve, both smart but casual, the jacket probably a blazer, the sort with brass buttons.

"Isn't it a wonderful day!" the man said presently. He leant back on the bench, stretching out long legs in front of him contentedly, and the bars rippled again beneath Rosemary, who shifted a little uncomfortably and agreed, rather feebly, she thought, in a surprisingly silly sort of high pitched voice; act your age, she told herself unkindly.

"Best Spring for years," said the man. He looked at ease. Rosemary looked at his profile, which was handsome. All his actions had been full of physical ease, of confidence, and this intimidated her a little. They sat for a while in silence, their eyes on the sea.

"Used to come here as a boy," said the man eventually. "There were so many boats then. Not just these monster ferries. Funny looking things, don't you think? More like floating tower blocks than ships!"

One of the ferries was heaving into view as he spoke, far out from the port several miles along the coast.

"They're quite nice in winter," said Rosemary shyly after a pause during which she had framed several possible versions of this remark, rejected them, and decided at last to take the first one after all, "you can

72

take day trips to France in them, very reasonable, and they're so quiet, half empty."

"Ah, you're a native. Of these parts, I mean," he added with a smile, and this made him look so dazzlingly handsome that Rosemary could only gaze at him, smiling.

"I've lived here all my life," she said at last.

"Lovely little place," said the man.

"Well it's mad at high season," said Rosemary with more of her usual animation. "Mind you it always was, 'cept then the trippers came by train, and now of course it's all cars." She fell silent, thinking she was being boring.

"We always came down by train when I was a kid," said the man. "The Riviera Express! Good old steam train, right beside the sea! We used to think it was wonderful." He crossed his legs, and sighed. "Didn't take much to please us," he added lightly.

"Our treat," said Rosemary, "was breakfast on the beach. Of course we were used to the seaside. But sometimes in the summer we used to get up very early, and walk right out round the point, that one, and we'd build a fire, and have a quick swim, so's you were, you know, good and cold, absolutely freezing, and then we'd boil a kettle and make tea and cook bacon and eggs and have a lovely breakfast on the beach."

"And go home just as the ordinary holiday crowd arrived," said the man.

"Oh, yes! Grockles, we called them."

They both laughed, and then there was a little pause. Rosemary watched the ferry, by now a tiny ship-shaped dot, disappear at last into the bright mingled blues.

The man moved suddenly, uncrossing his legs, turning towards her. He's off, thought Rosemary, with a little tremor of anticipatory sorrow. She smiled in farewell.

"My name's Gregory Banks," said the man, and he took off the trilby. The hair beneath was grey, thinning, and looked a little damp from the hat brim. He looked much more vulnerable bareheaded, altogether less jaunty. "I hope you don't mind me talking to you?"

"No, no of course not. Um, Rosemary Sholto. Hello!"

They shook hands.

"Now what I need, I don't mind telling you," said Gregory, "is a decent cup of tea. Do you happen to know a good place somewhere, not too far? And of course, would you care to join me? I should be so very grateful if you would."

"Oh. That would be nice," said Rosemary, and so it was.

CHAPTER
EIGHT

On the following day, Monday, Miss Troy received a letter from the city Eye Hospital twenty miles away, giving the date and time of her appointment with the specialist. She read it with some difficulty; it was one of her bad days. Even holding the letter up to the window, she was, she found, able to read it only one word at a time, and a further leaflet, detailing various ways of reaching the hospital, was in print so fine she had to put it away for later.

She went to sit by her window. The beech tree waved in blocks of colour, its trunk a dark blur. Shapes stood at the bus stop; at intervals mistier shapes collected by the zebra crossing and disappeared as they crossed the road.

For a moment Miss Troy allowed herself to despair. It seemed to her then that all her life she had wanted, consciously or otherwise, a room with a view, that she had forced herself to do without, told herself again and again that views after all did not really matter, that it was what one saw inside the room, what one felt and read and wrote, that mattered.

She had moved many times in her life, lived abroad, worked for many different people and companies, followed orders, done her best over and over again, asked little, never taken anything she was not prepared to give herself and now, at the end, when she by chance, by mere luck, had a view she loved, a view full of natural beauty and jolly human life, now, after just a few weeks, she could sit here and stare all she liked: she could see nothing.

They would make her move anyway; someone as blind as she was that morning would not be allowed to live at Cabotin Court, but would be sent instead to one of its two related nursing homes, where all the horrors of blankest senescence surely awaited, the rows of beds, the shared and public commode, the strangers, the handling.

Presently Miss Troy realised what she was doing and was able firmly to stop herself doing it. Pointless to agonise over these things before you had to. Suppose after all the doctors could do something? Suppose anyway it got better by itself, as it had before? And besides, Miss Troy told herself, you were right the first time, the View is merely symbolic. And I have been lucky; I have had all that it symbolises.

Though of course I was hardly as pretty as Lucy Honeychurch, Forster's heroine; Lucy with straight hair and spectacles, thought Miss Troy, with a snigger, at the same time suddenly remembering Rudolph, a tremendously good-looking and silly boy who had briefly worked at the film studios when she had been continuity girl. Who was it poor Rudolph had so incontinently compared her to? Some dizzily classical reference. Erato, Euterpe? Beauty, gentleness, and courtesy: the graces.

"I bought it for you."

"What is it?"

"It's just a little present."

"Rudy. I don't want a little present, I don't want anything."

"Please open it."

"Oh, very well, Rudy, this is all so, so . . ."

She disclosed a little plaster figurine, very delicate, slightly chipped.

"It's only Victorian," said Rudolph apologetically. "But look, don't you see?"

"See what?"

"Well it's you! Look! Isn't she! So beautiful!"

"Euphrosyne," said Miss Troy aloud now, with poor Rudolph. How embarrassed she had been! It was bewildering to realise how wrong someone could be about you; made you for a moment doubt all the great canon of literary and poetical love.

"Honestly, Rudy! She doesn't look a bit like me. Where's her glasses? Where's her shingle?"

Oh, but his face then! Such clumsy teasing.

"Actually I have a much better figure than that," she had said, flustered by the pain in his eyes, and realised as she spoke that she could hardly have hit on anything more apparently designed to inflame him, which was indeed the pattern of their relationship thus far.

Perhaps I really was doing it on purpose, thought Miss Troy, noting herself to be prepared to concede this point after the passage of some sixty-five years. Without knowing it, of course. I had no trust in my powers, and quite right too. It was still Euphrosyne he was in love with, not me. An idea of me. Though perhaps that would not have mattered to me if I had been in love with my idea of him. Appealing, his pretty child's face, but that was all.

For a little while Miss Troy thought of Charles, whom she had met and loved many years later, and of the great wealth of happiness he had brought her. All the View anyone needed.

Then she sat up straight, concentrating. Things were definitely clearer, she thought. Greyer, too, the sun had gone in. Evidently her sight was the worse for bright weather. I see only under grey skies, thought Miss Troy, now there's a bloody great symbol if you like. And I don't like.

I'll have to be jolly careful at lunch, that's all. And hope it's not spaghetti.

CHAPTER
NINE

Betty Potts, who had risen very early, had zipped
through her routine Monday morning duties, made a
few telephone calls, spent some time examining a street
map of the area, and then gone to catch a bus into
town. It was another fine sunny day and Betty felt very
well as she stood at the bus stop, full of energy and
strong intent. She admired the weathered brickwork of
Cabotin's back walls, and even gave a little wave to a
face she could just see through the leaves of the big tree
across the road, a second floor someone, Cameron?
Dobbs? The face made no response. Suit yourself,
thought Betty indifferently. For nothing, no madden-
ingly dopey inmate or tardy bus, could reach her today.
Her excitement was like armour.

To think!

After all this time!

Every so often Betty remembered again: that first
stunning shock, and then waking up dazed and
disbelieving, and dreadfully cold and wet from all that
milk, and the fuss:

"No, don't try to get up —"

"Deep breaths!"

"Should I call an ambulance?"

"Put her feet up, no, no, her feet, Betty, just putting your feet up a bit, how are you feeling now dear, any better, yes?"

Betty had never fainted before. She was immensely pleased with herself for doing something so dramatic. And of course as it happened fainting had got her out of a very tight corner. How on earth would she have managed any approach at normality faced with that woman? It would have been impossible, the Friends would all have thought she had gone mad. As it was the tea had been more or less abandoned and Betty presently left in peace to get over the first shock.

"Oh and I'm sorry, I didn't catch your name!," she had murmured to the new one, that one, as the last goodbyes and are-you-quite-sures were being said. Caught her eye, too, and known herself not recognised.

"I'm Valerie, Valerie Elliott."

Oh, no you're not!

The bus came panting up beside her, and Betty nipped lightly inside. What to do, what to do eventually, was still an open question. She sat back as the bus chugged heavily round the high garden walls of Cabotin, where once the inmates had toiled over vegetable patches. And there, the front elevation: the neat flagstones, the stone tablet commemorating the founder and set into the wall just above the arch of the double front doors, the robust fluted chimneys, showing where the cooking fires of the Great Hall once blazed, the pretty Victorian gas brackets, the Jakes-gate.

Oh yes, the gate. Well, thought Betty, that would be the first thing to go. If things went according to plan.

Not that there is a plan, thought Betty hastily. I'm just doing a bit of research. Just exploring possibilities. Like: if it's a big house, if it's one of the houses I think it is, out on the coast road, then that's money, that means real money.

She's married someone. Obviously.

Betty paused in her humming for a moment, struck by the possibility that the woman calling herself Valerie Elliott might have somehow made all the money herself. Well, some women did, of course. It was an uncomfortable thought. A successful business woman; Betty did not know any of those, had hardly met one. Wouldn't such a creature necessarily be a little hard-bitten, and resourceful, perhaps tricky to deal with? Such a person might somehow assume some upper hand over a mere employee. She thought back, remembering what she could of general appearance, not the face, which of course was vividly complete in her memory, but the clothes, the handbag, the pose.

No. That was no businesswoman, that was a Friend. The floaty dress, the heels. So soppy, thought Betty. And that smile, winsome. And you didn't combine Friendship with a working life. No; you were a Friend if you had nothing else to be.

And if you had money. The bus had reached the town centre, and began its long meandering circuit round the high street, which was now all pedestrian precinct. Already hordes of people were surging about, despite the hour. Consumers, thought Betty disgustedly. So much dross! Every one of them a Flora Jakes, greedy for new plastic. Everywhere the Flora Jakeses

81

were winning, they were covering England with roads and inexpressibly vulgar houses and giant malls and car-parks; they liked easy access; they liked toilet facilities. Betty sucked her teeth, enjoyably hot with hatred. This would be a small blow struck, perhaps. It would not take much, to de-Jakes Cabotin.

The bus, at last in higher gear, bowled along the promenade, and out beyond it to the town's quieter reaches. Two stops, and Betty, a little stiff but still rejoicing, descended, consulted her map, and walked on. Here the road was deeply fringed with tall old trees, the houses barely glimpsed through gates at the end of long gravelled twisting drives. Victorian, here, jolly and pointed, with occasional Gothic turrets and charming twiddley bits of metalwork ornamenting eaves and gables. Even longer gaps, now, between the houses; not gardens so much as grounds. This one? Betty stopped, her heart beating quite fast, and looked again at the little note she had made on her map's margin. No. The next one. She folded the map up again, and walked on. Several minutes passed.

At last she reached a gatepost, stone, with twin pineapples carved into their tops. A curved metal gate, very slender. Unlocked. Betty clicked it open, entered. And why not? Why shouldn't I?

The gravel crunched beneath her feet. Everything looked very neat. Must have a gardener, then. Apple trees. Laburnum. Lily pond. And there!

Betty stood still, looking. A Georgian house, a mellow beauty, with a nice little arch over its fan lit front door, windows of perfect symmetry, a graceful friendly human face. Creeper up one side. French doors at the back, thought Betty hungrily, opening out onto the gentle lawns and big shady trees.

This is where she lives. Well, well, well. Satisfied for now, Betty turned and started on the long trip back home again, telling herself that she could now go into all the possibilities; though really she knew that there was only one, and that she had already determined to act upon it.

CHAPTER
TEN

Mrs Derry noticed something straight away.

"Oh, are you quite well this morning?"

"Perfectly, thank you."

"Only I hope you don't mind my saying that you look a bit pale in fact."

"Too many late nights, I expect."

Mrs Derry tittered affably.

"What is it today, do you know?"

"Oh, er, chicken something, I think. Shall I pour you some water? There. It's by your hand.

"Thank you," said Miss Troy, rather impressed despite herself. She had no idea how Mrs Derry could have noticed her disability so quickly; but then she also had no real idea of the consuming and thus highly observant interest Mrs Derry felt in all her acquaintance. The chicken, she found with relief, was stewed and forkable. She ate carefully.

"Want some more mash? Sure? These big windows are a bit dazzley, aren't they, I can hardly see what I'm doing myself sometimes, you're not seeing arcs round lamps, are you dear, at night?"

"I'm sorry?"

"Because that would be glaucoma. You need to get that sorted out right away, I mean, delay can be dangerous, you know, are you seeing arcs?"

"I don't think so . . ."

"And if it's worse in sunlight, is it worse in sunlight?

"Well, I —"

". . . then it's probably cataract, you've seen your GP haven't you? What did he say? Have you seen your GP?'

This is communal living, Miss Troy reminded herself. This is a price one pays, graciously or otherwise.

"Oh, yes."

"What did he think?"

Wants to bore someone with me, thought Miss Troy. Well, that seems only fair. "He seemed unwilling to commit himself," she said.

"Oh, but you must see a specialist!"

"I'm going to, next week."

"Then I'll come with you, shall I? You'll need someone with you. I'd be glad to, what day is it?"

Miss Troy began to panic; she looked into the mental slot where plausible and courteous excuses were usually ready to hand, and groped, and found nothing.

"I'm afraid I, I can't quite . . ."

". . . remember the date, no, I'll pop in later shall I, when you've checked, there, that's settled!"

"Well, I —"

At this moment, seated on Miss Troy's other side, Annie Cameron had the blood-stained man digging flash again, so suddenly that she jumped, somehow sweeping her hands sideways in front of her, and knocking into Miss Troy's water glass, which spun round, hesitated for a moment, and then fell, emptying its contents over the table and into Miss Troy's lap.

"Crumbs," said Miss Troy weakly. She did not try to move. She looked down. There it lay, a neat triangle of cold water over her crotch. She sat motionless as it began to soak into the green tweed of her skirt.

"Oh dear," said Mrs Derry, whose face had been splashed, and who had make-up to consider. She dabbed at herself rather anxiously with a paper serviette.

"Take." Fidelis, unsmiling as usual, suddenly appeared beside Miss Troy's chair, proffering a tea-towel.

"Oh, actually I think I'd better —"

Fidelis put one hand under Miss Troy's arm, and pulled rather hard. Miss Troy rose shakily to her feet. Her armpit hurt where Fidelis had hauled her.

"Better change," said Fidelis, scanning the words almost into another language altogether. Still she did not smile, and Miss Troy, horrified, realised that she herself was near tears, wet and trembling and going blind, blind.

"That was me," said someone, briefly touching Miss Troy's arm. Miss Troy turned automatically, forgetting again that the machinery no longer worked, that she could no longer take in anything at a glance. A faceless blur addressed her. "I'm so sorry. I'm so clumsy," said the blur.

"Quite all right," said Miss Troy, jerkily brushing herself down with the tea-towel. She was calmed

86

instantly by her own voice, which sounded as it always did, light, amused, relaxed. "It's only water, after all."

"But so cold," remarked the blur. There was something in this that gave Miss Troy pause, a faint playful awareness.

"Jolly cold actually," she said, half-smiling.

"Come on," said Mrs Derry on the other side, recovered and clearly hoping to regain the initiative, "I'll come with you, you need to get yourself changed." She reached across and laid a proprietary arm round Miss Troy's shoulders.

"Anything wrong here? What's happening?" It was Rosemary Sholto, judging by the bulk. "D'you need to sit down, dear? Let her sit down please."

"I'm perfectly all right, really."

"Looks a bit . . ."

"Terribly pale, yes . . ."

"I'll come with you," said the blur. "It was my fault. No, I spilt my water that's all, it was me. Come on, I'm just opposite you anyway."

"So kind," murmured Miss Troy, trying to slide out from Mrs Derry's embrace in a natural casual manner, though on the whole she suspected that there was no hiding physical rejection, and that even someone as impenetrably dense as Kate Derry would feel it somehow in her heart.

In the relative darkness of the corridor she could see much better.

"Oh, it's you," she said aloud, as they stood beside the lift.

Annie took some seconds to work this out. "Who did you think it was?"

"I couldn't see."

"But you can now?"

"Well, I can see more."

"Would you like some coffee? When you're dry and all?"

"Um, well, yes, I would, thank you."

"Right, it's number fifteen, almost opposite. Just come in, I'll leave the door ajar."

"Thank you."

In her own flat Miss Troy felt her way through her wardrobe. She had only one other skirt suitable to the weather, and it would probably look very odd with the blouse she had on already, but she had no other ironed blouse, ironing being one of the many ordinary chores that required decent eyesight. Well, then; she would just have to look odd.

But, she found, she did not want to look odd. It was irritating, but she would just have to put her best dress on. After all, Annie Cameron would not know it was her best dress; no, indeed, thought Miss Troy, no one would ever guess that. She felt along the hangers for the velveteen collar, and realised as she fought the dress over her head that she actually felt a little excited. Going on a date, thought Miss Troy, wondering at herself.

The door of number fifteen, as promised, stood open. Outside it Miss Troy hesitated. It seemed quite wrong to go in without knocking, and yet she knew that

Annie would not hear a knock. Or would she? Had she had the hearing aid switched on before, or not?

"Hello?" Miss Troy pushed the door wide, and stood on the threshold. Annie was standing by her window. Her flat was like Miss Troy's seen through a mirror, though of course without the beech tree, which from Miss Troy's own doorway seemed to fill the view.

"Hello?"

Annie turned round. "Come in!"

"Thank you." Miss Troy closed the door behind her, aware as she did so of a delicious smell of real coffee. "I'm none the worse, as you can see." Most of this little speech, as Miss Troy turned away from the door, was invisible and thus unintelligible to Annie, who decided however that it was almost certainly of the small-talk-rhetorical variety that hearing people most hated being asked to say twice, and thus merely smiled encouragingly in reply.

For a moment Miss Troy felt slightly thrown. But of course, she thought, it is a question of what one thoughtlessly expects. I say, *none the worse, as you can see,* stoutly, playfully, and so expect her to say something like *good, good,* in the same tones. But she hasn't, and it's as if she's let me speak stoutly and playfully all on my own. Makes you feel rather a fool somehow. Best speak up a bit, she thought.

"Do you need me to close the curtains?" asked Annie.

Miss Troy considered. "I think not," she said loudly. "Diminishing returns. I'll be all right if it stays cloudy."

"Good," said Annie, "because if I make it any darker I won't be able to see you well enough to catch what you're saying. I need a good light, you see."

Light? wondered Miss Troy. So she's lip-reading, then. I suppose. "Between us we would make one reasonably effective human being, it seems," she said.

Annie laughed. "Who was it had one eye and one tooth between them? Please, sit down."

Miss Troy remembered remembering that she had once been compared to the Graces, and smiled to herself. "There were three of them, I think," she said. "The Grey Ones? The Grey Sisters?"

"Yes," said Annie, pouring coffee from the percolator. "And they get hoodwinked by someone in a cloak of invisibility, the old cloak-of-invisibility routine, you'd think a hero would have been able to get the better of such poor old folk without needing to pull tricks like that. Milk and sugar?"

"Just milk, please." Miss Troy looked about her, noting a pretty mirror-stand on a decent chest of drawers, a crammed bookshelf, and several library books in a pile on the coffee table, of a literary nature, judging by their covers, as of course you nearly always could these days.

"Have you been at Cabotin long?" she asked.

"Sorry, missed that."

"Have you been at Cabotin long?"

Annie hesitated. It was unfortunate that there seemed to be no inoffensive way of saying what she had to say. Somehow being given instructions, even in the mildest manner, generally seemed to put people's backs up, or maybe just made them self-conscious, so that conversation tended to die the death anyway; nevertheless it had to be said, and quickly:

"I'm sorry, it makes things worse if you shout, the machine can only take so much, it just turns everything into noise if there's too much sound."

"Oh. So, you're not lip-reading?"

"Yes, now that's just right, as if you were demonstrating pronunciation to a foreigner. Am I lip-reading? Well, yes, most of the time. But it helps to get the odd clue now and then. I know hearing people tend to assume that deaf people just learn to lip-read, well, it's not quite as simple as that. It's not like reading and writing. It's more like playing the violin. Everyone can try to learn. But not everybody will be able to play a tune."

"Can you?"

"I scrape by." They smiled at each other, Miss Troy suddenly relaxed, even cheerful.

"I'm just guessing, mainly," Annie went on. "If you know the context you can guess a good deal."

But that must rather limit conversation, thought Miss Troy.

"Books are so much easier. Someone says something, and you're told how, languidly, nonchalantly, slyly. But I can't get that in real life, I can't lip-read it. Can't always guess it either."

"And sometimes of course it completely alters the meaning of a speech."

"Yes. It's tough talking to deaf people. We can't take a joke."

"Only obvious ones."

"And they're not the best ones, are they?"

"I suppose not. Have you always been deaf?"

"Oh no. I know I sound a bit strange. A Scottish robot, I've been told. But if I'd been born deaf you probably wouldn't be able to understand me at all. My husband was born deaf, and anyone hearing him trying to speak tended to think he was defective. I was lucky, I was eight when I began to go deaf."

"Lucky?"

"Any younger and I would have forgotten how to speak. Well, maybe at seven you'd have hung onto some of it. But four or five, you'd forget."

There was a pause. Miss Troy saw a small girl sitting on a bed, the deafened child, slowly losing speech, knowing fewer and fewer words day by day, able still to join in with some of the games, smiling more, tentatively, saying less. Forgetting how to speak: the notion somehow made her stomach clench with fright. To lose not only hearing but language itself, the very stuff of humanity! What could be more terrifying, more lonely? And of course, she thought, live long enough and all these horrors get to have another go.

"Anyway I was sent away to deaf school. I got found out by the school inspector. I'd been trying to hide it. But all the doctor had to do was turn me round. Then I didn't know what she was saying. I know she said to my mother, You've a fine girl here, mother, but she's stone deaf. My mother wouldn't look at me, well, I know she had some idea that I was a judgement on her. She was very bitter that she'd tried so hard to be a

God-fearing woman and was actually a good deal more virtuous than a great many other women she could point the finger at, but all the same she's the one that gets landed with the stone-deaf child. She took it very hard."

"This was — when was it?"

"Just after the 14-18 War."

"Ah." Miss Troy put her cup down. "I was sent away to school too. When I was seven."

"I thought they only did that to boys."

Miss Troy thought. Annie's use of *they* had suddenly made it clear to her how great the divide had been between them, when they and the twentieth century were young. Our paths would never have crossed, she thought, and if they had I would not have been allowed to talk to her, and she would not have dared to talk to me. How strange it seems!

"I didn't have any brothers, or sisters," said Miss Troy. "My mother needed to recline a great deal, on sofas, and I rather got in the way."

"Was she ill, then?"

"Oh, hungover, probably. Neurotic, certainly."

"I was one of seven. We only had the two rooms," said Annie. She smiled. "It must have been a relief to everyone getting rid of me."

"I was sent to a very select academy in Shropshire."

"A Wentworth Home. Have you heard of those?"

Miss Troy shook her head.

"Used to be quite a few of them. Schooling and training for the blind and deaf."

"Not together, surely?"

"No no. Separate schools really. Just at the same place, that's all. Though it came in handy, of course. If they wanted to punish you they could send you over to the blind side. Or if one of the blind children misbehaved they got sent over to us, for a day, or for the morning."

"But that's . . ." Miss Troy was silent, working out for a moment the implications of being blind among the deaf, or deaf among the blind. "That was monstrous."

"Well, it's certainly something no one could inflict on a normal child. Does that make it worse? They didn't hit us very much. Which was fairly unusual in those days."

"Did it ever happen to you?"

"Once. But I was fourteen and not so fragile. I could talk to them, I could guess fairly well at what they were saying. It was much worse for the born-deaf, the ones who could hardly speak at all. The blind can't see you signing, and the deaf can't hear the blind speak. Quite neat, really. Symmetrical."

"Revolting."

"It was a long time ago. What was your school like?"

"It was very good. The headmistress was, oh, an HG Wells-ish, New Woman-type. Very energetic and principled. But kind and sensible, I was really very lucky."

"But you were only seven?"

"Yes. A little too young at first. I grew out of that." Oh, and it was myself I saw, sitting on the bed, not deaf but utterly bereft, lonely, speechless with misery and confusion, forgetting how to speak.

"I missed my nanny terribly."

She had meant this last to sound slightly ironic, but was surprised to hear her voice crack with emotion, as if it were acting on its own initiative. She remembered yesterday's powerful dream, and the lovely clear, stingingly clear, picture of Maisie's dear face.

But Annie will not have heard my voice break. How easy it would be to lie to her. Strange thought.

"What did you do when you left school, did you go to university?" What was it in this speech which implied so clearly that Annie would have liked to go there herself? The change in emphasis was so small, thought Miss Troy. And she won't actually have heard it herself. She can't hear transparency, not even her own. So can deaf people lie? Perhaps only to other deaf people?

"No," said Miss Troy aloud. "As a matter of fact I got a job. With a cousin of my father's, nepotism but I was jolly good so I always felt it didn't count. In the film industry."

"The what, sorry?"

Miss Troy smiled; hearing people tended to say that too. "My father's cousin's firm was a film studio. There was a fairly lively British film industry in the Twenties. The studios were in Putney, I think it was four houses in a row. Impossibly homespun these days. I had a marvellous time."

"What did you do?"

"Oh, lots of things. I started off in continuity, making sure that if the hero strode into the parlour in checked trousers he didn't wander out again in stripes. Ordering and numbering scenes. Later on I was in the script department. I really wanted to write, you see."

"And did you?"

"Reams," said Miss Troy shortly. "Were you a picture goer?"

"Well I was. Once I'd left school and got married. I'd no chance of going before that, there wasn't a cinema within reach and anyway everybody disapproved so much, there was a lot of Calvinism alive and kicking in those days, I think the idea was that enjoying something nice might somehow lead you on into enjoying something wicked, so it was best to stay away from any temptation to have a nice time at all, just to be on the safe side." Annie laughed. "So Edward and I used to go every week. Well, you know as well as I do: they were silent films. Films for deaf people. And now I've met someone that used to make them, I'm honoured!"

Miss Troy grinned. "Oh, I met all the stars."

"Yes?"

"Lorna McIntyre. Roderick Tremain. Evaline da Costa, no, no, don't worry, no one else has ever heard of them either. They were stars, but perhaps they did not twinkle for very long. Once I sat next to Evaline da Costa at lunch. We all used to eat together, director, lighting technicians, actors, everyone having the same hot dinner cooked in the back kitchen of number twelve! She was so beautiful, I could hardly look at her for fear of not being able to stop. Oh and the cook had a cat and sometimes if it jumped on your lap you would smell delicious perfume, because it had spent the morning lying on the lap of some exquisite actress

96

waiting for her call after a set change, I remember it so clearly, the perfumed fur."

"I expect there were some wonderful parties."

"Sometimes at the Savoy," said Miss Troy, happy to oblige, "in order to impress the distributors and sweeten the critics, well, that was the idea. And there would be people from all over the place, especially from the States, looking for talent, looking for anything or anyone they could use. We used to dress up, we were always dressing up in those days. I used to borrow jewellery from my mother, once a faux-pearl necklace broke on the dance-floor and all the cast and crew were grovelling for my pearls, made a game of it, and the best-looking young man in the world gave them back to me, wrapped up in his handkerchief, which I kept for years, because he was Ronald Colman."

"Oh my! Oh, I remember him! Did you dance with him?"

"No." Miss Troy began to laugh, it was still so funny even now, "I'll tell you who I did have a dance with, mind you I think he was a bit tight, but it was Clark Gable, when I was in Los Angeles, yes, me and Scarlett O'Hara, it's not everyone who can say they have waltzed with Rhett Butler!"

"Rhett Butler! He didn't give a damn."

"No, no he didn't, more's the pity, I wasn't his type at all, I'm afraid."

"Tell me all about it."

"There's really nothing more to tell," said Miss Troy. "I met lots of well-known people in the States, but really only to look at, you know, I was in the same room as them and that was about it."

"Who, though?"

Miss Troy leant forward, and began.

CHAPTER
ELEVEN

Mrs Dobbs, whose flatlet shared its bathroom with Miss Troy's, had been taken out for the afternoon by her youngest daughter. They had visited a garden centre, where Sheila had bought a very small azalea for the sort of money Mrs Dobbs' own father would have taken about a year to earn, as she had pointed out to Sheila, who had said, "Oh, mum!" in an exasperated voice. Mrs Dobbs was puzzled and hurt by this, for she was completely unaware of the many, many times she had already compared her father's earnings with various outgoings of her daughter's; usually Sheila was able to receive such information gracefully enough but she had worries of her own that afternoon.

Mrs Dobbs had come home tired and rather dispirited and had sat drooping on her bed for some time, unable to rouse herself so much as to take her coat off. But then, all of a sudden, she had remembered. She had sat up straight, then stood up almost quickly. How could she have forgotten? She hadn't thought of it once, all afternoon! Or perhaps she was wrong, and it wasn't today after all. Well, it was definitely Monday. Wasn't it? Yes. She riffled through her handbag, found her reading glasses, and checked with the *Radio Times*.

"10.00 City Pride Rosalind stands up to Ernest K. Delamar, and Frankie's ex-wife is called to the stand . . ."

Mrs Dobbs cheered up instantly. Oh, Jerry and Paula staking out the harbour, alone in their cramped little van, anything was possible. She checked her wristwatch: some four hours to go. She would go to bed early, she thought, and read until just before.

She washed her face and hands and made a thermos flask of tea and a hot water bottle. She put two curlers in her hair at the front, and a hairnet over all. Over her nightdress she put on a garment knitted by herself, an immensely lengthy rectangle of pale purple wool, its edges sewn together at either end into tubes, through which Mrs Dobbs inserted each arm: a sort of shawl with sleeves, and a very practical item, especially for reading or knitting in bed.

(Mrs Dobbs had no idea of the effect of this garment on her visiting children and grandchildren, but then, neither had they, really. None of them will discuss it or so much as mention it until Mrs Dobbs is dead, when they will be able tearfully to laugh at the horrors of her wardrobe in the poignant knowledge that they will never have to look at it again.)

But now, unaware of the depressions instantly inflicted by her bed jackets, Mrs Dobbs sits tensely upright in her bed, in the grip of passion. Not her own,

100

of course, or rather, not entirely her own; hers remembered, through the urgent medium of print.

The sea was very pale now, almost milky. Laura, looking out, thought that the very air seemed to be holding its breath.

"Laura!"

She turned. Knew, before she turned, who it was that stood waiting.

"Alistair!"

Impulsively she took a step forward. Then stopped, stricken with a sort of fear. She scanned his face, the face that, at last, she knew she loved. A terrible regret swept over her. This is what it will feel like, she thought. This is what it will feel like forever, because he should have been mine. He offered me everything and I threw it all away. This is just the beginning.

She began to tremble, her whole body seemed to recognise its loss. This is our parting, she told herself, and I must play my part, so that when I look back on the day when I lost everything, everything, I will at least still have a little pride.

"It's good to see you," she said at last. She sounded, she thought, cool, collected. "I'm so glad everything turned out so well for you. How is Helen?"

"Very well. As far as I know."

Her heart gave a great bound inside her. She felt suddenly that she could hardly breathe. She turned, and laid both her hands along the parapet, feeling the sun-warmed stone beneath her fingers. Dimly she heard footsteps, as he neared her. She raised her head, staring unseeingly out to sea.

"Laura," he said.

His voice broke. She turned. For a moment she felt paralysed, physically unable to move, unable to risk looking up into his eyes. What would she read there? Gentleness, forgiveness, friendship? Or the despairing passion she had, oh surely, heard in that broken whisper of her name?

Courage, she thought to herself, and looked up. His soul was in his eyes. She put up a hand to caress his cheek, and he caught the hand to kiss the palm.

"Oh, Alistair, I've been such a fool . . ."

Now she was in his arms, and their kiss seemed to last forever, and still to end too soon.

Cor, thought Mrs Dobbs happily, lying back on her pillows. She had read this one many times before. But though she knew the story, and all the time remembered Laura going off with Alistair at the end just as she, Violet Dobbs, had once come to what was in those days called an understanding with dear Joe, she could only remember Joe's first kiss, not experience it, as Laura and Alistair did, whenever Mrs Dobbs felt like setting them off again. Laura and Alistair were not remembering: it was always happening now, and their eternal present brought the past alive.

Not that Mrs Dobbs was really thinking of herself or of Joe. It was excitement she was summoning, and the thrilling hopefulness of love, to cheer her through a night alone at home, in her eighty-seventh year.

And very cheering it was. She checked her watch. Still only nine thirty-five. She hesitated for a little, then picked up the telephone on her bedside table, dialled, and by luck secured her youngest grandchild, who was fourteen and doing his Physics homework. Gladly they chatted for nearly twenty minutes, or rather, she listened happily while he talked, in his bold new tenor, to an extent that would have astonished and even rather vexed his mother, to whom he had for some time now answered only in monosyllables.

Though in the not too distant future he will remember, with a pang, how he has sent several of his friends into fits of giggles by describing his grandmother's intestinal rumblings and taste in knitwear.

For now Mrs Dobbs, satisfied, hung up carefully after her last "God bless," and, though there were still some minutes to go, picked up the remote, aimed it at the television, and switched on. If only she had one of those new video things like her daughter, that could record everything for you! Then you could watch the best bits over and over again. That might almost be too much.

Mrs Dobbs settled back, in thrilling hopefulness.

CHAPTER
TWELVE

The following week saw several appointments made, and kept, at Cabotin Court. Alethea Troy asked Annie Cameron in for coffee; Rosemary arranged to meet Gregory Banks for lunch at a little place on the sea-front; and Betty invited Valerie Elliott to take a little tour of Cabotin Court, to make up, she said, for the unfortunate cancellation of the usual Friends' tea.

Annie had had a few moments of uneasiness following her pleasant afternoon with Miss Troy. As soon as she was back in her own flat she had suddenly felt doubtful. Was it possible, she wondered, that Miss Troy might have, well, exaggerated a little? Embroidered? Or even made everything up completely out of some crazed desire to impress and entertain? If Miss Troy was really some sort of half-mad compulsive liar, then a dance with Clark Gable or a flirtation with Ronald Coleman was exactly the sort of thing half-mad compulsive liars might be expected to claim. Miss Troy had not of course seemed at all mad. But that might just be her cunning. Or due to Annie's own deafness; perhaps a hearing person would have noticed all sorts of obvious clues.

On the other hand it had been such fun, at the time. They had seemed in tune with one another. She had made Miss Troy laugh about the hapless manglers and Mary Jane Rawlings calling herself a lady's maid, and when she was leaving Miss Troy had said that there were not many people left who called her Alethea, and she would like it if Annie did, so would she, please?

Perhaps it had all been a fake. In which case all that sudden delightful feeling of friendship had also been false. It was somehow very tiring thinking such things. All the next day Annie kept largely to her flat, and had to lie down more than once. For a few days she had come down to lunch very late, since she had noticed how early Alethea always was, and kept to her flatlet instead of visiting the communal sitting room; but you could hardly hope to avoid someone for long in an institution.

On the Friday Alethea had simply approached her at the table, tapped her on the shoulder, and asked her to visit.

"Bib-bib?"

"Coffee," Alethea mouthed. "Do join me, please." Their eyes met as she smiled and Annie suddenly wondered if she hadn't been right the first time after all. Why shouldn't a young pretty Alethea have danced with Clark Gable? Somebody must have.

All the same, when they had admired the view and the beech tree, whose leaves were so gloriously mobile, and Annie had taken a quick look round, noting the rather surprising cheap modern dull furniture, the desk crammed with papers, the books everywhere, piled beside the bed, lining the windowsill, and at least two-deep on top of the kitchen cupboards, she had noticed several fat battered volumes all together at one end of a book shelf, and wondered if there could be any subtle way of proving things one way or the other without letting Miss Troy, Alethea, suspect there had ever been any doubt.

"Oh, are those photograph albums?"

"Which, those, well, yes, would you like to . . ."

"Are there any of your time in the film studios?"

"My glory days, well, yes, some; d'you want to see them?"

"Oh, yes, yes please."

Alethea had hesitated. Annie had held her breath. Was she thinking up some plausible lie to account for several albums of the sort of babies-at-the-seaside picnic stuff nearly everybody else had?

"That one's just family, I think," said Alethea, "I haven't looked at the things for years, is it this one?" She was really talking to herself, had quite forgotten, for the moment, that Annie needed to see her to understand, and Annie missed all of this speech, which gave her a few extra moments of suspense before Alethea sat down beside her with the second of the albums, and opened it on her lap.

"Here you are. I'm afraid none of them are very good, I never was much of a hand with a camera. I didn't take them all, of course."

"Is that you?"

"Yes. Frightful hat."

Miss Troy, Alethea, a small curvy young woman, grinned a little awkwardly beneath an arched ironwork Wayward Bros over a doorway, held a clapperboard on which was chalked *Hard Going 13 take two*, offered a cup of tea to a woman dressed in a curious slack-waisted Twenties approximation of Elizabethan costume, ("that's Lorna McIntyre"), and smirked into the camera in front of what appeared to be an eighteenth century sailing shipful of waving deckhands, midshipmen, and full-dress Admirals.

"Wayward Brothers were simply nuts about Nelson," said Alethea. "Harry Wayward had an enormous flotation tank built somewhere out in Kent, on the marshes, to shoot the battle scenes. Like a huge paddling pool. Cost a fortune. It was Harry who was my father's cousin."

"Is that him?"

"Yes. Those are the main cameramen. That's me again. That dress. I look like a roll of carpet. That's Evaline da Costa, a publicity still. See what I mean? That's Studio Three, from the lighting gantry, oh, a sliding thing, high up, so you could move the lights without disconnecting everything. I don't know what that is. I think that one's Studio Two, I used to know which set it was . . . That's Forbes Campbell, one of the directors. That's from my first, no, second film, that was on location on Dartmoor, such a disaster, all sorts of things got broken or left behind in London, I was chasing up and down on the train almost every day, oh, that's a party, let me see, just before *Open Fire*, which was rather a hit, I'd have you know. I think."

"Who's that?"

"Oh. Oh yes. That's . . . Sally," said Alethea, and her tone would have made anyone hearing it sit up and take notice; hearing it herself, she had a moment's anxiety before remembering that of course poor Annie would be oblivious; not realising, naturally enough, how completely her face had mirrored her words, so that Annie, practised at reading the smallest of signs, had in fact missed nothing at all.

"An actress?"

"No," said Alethea after a pause. "Another continuity girl."

"Oh, who's that?" asked Annie, to change what was clearly a rather painful subject. "He looks like trouble."

"Now that was Stuart Tregear, a leading man, and he was lovely, unassuming, rather a wit, I agree he looks like Mr Rochester. Knickerbockers. And a Norfolk jacket. Those were some gardens, I can't remember why were we there. Oh crumbs, that's Rudy . . ."

The photographs were very small, and, as Alethea had said, rather blurred more often than not.

"Oh, that's it, that's the paddling pool thing. Very brief battle scenes and lots of swooning with Lady Hamilton. Love scenes come so much cheaper, you see."

Alethea, who had really not looked at her photographs for many years, was a little taken aback to find herself vexed, as of old, by her own appearance in them. Didn't one generally look back at one's younger self, and see at last the youthful beauty one had simply not believed in at the time?

Owlish and dowdy, thought Alethea now: clearly looking back didn't work for everyone, she concluded, with some amusement. Though of course the dresses of the nineteen-twenties could not have done less for the small and buxom. And gosh poor Rudolph looked not so much childish as actually a child; her memory, she noticed, had quietly matured him, presumably to make the remembrance of his lovelorn attentions more flattering to whichever small craven part of her still seemed to need that sort of thing.

And this one: she remembered that dress, a rather daring backless pale yellow shantung, could even remember checking herself earlier that evening before her mother's full-length looking-glass, when she had seen Billy Bunter in drag. (She had had no idea then how vividly the sight of her smooth milk-white shoulders had made any heterosexual male within range imagine the rest of her, creamily naked and inviting. Even now, confronted with the evidence, she sees the girl with her own mother's eyes.)

"Such a plain Jane. Not really up to much, are they? I didn't even put them in an album until —" Until when? When she had retired, and left London: more than twenty years ago.

"Oh, but they're really interesting," said Annie, in truth completely captivated. She had quite forgotten why she had wanted to see the photographs in the first place. Like the Cabotin notebook the pictures were history in themselves. And in layers. This Victorian street-scene, for example: it was a set, a mock-up, fascinating in itself; but the people walking about in it, some of the actors, most of the film crew, had really been Victorians, born well before the old queen's death. There they were, jokily posing in their crinolines or enormous top hats, cheerfully summoning up the past; yet the past had slowly engulfed them, and drawn them completely into itself.

Annie would have liked to take the album home with her, to study details as well: the Twenties shoe-styles, the headgear, the make-up, the handbags; and to memorise the incidental backgrounds, the sooty-black bits of London, a village street clearly of hardened earth, the glint of tramlines, the scruffy half-rural look of so many pre-War roads, where there were no parked cars, no white lines, no chevrons, no traffic islands. No traffic.

And in the foregrounds of these casual fragments of history, such interesting faces! Unfamiliar, all of them, but often startlingly good-looking, with the mysterious vehemence of glamour (*stars*, thought Annie reverently), and yet snapped unawares, unposed, in private: the beautiful Evaline da Costa hunched over a magazine, with all her hair at the front tied up in a row of little rags; a dreamboat of a Rear Admiral Nelson, limp in a deckchair, smoking a cigarette; a tableful at a supper party, vivid against a background of blur from the crowded dance floor behind them.

Why ever did you leave? Annie would have liked to ask, had it not seemed too direct.

"Were you working there long?"

"Five years. Then I felt like a change. That was when I went to America, I was a private secretary. To

110

Meredith Pope. Meredith and Nancy. Does that ring any bells?"

"Say again, sorry."

"Meredith and Nancy Pope, they were —"

"Did they write whodunits?"

"Yes, that's them, though actually I think they had a bash at everything at one time or another. Anyway they went to Hollywood in 1931, under contract, to make screenplays out of Sherlock Holmes. And I went with them. For a change."

"Did they —" began Annie, then stopped short. For a second she thought she was still looking at Alethea's photographs, at an unaccountable shot of Alethea herself, wrapped in a small towel, and crouching under a table, until the calm familiar voice spoke within, giving the picture a title: "*Six point eight.*"

"Bib-bib?" asked Annie aloud, in confusion. Six point eight? What was that supposed to mean? Oh, leave me alone, you bloody nuisance, thought Annie to the voice, not for the first time.

"Are you all right? Annie?"

What on earth had Alethea been doing half-naked under a table anyway? The likelihood of never finding out was such a distraction: she knew from experience that the small irritant mystery of it would get in the way of all attempts at normal conversation for some time.

"Och, a dizzy spell, it's nothing, sorry, there, I'm fine now. Meredith and Nancy Pope, I think I've read some of theirs. What did you have to do?"

"Oh, look after them, mainly. They were a very skittish pair. I did all the dull legal stuff, documentation, tickets, passports, luggage. And typing, of course. We went across America by train. From New York to the West Coast. That was how you got there from Europe, in those days. It took five days. I think. Greta Garbo was on the train too, in her own carriage, at least that's what we heard. She wouldn't come out."

"Wanted to be alone."

"Needed complete rest, we were told. But there were lots of other Hollywood people around. Technicians, producers. There were lots of parties, several going on at once, usually. It was really a very curious interlude, one felt life was almost suspended, in a particularly jolly and sociable limbo."

Alethea fell silent for a moment. Everything she had just said had been perfectly true, but so far from the whole truth that saying it had felt like a lie. She shrugged: it hardly mattered, after all.

"It was strange," she went on, "because the rhythm of the train after a day or two seems to get right inside you. I kept noticing myself wanting to talk in time to it, and once or twice I thought I noticed other people doing it, too. As one begins to copy someone else's accent, perhaps you can't grasp this? It's not exactly on purpose, it's as if some accents are catching, and the train was infectious . . ."

("Oh, Ilium dear, oh listen to this, listen to me, what shall I do? I just can't stop, oh help me please, you know what I've done, *I've caught the train!*"

112

Meredith, always so facetious. She had not known him well enough then to have kept her observations to herself; in Meredith's company only Meredith was allowed even the smallest spark of originality, and he had teased her about talking in Train as relentlessly as he had punned her surname; it was months before he had stopped lapsing into rhythm whenever he addressed her, but she had hardly been surprised when, leafing idly through the latest Meredith and Nancy Pope Inspector Henri mystery several years later, she had come across her own light-hearted speech, reproduced verbatim, and put into the mouth of the fluffy young ingénue who was clearly going to be Victim Number Two just before the end, Pope mysteries tending to run along regular tracks almost as closely, thought Alethea, as ever any train did.)

"Was it difficult, working for two people like that, I mean, married to each other?"

Alethea shook her head. "We all did whatever Meredith told us to. I suspected Nancy of being the better writer, but it was hard to tell, she had subsumed herself in him. He could be very charming, of course. He was terribly camp; it was rather a fashion at the time."

("Ilium darling. My very own Topless Towers. Just look at this beastly story. It's such a worry, and no one but me has ever noticed!"

"Noticed what, Meredith?"

"The Copper Beeches. The little boy. He's so unlovable. You know, his head's too big, and you should see him killing cockroaches with a slipper, three gone

113

before you could wink split splat splot, or words to that effect."

"Yes?"

"Well, this wretched big-bonced child has been taught by his disgusting papa to enjoy cruelty, and I suspect it's all so that you and I and all the other gentle readers don't care tuppence what happens to him at the end. We don't give him a thought. Conan Doyle clearly didn't. Kills off the kid's mother, loses him his nice new governess, shoots his dog, gets the disgusting old dad thrown in jail, and not a word, at the end, about what happens to him! There's nobody left to look after him anyway. And no one to care, because after all he's such a nasty little oik, and I call it irresponsible at the very least. What's he playing at, inventing children so nasty that no one will want to look after them? And all to get himself out of tying up a few loose ends, lazy sod. I've a good mind to insert a scene at the end showing the child sobbing and heartless Holmes giving him a clip round the earhole, just to make my feelings plain. What d'you think, Ilium?")

"He had such a lot of props, Meredith," said Alethea. "A silver filigree cigarette case, from Egypt. And a lighter with his initials engraved on it, people don't have these things any more, do they? He made great play with them, he knew he had beautiful hands." Then she yawned suddenly, helplessly; it had been some years since she had managed to stay awake for an entire afternoon.

Annie, noticing, peered at her watch, and exclaimed in surprise, and presently the visit was at an end.

"Oh, good luck at the hospital," she added at the door. "When is it again?"

"Next Monday."

"Not much notice!"

"A cancellation, I think."

"And Kate Derry's going with you."

"Well, no, actually. It turned out she had a prior engagement."

Their eyes met briefly, with very small smiles. There was a pause.

"Would it help if I came with you?"

"That's very kind of you, thank you, but I should hate to put you to so much trouble."

Annie hesitated. It was, she thought, impossible to tell what this really meant. Wasn't it the sort of thing Miss Troy's sort said when they really didn't want you? Wouldn't she have said just that to Kate Derry? Oh, I wonder what she was doing under the table, six point eight what, exactly?

"It wouldn't be any trouble," she said. "I'd quite like the ride, actually."

"Would you?"

"It's a bus, right?"

"Yes."

"Double-decker. We could sit on the top. Take a picnic."

Alethea laughed. "Well, if you're sure . . ."

"I might not be any use, mind."

"We've eyes and ears between us."

"Oh aye. The Grey Sisters. Right, then, that's a date!"

"Good," said Alethea.

CHAPTER
THIRTEEN

Betty had done what homework she could. She had telephoned Melanie Hapgood, and discovered that the new Friend was a widow, which was a little disappointing, but not necessarily a big drawback; that she had three children, all of whom were most satisfactorily engaged in various delightfully respectable professions; and that she had spent much of her married life abroad, as her husband had been, as Melanie put it, in oil.

"Left her very comfortably off."

Oh good, thought Betty, who had been considering her needs. The carpet would have to go, of course; if there were flagstones underneath it well and good, but if there were not the office should have some kind of hardwood floor. Oak would be very nice. The walls should be stripped and re-plastered, and the false ceiling of course removed and properly resurfaced. The furniture would be sent to Oxfam piecemeal, as suitable replacements were found for each item; I'm not insisting on antiques, thought Betty, knowing herself to be a reasonable person, just something solid, well-made and dignified without being heavy. Perhaps one really nice piece, a walnut corner cupboard, something like that. And the fire. Again, simple, nothing too ornate. Not a range, of course; one somehow could not replace something so specific and so obsolete. But a fireplace was different.

A few months earlier Betty had visited an old friend who had recently moved house. The new house had been large and Edwardian and not Betty's cup of tea at all, luckily, or the visit might not have gone off so well. As it was she could admire the big square rooms, the huge bay windows, the tiled hall and what was left of the stained glass with light-hearted insincerity.

One feature of the house, however, had given her pause. The main sitting room was dominated by an enormous fireplace of veined black marble, which Betty had gleefully thought quite hideous.

"Oh, lovely!" she had exclaimed, running her hand over its jetty mantelpiece, but felt all the same a familiar pang, for the lost little grates of Cabotin, ripped out and destroyed by that vandal Jakes while Gothic monsters like this survived.

"You know, you're lucky no one tore this out!"

Betty's friend had exchanged a happy little glance with her husband.

"It's not original!"

"What? D'you mean —"

"Yes, isn't it funny! I mean in our first house, d'you remember? We took all the fireplaces out, didn't we, George! And now here we are putting them all back in again."

"Focal point," said Betty.

"Yes, yes, it's a focal point. But look at this though . . ." And she had reached down, turned a knob, held it for a moment, and then clicked something else, and then lo! with a soft *whump* of ignition, the fire had lit itself.

"It's gas!"

"But —"

"Isn't it wonderful! See, you get all these flames! Looks completely real, doesn't it!"

"But what about the coal, won't it —"

"S'not coal! It's fibreglass. It doesn't burn, it just gets all red-hot looking, it glows, doesn't it, George! We got this firm in, they did everything, we just chose the fireplace, George keeps going to chuck things on it, don't you, George, orange peel and so on, 'course you can't, not really."

But there it was, the perfect answer. The awkward gap was even piped for gas already; all Betty had to do was get a firm in and choose her fireplace.

"I know it's foolish," she would say, lightly, "but it does look cosy, doesn't it?"

Perhaps, later on, the question of the gates might come up. Betty had not fully made up her mind. Even as it was, restraining herself to her office, she was most uncomfortably subject to sudden mysterious fits of trembling. She would be working away as calmly and purposefully as usual on some ordinary routine task and suddenly have to stop altogether, struck, it seemed, with the physical symptoms of terror, as if she had looked up from her word processor to find that a tiger had silently padded in through the office door.

118

Betty put these attacks down to excitement. She certainly was very excited, too excited to sleep very well. Often, sitting down to lunch or even in the act of raising a piece of toast to her lips at breakfast time, she would remember again the extraordinary chance that had befallen her, and feel far too excited to eat either. But this, she thought, was natural considering the admittedly unpleasant task that lay before her.

Firstly, she must entice Valerie Elliot into her office, on her own; then, she must apprise the woman of certain facts; then (obviously the worst part) make certain threats, sounding all the while like someone fully prepared to carry them out; and then name the sum involved. Betty had arrived at the sum involved after much research among local decorating firms; she had scrupulously gone for value-for-money, and tried to arrive at a total anyone would think was fair considering the work involved.

The amount calculated was, Betty felt sure, well within Valerie Eliot's affluent reach. A woman who could on her own buy a house like Valerie Elliot's would have no trouble finding so essentially modest a sum. The whole business was perfectly reasonable. After all, Valerie Elliot had come forward, had volunteered to come to the aid of a charitable institution; all Betty was doing, in a way, was helping her to give her money where it would do most good. And if the money was, yes, a little more than Valerie had initially intended to give, well, who was to say how much she might have ended up donating as time went by? She might well have been writing out healthy cheques for years; giving it all at once like this, instead of in less useful dribs and drabs, she could in the long run actually turn out to be saving herself quite a bit.

At night Betty lay awake for hours running through various versions of these arguments, and trying further to prepare herself by imagining every possible response. Tears, of course, were likely, once the shock had worn off. Anger would be easier to deal with; threats about going to the police she must ignore. And whether they were mentioned or not she must behave in any subsequent interviews as if she knew the police were listening.

"It's so kind of you to make this generous donation! Do have another scone, I made them myself. Cream?"

That sort of thing. That would stymie them. And if they tried to question her she would of course instantly volunteer the connection, show them (reluctantly: when asked) her newspaper cuttings, and suggest gently that perhaps these wild accusations were, under the circumstances, only to be expected, as the products of a weak and guilty mind; that, while it had upset her very much to see Valerie again, Valerie herself (poor tortured soul) had clearly gone completely off the rails.

As a further precaution she would, when opening proceedings, show Valerie just one selected newspaper cutting, chosen for its catchy headline; allowed to study it Valerie would, almost certainly, remember the form of words it began with, and quote them later on if she really went to the police; Betty would then destroy the cutting, but be able when required to show the police the other two, which covered the story in quite different

120

words. It was a small ruse, but one of which Betty felt rather proud. It was subtle, she thought; it would cast doubt just where doubt was required.

No court case, surely. Not if she kept on her toes. But how would the Board react to rumour, or gossip, or outright scandal? If Valerie made accusations they would be sure to spread. But if the police had no proof, the Board would have none either; after three years they could hardly sack her without proper cause. In any case they would be so busy, being shocked and horrified by Valerie Elliot's past. Presented in their turn with the envelope-full of newspaper cuttings they would, thought Betty, have no choice but to accept her own account of things.

"Blackmail, me? Do I look like a blackmailer?"

In this imagined scene Betty was always wearing a soft flowery dress, pale pinkish make-up and a gentle smile; it was a perfectly reasonable line, in the circumstances. But sometimes in the mornings, after yet another night of scheming insomnia, she would eye her raddled hot-eyed reflection in the mirror over the sink, and wonder.

It was a word only the blackmailed ever used. At least it was in films and television stuff.

"D'you mean — you're blackmailing me?"

And then the blackmailer, depending on his or her mood or frame of mind, would either quibble and prevaricate — "That's a very nasty word!" or scornfully agree, sometimes with a touch of hysteria: "Yes! Yes! and you're going to pay and pay!"

Either way the blackmailers usually got themselves murdered. Blackmailing was a very high-risk occupation in films. Would Valerie Elliot consider this desperate alternative? It could hardly be ruled out, remembering the part she had played forty years earlier. Steps would have to be taken, to ensure that she did not. A letter locked away in the office safe, perhaps. Addressed, say, to Rosemary, honest if dim-witted deputy.

In the event of my death . . . under any circumstances. Any, Valerie. You'll just have to hope I don't fall under a bus, won't you? Or it will all come out anyway.

Blackmail.

"That's a very nasty word!"

Hadn't she sat through some largely incomprehensible television comedy programme once, where the blackmailer, politely agreeing as to the nastiness of the word in question, had offered to call it something else, something facetious? Shampoo, perhaps, or gelatine, something like that, it was maddening, thought Betty as she held a wet flannel over her puffy eyes, not being able to remember exactly what ridiculous word it was.

Blackmail. A perfectly straightforward word. Betty intended to get in first with it. Not long to go now. One more day, and then tonight and tomorrow morning, and then it would at last be time to begin. It would be quite a relief, she thought.

CHAPTER
FOURTEEN

Rosemary had had a lovely afternoon. Gregory Banks had been sitting at the table when she arrived, and he had stood up to greet her, and pulled her chair out for her. They had both had the fish soup, which was very nice, though perhaps a little too garlicky, with a glass of white wine and a nice enough salad.

The unaccustomed wine went straight to Rosemary's head, and she talked a great deal, about Cabotin Court, its inmates, its bossy and unpredictable warden; about her daughter Maureen, so independent, such a career girl; and about cookery, her hobby.

"Your passion," corrected Gregory.

Rosemary blushed. "It's true, I do feel strongly about it. I think most people don't know what food's *meant* to taste like. Say, pastry. You have to make pastry with white flour. There's this idea about nowadays that everything you eat has got to be good for you. My point is this: pastry isn't meant to be good for you. Either it's to help fill you up, make something go a bit further, like in a meat pie or a fruit pie. Or it's to be a sort of background to something special, to hold something delicate together. Either way it's not the main thing, d'you see? It's got to be good, it's got to be light and moist. But it doesn't matter, it's only pastry. And yet you go down the High Street, you'll see shops selling pastry made with wholemeal flour! Looking like nothing on earth! Thick and heavy, sticks to the roof of your mouth! It's diabolical, and what gets me is that all sorts of young people are going to go around thinking that pastry is this thick heavy brown stuff that sticks to the roof of your mouth. And the idea is, it's good for you, so it doesn't matter how horrible it is! Crazy, isn't it! I mean, this country, it's chips with everything, or it's the whole meal cooked for you in a box and all of it just vile rubbish really bad for you, or, it's good for you, and it's so good for you there isn't any room for it to be anything else, like flaming well nice to eat!"

"Absolutely," said Gregory, while Rosemary seized her glass and drained it. "Now, I don't know anything about cookery. Boiled egg's about my limit. But I'll say one thing to you, Rosemary: buns."

Rosemary giggled. "Yes?"

"I have noticed," said Gregory, playfully serious, "a terrible decline in the quality of shop-bought buns, in fact they can be quite difficult to track down at all. Currant buns, I mean. Sticky on top. Dark brown sticky. Very light inside, but damp, and a bit chewy. Lots of fruit. Preferably one slightly burnt raisin buried in the sticky stuff on top. That is my idea of a good bun." He spread his hands. "Where have all the good buns gone?" Ou sont les buns d'antan, he thought to himself, and smiled.

"Well it's yeast cookery," said Rosemary, not smiling back, this was nothing to be playful about. "Yeast

124

cookery is in complete decline. You can't get a decent loaf of bread nowadays unless you make it yourself."

"Oh, I thought the supermarkets were —"

"Oh, no, you can't get good bread in supermarkets, they all put flour improver in and pump the dough full of air, you can always tell: the bread's too light. Good bread has a heft to it. Like your buns. People don't know how to use yeast properly anymore, that's what it comes down to. You can't buy buns but you can buy muffins, have you noticed those? These little sort of American cakes. Easy to make with brown flour of course and lots of baking powder to make them rise, sometimes they even put bran in them, to help you go to the toilet, that's the only reason you're meant to eat them, I reckon, they're as horrible as wholemeal pastry and just as good for you," finished Rosemary, bitterly.

In the short silence that followed she realised that she had said the word toilet aloud and at the table, and to a man she hardly knew, and felt almost too desperate to breathe for a while.

"Shall we have a pudding?" said Gregory lightly. "I rather fancy the sticky toffee pud myself."

"Oh don't," said Rosemary. "No, honestly it's not that good, I do a much better one myself. Their profiteroles aren't bad."

"But not as good as yours?"

Rosemary smiled back, shaking her head. "Bighead, aren't I?"

"You're an artist. You are bound to have a proper opinion of your own work."

Even though she was sitting down Rosemary's knees began to tremble.

And thus the whole afternoon had pleasantly passed, Rosemary talking a great deal, Gregory far less, but so agreeably; he had gently insisted on paying the bill, and then they had strolled for a while along the still sunny prom, and even had a quick cup of tea together before he had walked her all the way back to the bungalow, where he had taken his leave. She was going to give him lunch next time. At home. Well, lunch was all right, no worries there. Some meaty stew would be best, something slow-cooked and succulent. No! A pie, of course. Steak and mushroom, perhaps, or better still rabbit, and with a spectacular pudding to follow. The fabulously light toffee, perhaps.

Her head full of these delightful plans, Rosemary went out into her long narrow back garden, to consider herbs for a bouquet garni, and so missed the very last telephone call from the ward sister at the hospital in London, who had been phoning her all afternoon, and who was now officially off-duty. Before going home she of course passed on to her successor on the evening shift that she had been unable to contact the next-of-kin for Molly Sholto, but the ward was particularly busy that night and the staff nurse in charge forgot to try again, and the next day's ward sister happened not to notice the un-ticked next-of-kin box on the notes. By then the notes were onto the following page, so no one else noticed either.

Over the next few days Rosemary rang her daughter's number once or twice, but was not surprised to find her out, and in fact was a little relieved. Normally she would have called the office, and put up with Maureen being a bit off-hand, just to be on the safe side, after all Maureen would insist on living alone in the city; but for now she decided not to. She wanted to keep her new friendship to herself for a little while. And once she got talking to Maureen, she would be sure to start on about him, she just wouldn't be able to stop herself.

So good-looking! So charming, such a real old-style gentleman!

And as for what Maureen herself would think or say about her mother finding herself a boyfriend — well, Rosemary was not at all sure she really wanted to find out.

She doesn't want me bothering her at work, thought Rosemary. Which was entirely accurate, as far as it went.

CHAPTER
FIFTEEN

Alethea Troy slept very badly the night before the appointment, waking at five and worrying seriously for some time over whether she would be able to climb up to the top deck of a double-decker, and how long it would take her if she tried, and what sort of grotesque accident would ensue when she was forced to attempt the impossible and climb back down again.

But if they had to stay downstairs Annie would be so disappointed. You saw so much more from the upper deck. You were in a bus with a view, thought Alethea, and then told herself firmly that if she was going to lie here agonising she might as well do it properly and worry about the real central issue, which was whether or not she was going to go blind, rather than which seat she ought to choose on a bus.

This was so cruel a thought that Alethea was instantly distracted by memories of her mother, for it was just the sort of thing that she used to say, in her high, rather weak voice.

"Oh God, I never saw a child look more like a toad," she had wailed once, from her sofa, when presented with the five-year-old Alethea in her best silk velvet, dressed for a party.

How she hated me, thought Alethea now, getting up and going to the window.

It was a grey dawn, so everything looked beautifully clear, the empty road, the deserted bus stop. I remember the party. How I tried to pretend she had not said it, how for several minutes at a time I was able to; how strangely frantic my stomach felt, all empty and yet buzzing inside; how many jellies I gobbled, as if I could still it. How sick I was.

"You disgusting child!"

Well and it's very interesting, thought Alethea suddenly, but it's clear to me that Annie's mother didn't like Annie very much either. Is that why we are drawn to one another, I wonder? Could it be? What was it that I saw in her, and she in me, is there some mark, some tic we both have? A psychic tic? I'll ask her; why not; you can say that sort of thing to Annie; it will be very interesting to hear her reaction.

And of course she won't mind if we sit on the lower deck. Of course she won't.

Alethea felt much more cheerful by now and went to put the kettle on, but before she could make the tea she was surprised by a knock at her door. She peered at her watch; it was barely six.

"Hello?"

"It's me, sorry," said Annie's voice, very loudly considering the hour, but then of course she's hardly going to think of something like that, thought Alethea, opening the door wider.

Annie was in a nightdress and a rather smart dark green velour dressing gown, her soft white hair a little disordered at the front.

"I saw your light, I always wake early. I was wondering if you'd like to have breakfast with me. Everything's ready, come as you are. If you want to."

She smiled, and Alethea decided that she did want to, very much.

"Best time of day, this," said Annie, pouring tea.

"People usually say it's because it's so quiet," said Alethea.

"The world is always quiet," said Annie. "There's a different feel to the air. I feel rush and hurry, you can see those. Perhaps it's just traffic I'm talking about."

"That's odd!"

"Sorry, missed that."

"I saw Miss Potts. Look. There she is."

Annie half-rose in her chair.

"She was up early yesterday as well," she said. They watched as Betty, hunched in a grey raincoat, crossed the courtyard, paused for a moment at the open gateway, turned the corner, and disappeared.

"D'you think she's all right?"

"What, in general?" Annie shrugged. "Seems okay. Well. I think she's the sort of person who'd never say, 'I don't see why not' — because she always can see why not."

Alethea laughed. "Oh, that's it exactly!"

"I wonder how she lost all that weight" said Annie.

"What?"

"Oh, I heard she used to look very different . . ." said Annie vaguely, and untruthfully, for once on a Sunday, as Miss Potts had put her bony hands together and begun, "Oh most merciful Lord, consider now we beg these thy poorest servants that here resteth," Annie had been startled to see, sitting sullenly on Miss Potts's right, Miss Potts's own large teenaged self, looking very bored, and swinging her big legs in brown woolly knee socks. "*Fourteen stone*" the voice had announced: which at least made sense.

It was a little careless of her, she thought, to have mentioned it to Alethea. Perhaps it is because I feel at home with her somehow; it is the sort of thing I used to say to Edward.

For once he knew, it had become something of a hobby with Edward, noting his wife's mysterious pronouncements and trying to help her work out what they were about. Not that he had succeeded very often. But they had both come to enjoy these surreal discussions. They had been so private, thought Annie now.

I would have told Edward about this morning's too. It was Betty Potts all right. A long time ago, fat and young and frightened on a bicycle. *Only a façade*, had been the title to this one, and what could anyone make of that?

"She's certainly not fat at the moment," said Alethea carelessly. "Is that honey there please, or marmalade?"

CHAPTER
SIXTEEN

Presently Betty began to feel very cold, and drew the belt of her raincoat more tightly about her. She had planned to walk as far as the sea front, and then catch an early bus back. Perhaps she wouldn't bother, with the wind so chill. But the thought of going back to her room and hanging about there was simply unendurable. Perhaps she would have a cup of tea at one of the little places on the front, if any of them were open. She strode on, head down into the wind.

It was just nerves, that was all. Such as an actress might feel before an important performance. Even the best, the most famous actors and actresses suffered from stage fright. And with this there would be no rehearsal.

Well, she knew her part. All that remained was to play it as well as she could.

She walked on. But as she reached the first of the quiet Edwardian squares behind the front the horrible feeling stirred again inside her. It felt like something alive, uncoiling. The feeling formed itself into an idea:

you are committing a sin

and it spoke from so deep within that Betty had to sit down for a minute or two on a nearby bench until the fit of trembling resulting from it had died down a little. Then she got up and walked on again, arguing with herself.

What was so bad, then, about blackmail? No lies were involved. Blackmail was about revealing the truth, the truth about someone else's sins, not your own. And if anyone suffered, wasn't that as it should be? Let those who had got away with their crimes be punished. That's all I'm doing, thought Betty. I'm punishing her, for what she did. Someone ought to. She ought to make some retribution, for her own good. I am allowing her to do so, and I am not being harsh.

And this was a chance to be taken. Money won on this courageous gamble would be all well-spent, not a penny on herself. She was simply seizing an opportunity: and didn't the world usually praise such risk-taking?

All this is true, said Betty to herself stoutly, more calmly. She was right on the sea-front, she realised. And she felt fine, just excited and hopeful and actually rather hungry. She sniffed the air, her wide nostrils flaring. She could smell bacon frying from somewhere, perhaps one of the seafront guesthouses, perhaps from a café. She went to find out.

CHAPTER
SEVENTEEN

The doctor did not look up as Alethea entered. For several minutes he went on murmuring into a very small tape recorder, and once, apparently stuck for words, lifted his head to gaze moodily out of the small window high on the wall beside him. Alethea looked up too, and caught a glimpse of a quick passing darkness, which she soon realised had been feet as someone walked by outside. She tracked the buzzing noise down to the neon strip lighting, and the intermittent resonant vibrations, deep enough to set the empty teacup on the doctor's desk rattling in its saucer, to the bus station across the road.

What a nasty place, thought Alethea cheerfully. She had very much enjoyed the morning so far. The bus had turned out to be a single-decker, the journey pleasant and companionable, the long wait so far a perfectly comfortable rest. Moreover she had noticed an elderly couple also waiting. Not once, in an hour, had they looked at one another or exchanged a word, except when the man began to fidget a little and his wife hissed sharply at him,

"*Now* what?" in tones of startling malevolence. But then, thought Alethea, perhaps he was not always blind and dependent. Perhaps she is taking revenge for the life he led her. Perhaps she is what he made her.

She looked at the poster above their heads, about the new YAG laser, and deciphered it again, and thought of the light that could, it seemed, shear away blindness. If only there was a laser for memory, thought Alethea, for bitterness or regret, those generally useless accretions; perhaps those two could have used one, a life-laser, a kindly piercing point of light to shear away the past.

Mentally trying to turn this idea into a poem had occupied her, or rather intensely gripped her, until the fat young man had at last approached her again and asked her to follow him. He wore a white coat, with epaulettes of palest blue, and an illegibly small name badge, though as she had pointed out to Annie, any badge actually large enough for her to read would have had to be about the size of a sandwich board.

Another bus heaved forward outside; the room drummed and rang. Alethea herself, though she would have liked to clear her throat, did not do so, in case the doctor heard the sound as a hint. She felt she had no right to impatience. Besides, she felt none. She would have liked to convey this positively to the doctor, who was now scribbling noisily with a felt tip, and whose posture, hunched over his desk with one hand clamped over the nape of his neck, clearly conveyed an urgent desire to be left alone. Accordingly Alethea sat very still and quiet, and presently fell to thinking about the life-laser again, and so jumped when the doctor suddenly looked up and loudly spoke.

"Right, sorry about that, Miss Troy, morning, right, will you sit here please, here, and just put your chin here, no here, very still now, just a light shining, no, open your eyes . . . no, close your mouth and open your eyes . . . look left, no, left, left, yes, now right, right please, thank you, good, other one, no, close your mouth, yes, left, no, left. Left, good, right, good, thank you very much, now, what seems to be the trouble, not seeing so well, right?"

"Er . . ." said Alethea.

"Hang on," said the doctor, and took up a small black instrument with a fine light in it, like a torch, which he shone rather painfully into Alethea's eyes.

"Right." He sat down again, and scribbled some more. Alethea, her vision flecked with great shifting bars of blackness, peered through them across the desk, and began to tremble. This brisk young man, with his knobbly hands and his freckles and his faint Northern accent: already he knew. He could look up at any minute and say the words she most dreaded to hear, and at this thought all the careful barricades Alethea had erected between herself and the terror of blindness instantly counted for nothing.

She sat very still again, her heart seeming to pound in her ears. Some time slowly passed. Then the doctor looked up, and spoke, but Alethea, though she heard what was said, somehow could make no sense of it.

"What, I'm sorry, what?"

The doctor sighed.

(The clinic was running nearly two hours late, because that lazy bastard Barry hadn't turned up again,

136

he had already missed the lunchtime meeting as well as lunch and he had an operating list of several none-too-simple cases ahead of him all afternoon. His stomach was rumbling and Miss Troy was his thirteenth patient that morning and ninth old lady with cataracts. Eight times the doctor had already examined, explained, instructed, reassured; eight times he had repeated everything at least twice, because old folk with failing vision tend to have failing hearing as well; and all the time in this bloody interrogation cell, day after day shut up in this basement bawling at an ever-changing series of half-deaf half-blind miserable old bags; and he was still feeling upset anyway because of the fierce row he'd had with Cathy that morning, as well as worn out because she would keep letting Tasha into their bed every bloody night and of course he wouldn't mind if she'd just go to sleep but she just kept on kicking him all the time, and how was he supposed to put up with that?)

"You have quite dense cataracts in both eyes. We can operate easily and you'll be able to see as well as ever. Right?" He managed to sound encouraging, but Miss . . . what was it . . . Troy, suddenly tilted her head towards the ceiling, giving a little gasp. Tears ran from beneath her closed lids.

"Oh, thank you so much!"

There was a short silence while the doctor eyed her with some discomfort. He felt caught out, and unfairly. After all the last four old crones had hardly been compos mentis and if they all looked the same and acted the same and sounded the same how was he supposed to know when one finally turned up in full working order?

"Sorry," said Alethea, rummaging in her handbag. "Idiotic . . ."

"Not at all," said the doctor. His voice was tight, for adding guilt to his existing difficulties had made the cumulative weight of these suddenly so unbearable that for a moment he felt ready to sob along with his patient. And I'm so hungry, he told himself plaintively.

"I'm so relieved, you see. That it's something you can treat."

Warm and reassuring, come on. You can do it. "Of course we can treat it."

Alethea dried her eyes. "There. I'm so sorry. Do go on, please."

The doctor opened his mouth to speak, and closed it again as another bus, perhaps with some fault in its engine or a particularly heavy load, drew level outside and for a moment the whole room seemed to throb along with it in steady time.

Oh for fuck's sake, thought the doctor furiously, clutching at his vibrating desk, but as he looked up he caught Alethea's eye, and in the sudden silence as the bus left she laughed, and presently he had to join in.

"Sorry about that."

"Like a minor earthquake," said Alethea gaily. "Are you in here every day?"

"Well, not every day. We take it in turns."

"How democratic. Is it only cataract, that I have? Nothing else wrong as well?"

138

"No. Not as far as I can see."

"And you take out the worn-out lens, and replace it with a nice new plastic one?"

"You've been reading this up."

"Yes. Very slowly, one word at a time. I can read. But like a rather dim six-year-old. I can quite understand now why poor readers so dislike reading, by the time you've reached the end of the sentence you've generally forgotten what the beginning of it was, it's very tedious. Which eye will you do?"

"Both. Eventually. Right one first. Under local."

"I don't understand."

"We don't need to put you to sleep. These days. Just local anaesthetic. Much better for you. I'll just freeze the eye. You don't feel a thing. You just have to lie on the table covered in sterile drapes, listening to my conversation. That's the worst bit."

"The conversation?"

"So I'm told," said the doctor, deadpan. He was feeling a little better, he noticed. He thought: I've just got to let them talk a bit, like this one, I've got to risk them going on and on, because the fact is putting up with a bit of them rabbiting on is somehow less awful than trying to shut them up all the time, of course it slows things down but swings and roundabouts, it's how I feel that counts. It's just treating them like human beings after all. For my own sake as well as for theirs.

But God, look at the time now!

"Oh, did I give you the leaflet? No, I didn't, did I, here, take this, if you've any further questions there's a number to ring, look, there, and I'm putting you down as urgent, I can't promise anything but with any luck it will be weeks rather than months, okay?"

CHAPTER
EIGHTEEN

"That one? That one there?"

"Yes," said Alethea, leaning forward as the bus slowed, "I think it's the traffic lights, when the buses have to stop just about here the whole room shakes, it must be maddening."

"You were very quick," said Annie.

"He was jolly quick. He was in a tearing hurry. And assumed I was senile, so I felt obliged to try to convince him otherwise, which is slightly senile in itself, don't you think? I may have jabbered."

"Want a mint?"

"Mm, thank you. It really reminded me, that room. There was an earthquake, when I was living in Los Angeles. I'd hardly thought of it for years."

"An earthquake? You were in an earthquake?"

"Yes, when was it, '33? '34?"

"Oh, what was it like?"

"Well . . ." Alethea thought. It was a long time since she had told anyone her earthquake story, and she could not for an instant remember why she had always had to alter it a little.

Ah. Oh yes, of course!

"I'd just got out of my bath," she said. "And I saw something I would not have thought was possible, I saw the floor, which was carpeted, over floorboards I suppose, I saw it move in a series of little waves, like water. I had just an instant to think *what?* What did I think I saw just then? And then the light fitting over my head began to swing, suddenly, hard, as if someone had taken a great bash at it, and then there was a noise, a tremendous roaring from deep under the ground, it seemed, a roar that seemed to be coming closer, right at you, as if there was an express train coming but under the ground, and it seemed as if every brick in the house was rattling against its neighbour, and the roaring from under the ground grew louder and louder until the whole world seemed to be full of this terrible grinding deafening sound, and I screamed out loud with terror, you see, one minute I was idling about in a towel and fifteen seconds later, that's all it was, I was screaming with terror, as I never had before or since. And then it stopped."

"It was a bad one, then, was anyone killed?"

"Oh yes," said Alethea, remembering. "A house further down the valley collapsed, and a baby was killed in its cot. We didn't know that then. We went outside, it was so quiet! And all the trees looked normal, everything natural we could see looked normal, but the house was wrecked. Every single thing that had been on a shelf had fallen off and broken. You couldn't get into the kitchen at all. It made you think: we simply should not be in this wilderness. And just beforehand I'd called through to Merry — you remember, Meredith Pope, I

142

was his secretary out there — I'd just called through to him, I'm afraid in stage cockney, we were going through a phase, "Merry, ja fancy a cuppa tea?" Alethea giggled, "and I remember thinking afterwards how nearly those might have been my last words, fitting enough, perhaps. The patio had rippled like the carpet, but frozen in its waves, a little terracotta sea. I can't remember what it was," Alethea added vaguely, "I used to know what it was on the, you know, measures seismic activity, Richter scale, now, what was it . . .?"

"Six point eight!" cried Annie suddenly, in triumph.

Alethea stared. "How on earth did you know that? You're absolutely right. How did you know?"

Annie smiled and shrugged. "I don't know. Telepathy?"

Oops, she thought cheerfully. Very careless there, just wasn't thinking. Yippee though.

Funny, hadn't looked like a bathroom. More like a dining room. And offering your employer tea, from the bathroom. Whilst in a towel. A likely story, thought Annie hopefully; for without thinking about it too much she rather wanted Alethea to have had some preferably varied and exciting love-life to make up for its not having been a long secure one like her own; it was a sort of retrospective well-wishing.

"Telepathy?"

"It just popped into my mind," said Annie, with perfect truth. Alethea went on looking puzzled.

"Extraordinary!"

Puzzled but impressed, thought Annie. Funny how people are happy enough with telepathy nowadays.

Most people seem to believe in it. If I'd told her the truth she'd have thought I was mad. Hearing other people's thoughts is perfectly all right, but hearing other people's voices is bananas. Joan of Arc stuff. And I bet she had what I've got. But a nicer class of picture, thought Annie, smiling to herself.

"It's nothing. Want another mint?"

CHAPTER
NINETEEN

As the hour approached Betty got into rather a state. She couldn't decide what to wear. The pleated skirt she had chosen earlier looked somehow peculiar once she had it on, as if someone else had been wearing it, and everything else in her wardrobe, as she drew it all out bit by bit, seemed to have aged terribly since the last time she'd looked. Betty began to panic. She should, of course, have bought herself something new to wear, just for this important occasion. Why hadn't she realised? But there was no time for that now, even if the town had any decent shops, which of course it hadn't.

Surrounded by heaps of shabby unsuitable clothing Betty sank to her knees on her bedroom floor, and despaired for a minute or two, before remembering her blue suit with the white stripe on the lapel, which — yes! she had hung on the back of the door when she'd got it back from the cleaners, and then forgotten about, because she had then hung her dressing-gown over it. There, still in its plastic. Not as good as new, of course, but better by far than anything else, and (Betty giggled nervously) just right for embarking on one's first serious crime.

There were competitions like that, she thought, as she climbed shakily into the skirt, in women's magazines. Match a set of outfits to a set of occasions, suits and dresses, high heels and hats, to the Formal Wedding, or a Trip to Ascot, or a Night at the Opera. As if it mattered. An Attempt at Drug-Smuggling, one's First Stab at Embezzlement, a Venture into Insider Dealing: didn't go into those, did they? Though of course the right outfit under such circumstances was obviously far more important than for any mere social gathering.

A Visit from One's Lawyer, thought Betty, a Trip to the Police Station, an Appearance in Court.

It's not too late, she told herself, as she zipped up the skirt. I don't have to do it. I can just forget the whole thing. If ever I regret it, she thought, this is the time I will most think of, the time when it hadn't happened and I still had a choice.

What shall I choose?

Say you didn't go through with it. There you are going to bed tonight: not having done it, what does it feel like? Betty stood still for a moment with her eyes closed, trying to imagine. All she could make out was a great weight of disappointment. It seemed to her that she would never be able to forgive herself if she backed down now. That was how she put it to herself. You can't back down now, she thought, not now you've thought it all out. Just thinking of it in the first place. That was enough. You can't not do it, now.

Come on, head up! Courage, that's all it took. Courage, to go downstairs, now, and go to the kitchen to make the tea. A tray, just as normal. Slice and butter: cucumber sandwiches, a touch of elegance. And some of the Sholto's fruit loaf. Cups, plates, milk, sugar. There. Very nice.

If only there was someone to answer the door, though! If this was a film someone would announce her.

"Mrs Elliott!"

And I would look up from my desk, "Ah! Valerie! Do come in, please," and she would have to walk in, while I sat, perhaps coolly finishing off a bit of office business, much better than having to go to the door and let her in myself. I won't feel safe somehow. I won't start until I'm back behind my desk. She can have that low chair, of course. Tray on the desk here. So I look calm. I am calm.

I'm ready.

CHAPTER
TWENTY

While Rosemary was making them both another cup of coffee Gregory leant back in his armchair and considered possibilities. It was hard going because he had eaten so much. All of it very nice too. The nutty flesh of the rabbit, so tender yet so delightfully resilient to the bite! The picture-book pastry, golden brown, crisp on top and moist within! Good plain cooking, that's what it had been. Jolly good, in fact. Possibilities, now, he reminded himself. Where to go from here? Finances perfectly in order for now, all right, but for how much longer? He did not like to think of such things. He closed his eyes.

Though he had in fact told her almost nothing about himself Gregory had allowed Rosemary to assume a certain amount. It was not the first time Gregory had allowed a woman to construct him. The upper middleclass background, the hint somewhere of long lost old money, of a gentlemanly Oxford and the military, all these were familiar roles. He had played them, in fact, in a variety of stage and television productions, generally getting shot early on in war films, or cuckolded in peacetime; sometimes both. Decent losers were his speciality.

There were few such parts going nowadays, of course. And competition was pretty fierce. It was four years since Gregory had done any telly at all, and that had been children's stuff, a crude parody in fact of the gentle ineffectives he usually played. He would hardly be able to think of himself an actor still had it not been for the small but steady repeat fees for a fairly successful drama series he could almost be said to have starred in during the late 1960s, programmes which were now spreading the notion of honourable British upper class ineptitude halfway round the world.

Not that it needed much spreading, in Gregory's view. What a persona to get yourself stuck with! So out of date for a start. It was surprising really, considering how old-fashioned a stereotype it was, that Rosemary had so unhesitatingly pinned it, as it were, to his bosom. Presumably she'd never met any real aristocratic military types, any more than he had himself. She could only recognise the dramatised version.

Gregory sighed, or rather, tried to, but his trouser band was too tight. Oh, that pudding! Serve him any more meals like that, he thought, and she could natter on about pastry all night if she wanted to. And that was another thing. There'd be no worries with Rosemary. She was a gentlemanly-companionship type if ever there was one. She wouldn't think of starting anything anyway. She'd leave all that to him, and quite right too. Be a bit of a long wait, that was all. Because although he had in the past been perfectly happy to oblige women with even fewer physical charms than poor old Rosemary he was well past that sort of thing these days.

It had occurred to him, though, that he might just be able to get a bit more out of Rosemary than a few admittedly decent square meals. Not very much, of course; real money didn't live in bungalows. But she almost certainly had a little something tucked away, more than a little, if one or two hints of hers had meant anything at all. And every little helped. He would have to proceed very slowly, though; she had a sharp look to her sometimes. Over several months, probably; would it really be worth his while?

Cookery was the key though. They all had one. So. Praise her up a bit. Make out she was a natural genius, well, she was a decent little cook after all. Then come up with the business proposition. Your skills, my management, thought Gregory drowsily. Select little place just off the front. Lunches and teas. Get those talents to a wider audience. Go like a bomb.

For a moment Gregory roused himself to wonder whether the thing might not actually work after all. Food like that . . . they'd flock in, wouldn't they?

Then he thought of all the god-awful grind of it, and knew he would never want to find out. No, set up the collateral and quietly disappear; and in the meantime be the person Rosemary wanted him to be. Not that he wasn't quite fond of the old josser himself, in a way. He stretched his legs out comfortably, and Rosemary, coming in from the kitchen with the coffee on a tray, was rather touched to find him so unguardedly asleep.

CHAPTER
TWENTY-ONE

As the bus neared home Annie fell asleep, but Miss Troy, though she was very tired, was too keyed up to doze. The earthquake went on vividly presenting itself. She thought too of the number of times she had changed her mind about Meredith Pope, and how easy it had been to hold several conflicting opinions about him at once. How exotic he had seemed at that first interview.

And of course I was quite used to exotics, at the time.

"Really? We thought it a nom de guerre, didn't we, Nan? Alethea, my dear Miss Troy; how frightfully Pontifex!"

"I'm sorry, I don't think I . . ."

"Butler. *Way of All Flesh*, yes?"

"Merry, please leave this to me."

"Such a mystery woman, Alethea," said Meredith, ignoring his wife. "Pontifex, I mean." For a moment he held up one beautiful hand and closed his eyes. "Ah. Yes: 'It is impossible,' he went on, declaiming, " 'to explain how it was that she and I never married. We two knew perfectly well, and that must suffice for the reader.' What a nerve, don't you think!

Nancy, my darling, don't you agree? What a cheek! Couldn't be bothered to come up with a decent explanation, and doesn't notice or care that for at least the next few paragraphs we gentle readers can't concentrate at all for coming up with our own ingenious and discreditable or I dare say even revolting explanations, which of course suffice even less, somehow, don't you find?"

"You are showing off, Merry."

"And why couldn't either of them marry anyone else? After all, they're cousins, aren't they, so you can't help suspecting that both of them have got something horribly wrong with their insides, though why that should stop them getting horribly together in private I can't imagine."

"Meredith, please! You are embarrassing Miss Troy. And I've forgotten where we were. Where were we, Miss Troy?"

"I was leaving Wayward Brothers."

"Ah, yes, do go on, please." Nancy Pope, plump and dishevelled in her dark blue draperies.

"I'd been working there for nearly six years. It seemed like a good time for a change."

"But you didn't find another job first. You just left. May one ask why?"

Alethea had hesitated. Really she had left because of Sally, pretty Sally, whose photograph a lifetime later would still make her heart constrict with pain. May one ask why? No, thought Alethea, it so happens one may not.

152

"To be honest," she said lightly, for she very much wanted the job, "My uncle told me about you, and I decided to take the risk."

"Well, he told us about you, of course," said Meredith. "So here we are. Uncomfortably interviewing one another."

"I hadn't thought that I was interviewing you, Mr Pope."

"Well, you ought to. After all, you are going to follow us to the ends of the earth. Hollywood anyway. Near as dammit. Don't you think? It's Meredith anyway. No popery here, thank you. *Or wooden shoes.*"

Sally Hargreaves, thought Miss Troy, as the bus turned slowly onto the promenade. She yawned. Of course I could never trust anyone after Sally. Couldn't trust myself. But then wasn't I pretty well like that beforehand, anyway?

Then she remembered the sad couple in the clinic, and the life-laser, and the beginning of her poem, and was able to stop thinking about herself altogether.

Annie had fought sleep as long as she could. But the warmth, and the steady thrum of the engine, were too much for her. Her head drooped uncomfortably, nodded twice, and then she was away. She dreamt that Rosemary Sholto, in a tulle dress like a ballerina, was tightrope walking above the cobbled courtyard of Cabotin.

"Shouldn't she have a safety net?" she asked someone next to her.

"She thinks there *is* a safety net," said someone else, with a sneering guffaw.

Annie realised with a pang that Rosemary, feeling her way high above their heads with pointed toe and wobbling bar, was stone-blind, had been blind all the time! She nearly awoke, but the scene changed so abruptly to something to do with sea-lions that she was soothed, and sank back still more deeply. Soon she returned to a place she recognised.

It was very dark. She was inside the house now. He had his back to her, his head bent over his work. What was he doing?

Why, he was sewing. The flash of a needle. Very thick thread. More like rope.

I don't want to see what he is sewing, thought Annie in her dream. Please don't make me look.

Not in front of her now, but sideways on, and by the light of his candle Annie saw the blood on his hands, and on the drenched rope he was forcing through the slack dripping pile of raw meat before him on the table.

"*It is human flesh*," said the voice, and Annie awoke shuddering.

For a second nothing she could see made sense. Then someone patted her arm, and possibly spoke.

"Oh, Alethea!" said Annie, realising where she was. Oh, of course, the clinic, the bus — and it was as if gathering this reality meant that there was instantly no room in her mind for anything else; she felt some other piece of information being shunted abruptly away, out of reach. For a second, her heart still beating fast, she

154

tried to recall it, but the more she tried to remember it the faster it slipped and coiled and vanished.

No. Whatever it was had gone completely. Just a bad dream anyway, thought Annie. Sleeping sitting up, what else d'you expect?

"Next stop," said Alethea, almost certainly, for she had turned her face away as she spoke, scanning the windows for the big clues she needed. Something about blindness clicked in Annie's head, and, feeling completely recovered now, she laughed at the absurd picture memory showed her.

"I dreamt Rosemary Sholto was a ballerina," she said.

CHAPTER
TWENTY-TWO

"Betty?"

Valerie Elliott met Betty's eyes so briefly that Betty knew instantly that she had been recognised. So much for the element of surprise, she thought, but now the hour had come she felt herself to be full of a pleasant sensation of controlled recklessness. Though Valerie Elliott's clothes gave her a moment's fright, for Valerie was wearing an elegant pale fawn trouser suit with a long graceful jacket, and her hair looked professional, so that for a moment Betty remembered the sophisticated businesswoman she had pictured earlier, and quaked a little.

Still she sat unquestioningly in the low chair in front of Betty's desk, and was clearly looking anywhere but at Betty. Nervous, thought Betty, feeling smooth and yet hot inside. She let the silence prolong itself until Valerie looked up and tried a small half-smile. Then, without returning it, she began:

"You know who I am, don't you?"

Valerie Elliott nodded, looking up just long enough for Betty to see how pale she was. Pale but still pretty.

How, why, was that? Long ago Betty, looking in the mirror, had been able to note how very small the differences were between her own face and that of, say, Rita Heyworth; tiny differences measurable in fractions of an inch here, the slightest degree of curve there more, or less; and yet Rita was beautiful, and she, Betty, was not, was so far not beautiful that never in her life had any man awarded her the earnest searching glance she had seen them give to other girls. No one had so much as looked at her twice to make sure. How bitter the knowledge was!

Despite the pallor Valerie seemed to be wearing no make-up. White as a mushroom, thought Betty savagely.

"D'you know why I asked you here?"

A shake of the head, this time. "I've . . ." Her voice was very low.

"What?" said Betty briskly.

"I've often thought of you."

"Have you indeed."

"I've so often wanted to say to you, how much I — how grateful I have always been to you." The voice quavered away completely.

Betty eyed her in some perplexity. While she had imagined a wide variety of initial reactions and thought out all sorts of devastating replies to anything her imaginary victim might come up with, she had not for a moment considered gratitude.

"I have so much to thank you for. You know, I've tried to find you, but —"

"You just listen to me," interrupted Betty brutally. "I don't care how grateful you are. I don't need gratitude." She paused, dimly recognising a moment of drama. "I don't want gratitude. I want you to give me some money."

"Oh."

"Yes. That's all right, isn't it? Seems fair enough to me. You're grateful, well, you can pay up."

"Well, I . . ."

"Or I'll tell everyone what happened."

"Oh! Do you mean — blackmail?"

Betty's eyes widened suddenly. All right then, call it fishpaste, she thought, and was unable to prevent herself from giving a sudden wild bursting snort, as of laughter.

"I'll show them all this!" she said weakly, prodding the big brown envelope over the desk. There was a pause while Valerie opened the envelope, drew out the cutting inside, opened her handbag, found her glasses case, opened it, put on her spectacles, and read.

"Well?" said Betty sharply, when Valerie at last looked up.

"Well what?"

"I want twenty thousand pounds."

"I see."

"Well?" said Betty again.

"I just can't answer straight away. You must see that," said Valerie, her tone almost conversational. She looked down at the cutting again. "Haven't you lost a lot of weight!"

There seemed no sensible answer to this.

"It was because you fainted," said Valerie. "And then, on the way home actually, I suddenly realised . . . your eyes haven't changed. You know I wanted to attend the

158

hearings, but they wouldn't let me. I wanted to testify. But they said I wouldn't be any use. That was very hard."

"You weren't any use," Betty pointed out, unkindly; it had given her a pang to be told her eyes had not changed. She felt thrown a little off-balance, though she had no idea as yet what the pang had actually consisted of.

"I did tell you, though, didn't I. I tried, I know I did."

Betty shrugged.

"Did you know he died, quite soon after, my father? He died of pneumonia. They found him dead in his cell. It was a relief."

"I'm sure it was," said Betty drily.

"You don't think I agreed to it, do you? I had no idea what he was doing."

"Look." Betty sighed. "I'm not interested. I don't care. I want payment. Or I'll tell everyone what happened."

"But surely — why d'you think they'd be interested?"

"Oh, they would be. Don't you worry about that. It's front page stuff, this. It was then, you were just lucky there was a war on. And the papers had standards in those days, they wouldn't have printed a lot of it. Not the details. They would now. I'd be in all the magazines. So would you. And your children. Like them to know all about it, would you? Think about that. And all their friends and bosses and people at work and so on. All knowing. And all your friends. And your husband's friends. And his family. And your neighbours. You just think about it. Think about walking down the street knowing every single person in it knows all about your very nasty little secrets. I think all that's worth twenty thousand pounds, don't you?"

There was another long pause.

"Is there tea in that pot?"

"What?"

"Tea. In that pot, can I have a cup, please?"

The hand that took the cup was trembling; Betty noted that, though she felt not a twinge of pity at the time. She was conscious though of the image being as it were filed away somewhere inside her, and had a moment's uneasiness on her own account.

For several minutes they sat in silence, sipping. Then Valerie spoke:

"Are you . . . I mean, are you really sure about this?" Her tone was very odd, gentle; Betty could not fathom it at all. "Is it really what you want?"

"I'm not going to go on making demands," said Betty, "if that's what's worrying you. You won't hear from me again, after this. Not once you've paid, I mean."

"No, no, I meant — look, why don't we just forget about this? I'm sure it's not right, for you. This isn't you. Is it? I know what sort of person you are. I've looked up to you, all these years. Please don't do this. It's all wrong for you."

Betty knew a moment's quivering doubt before she took refuge in fury. She put her cup down very carefully, without making a sound.

160

"All I want from you," she said icily, "is twenty thousand pounds. I don't want advice, I don't care what you think is right for me. I don't want anything from you but the money."

For a moment Valerie went on staring at her. Betty had a sudden memory of the white desperate girl's face looking up at her from the soiled ticking pillow.

Who are you?

I'm the nurse.

Help me, help me!

"I'm giving you a week," said Betty, "to think about it. I've opened a special account. All you have to do is organise yourself and write a cheque. That's it: all over. Okay?"

"Well, I . . ."

"And I wouldn't bother with the police if I were you. You can't prove anything. And everything would get out straight away. You don't want that, do you?"

Valerie Elliott stood up. "I'll let you know what I decide," she said, and she spoke so composedly that Betty grew frightened, and jumped up herself.

"There's a letter with my solicitor," she cried, "all about all this, which he's going to open if anything happens to me, so don't get any ideas!"

Valerie made no reply, except that she blushed. Even her ears went red, Betty noticed. "Goodbye," said Valerie, her eyes averted. She picked up her bag, a nice soft brown leather one.

"Right then," said Betty, still looking at the bag. Oh, go away, go away!

"I wouldn't dream of hurting you," said Valerie, and went.

Betty sat down very shakily.

There. That had all gone pretty well, hadn't it? She had missed out one or two things but she could always say them later if need be. Funny woman though. Hadn't got angry. Hadn't got anything really.

Except soppy. "I'm sure it's not right for you." Ugh! Bloody cheeky too.

And "I wouldn't dream of hurting you." Huh, thought Betty scornfully, and she tried to remember this speech as prissy and affected; but it went on sounding simply genuine, so she made a fierce effort and thought about something else.

Alethea May Troy, d.o.b. April 6 1897. Shouldn't she be back by now? With the deaf one. Anne Cameron, d.o.b. October 12 1902. Right.

Betty put the teacups back on the tray, carried everything back to the kitchen, and resolutely went to find out.

CHAPTER
TWENTY-THREE

For the next month there was much waiting, at Cabotin Court and elsewhere.

Rosemary waited, with increasing indignation and resentment, to hear from her daughter Maureen, though the same shyness about Gregory Banks, whom she was by now seeing almost every day, still prevented her from picking up the telephone herself.

Gregory waited too, until the time felt right.

Alethea waited to hear from the hospital, and in the second week scalded her hand whilst making tea. Betty took her to the local hospital, waited with her until she was seen by a doctor and bandaged up, and then telephoned the Cabotin GP, whom she ordered to write to the Eye Hospital to point out that Miss Troy's painful injury, due entirely to her increasing blindness, had taken place while she was on their waiting list; meanwhile, in case he dawdled or disobeyed, she wrote quite a stinger herself, in triplicate, to the consultant, to his registrar, and to the hospital manager. It took her mind off things.

For Betty had hardly had to wait at all. Three days after their interview Valerie had sent her a cheque. The cheque. There had been no letter with it, Betty had been very glad to see. She had banked it, made a few telephone calls, and even got up and yanked at the carpet in one corner of her office, disclosing what looked like hardboard. And what was underneath that? Betty could not pry anything further loose at all, but the flooring company of course would find out soon enough. First thing Monday morning. No time at all.

"It's sprouts, shall I help you to some?"

"Erm, yes, thank you —"

"There. Mash at seven o'clock. Sprouts at noon."

Alethea giggled. "Sprouts at Noon, wasn't that a Western?"

Mrs Derry made no reply, thought the quality of her silence was clear enough.

"Thank you," added Alethea.

"It really is shocking making you go on like this," went on Mrs Derry, as if there had been no interruption. "A neighbour of mine who used to work for the civil service actually died on the waiting list, he was waiting for heart surgery, years he waited. His widow got the letter the day after the funeral, you know, telling him to come in."

A familiar story, since it combined so many of Mrs Derry's favourite themes. Alethea, her mouth full, tried to register disparagement.

"But then he wasn't actually disabled, you see, he could get about all right, go for little walks and so on, whereas you, well, you really are a bit stuck, aren't you? Of course," Mrs Derry went on bitterly, "it would be different if your name was Singh or Patel, they'd have got you straight in then. You didn't want gravy, did you?"

"Oh, no, thank you."

"Gravy, Violet? Violet! Yoo-hoo!" called Mrs Derry gaily across the table.

Mrs Dobbs jumped. She was not really sitting at the table in the Great Hall at Cabotin, she was not in England at all, she was in America, in some great and terrible city, with Jerry and Paula.

Jerry and Paula had made so little progress on television that Mrs Dobbs had been forced to make up a whole series of scenes for them in all sorts of different places, first dates, early significant looks, and, best of all, long first trembling passionate kisses. She had gone over and over these scenes, enjoyably polishing and refining them and re-writing little bits of dialogue until everything sounded exactly as she wanted it to, and then! Then, last night, she had switched on as usual without, by now, any hope that their romance would, as she put it to herself, *come true*, when halfway through the story had suddenly shifted to Jerry's apartment, and Jerry himself, rather dishevelled and unshaven in a dressing gown, making coffee; but before she'd had time properly to take in this delightful and unprecedented glimpse of her hero at home he had poured two mugfuls, taken them through to the bedroom, looked down at his bed and said tenderly,

"Hi!"

and the camera had then stepped back to show Mrs Dobbs what he was looking at, and it was Paula, asleep, with the sheet tucked round her naked shoulders!

For a moment Mrs Dobbs had felt quite dizzy with shock. She had a sensation of somersaults being lightly turned inside her, and her heart held its breath, then banged away like mad.

"Hi," said Paula, smiling a little shyly up at Jerry, and he put the mugs down so that she could pull him close, and Mrs Dobbs had actually been forced to look away for a second.

"Well!" she had exclaimed aloud, to Joe's chair. And then it had transpired that Jerry and Paula had been an item for weeks, actually weeks, but that they had decided to keep it a secret for a while from all the other police, which was fair enough, thought Mrs Dobbs, but why had all their viewers needed to be kept in the dark as well? It was such a waste. Not a single romantic touch or look, just straight into bed! On the other hand it had actually been terribly exciting, thought Mrs Dobbs, and remembering the shock and picturing the scene again gave her a sudden reprise of the pleasant internal somersaults she had felt at the time.

And of course it put a different slant, retrospectively, on so many of their scenes together during the previous few weeks; all those indifferent exchanges and abrupt Goodnights, which had so baffled and frustrated her at the time, were charged now with significance, in fact it was obvious, looking back, that there had been one or two hints she was somehow rather glad not to have

166

noticed. In bed that night she had replayed the scene many times, and found it worked every time.

"Yoo-hoo! Violet, gravy?"

"Oh! Oh, no thank you, Kate . . ."

"So, was it the earthquake that made you come back to England, then?"

"Well. I suppose it was, in a way." Alethea hesitated. "I didn't think so at the time. I suppose I just felt I wasn't getting anywhere. It was the same problem as before: I wasn't doing my own work, you see, I was just doing Merry's."

"You mean Meredith Pope?"

"Mmm,. Yes. I did get quite fond of him actually, oh, look, Annie. There. Is that the nurse?"

Annie stood up and looked out of her window, where the car Alethea had heard, but could not see, had pulled up in the courtyard.

"No, sorry, it's just Violet and her daughter. Is she due yet, it's only three o'clock."

"You did put the note on my door again anyway, didn't you, so she'll know I'm here? I'm sorry, I don't know why I'm so anxious about her."

"You've so much to be anxious about, I think that's the trouble."

Alethea nodded. "D'you know, I haven't longed for something so much for years. This operation. I feel taken up by it. I've been trying to think of it as a sort of prison sentence: that I have to serve a certain amount of time behind these bars.

"You know I can't write now, I can't see what I've written. I've been trying with the tape recorder but it's all so different, I can't somehow tell if it works, if I can't see what it looks like. And I hadn't realised how much I enjoy the actual shape of print on paper, I mean, obviously some things are only funny on paper, you read them out to someone and it just doesn't work, I mean I've always been aware of that. But somehow for serious things it's the other way round. Well of course, you know, novels and so on, on tape, they're all read by professional actors, who put their own reality into what they are reading, and so make almost anything palatable. It's actually much harder for me to judge when a book is dishonest or even downright feeble, the voice of the actor disguises the voice of the author, gives it a depth or resonance that the words themselves on the page might never have achieved.

"And even if it's a book you know, one you know is good, the other voice is still interpreting for you and getting in the way. It's a bit like reading nothing but translations from another language that you don't at all know. And you see all my life I've been, oh, addicted to reading, wherever I was the library was always the first place I went out to find, I've always had huge handbags to be sure I could always carry the current novel wherever I was, I really cannot remember not being able to read, I've always lost myself in other people's lives in that way and needed to, and more than anything else it matters, it matters to me so much! And I don't care if I never make myself a pot of tea again or look out of my window at the beastly view it's just this loss of escape and not being able to listen in that direct profound way to the voice the real living voice of the author that I really can hardly bear."

Most of this was too wild and too unexpected for Annie to follow, though the distress of course was clear enough. She leant across and tentatively touched Alethea's unbandaged hand, and presently, without thinking about it at all, broke the habit of a lifetime.

"You'll see again very soon. I know it. Don't you fret. Not long now."

Alethea found a handkerchief and blew her nose. "Yes, I'm sorry."

"No, no, I'm not just saying it. I saw it. I saw you seeing someone, someone you used to know. It just popped into my head, the way things do sometimes. Honest. You'll be all right."

She smiled so encouragingly that Alethea had to smile back, though in her turn she had not really taken in what Annie was saying. Already she was ashamed. Whining on like that, and to Annie too! But the scalded hand was hurting her so much, and soon the nurse, for all her gentleness, would hurt her a great deal more.

"Sorry about that. Though I must say I feel rather better for it."

"Good," said Annie. Wasn't listening, she thought. Strange how the hearing seemed able to choose. Still, in this case it was probably just as well. Wonder who it was, though, such a young cheerful face, and poor

Alethea so happy to see her, starting up from her bed with delight, as bouncy almost as a child. Something nice for her anyway.

"Would you like another cup of tea?" said Annie.

CHAPTER
TWENTY-FOUR

Late one night, Betty, who had been restlessly watching Inspector Morse, switched off with a curious mixture of emotions when the murder victim turned out to have been a blackmailer, emerged from her bedsit and stalked along the corridors sniffing the air. The whole place seemed to reek of paint, even though the workmen had of course only been in her office. And the mess, the footprints they had tracked into the hallway carpeting! Twice that very day she had again had to ask them to turn down their radio, which was permanently tuned to the local station and turned up very high even during the phone-ins and quiz shows which, it appeared, occasionally took over from the otherwise non-stop pop stuff. And all of them smoked, all of the time. She was sure of it.

"I'm afraid you really can't smoke in here. Fire rules," said Betty, on the first morning.

"Right you are," said the tall one with the flat cap, who seemed to be in charge. He took out his roll-up and pinched it out between his great hard fingers. But when she had next passed she had smelt smoke again, and opened the office door very suddenly, to catch them at it, and accidentally struck the youngest one, who had been standing just inside, quite hard on the temple. No one seemed to have been smoking, either.

After that Betty thought she smelt smoke quite often, but there was never anything to see by the time she had knocked and looked inside to check. Once, in the evening, she had found a definite dog-end in a corner, underneath the sheeting the men were using to protect the floor, but when she had confronted the tall man with it the next day he had appeared perfectly unconcerned, pretending with maddening indifference that the end must be an old one, which she knew was a lie, for had she not checked for them every single evening?

But when she had charged him with this obvious falsehood, he had become downright abusive, and made personal remarks, so that she had had no choice but to sack him immediately. Finding replacements, however, soon proved difficult. No one, it seemed, wanted to take over a job half done.

Betty had at length been compelled to ask the horrible men to come back, and they had agreed with an insulting indifference, though they had not actually started work again for another six weeks, since by then they had, it seemed, started another job somewhere else, and felt obliged to complete it before returning to Cabotin Court. Betty, by now rather demoralised, had agreed, and though she had tried to assuage her feelings by forbidding Rosemary to offer them so much as a drink of water, she was certain that even in this her wishes were being flagrantly ignored, and that Cabotin funds, in the shape of endless fruit cake and great gouts

172

of well-sugared tea, were vanishing down the ever-open maws of that disgusting trio of men in dirty whites.

This afternoon, though, they had announced themselves finished, and immediately disappeared in their lorry, mysteriously leaving behind them three wooden ladders, several half-finished tins of paint, and a big heap of stained and grimy sheeting. Gingerly, for earlier the gloss on the door had still been tacky, Betty entered the office and looked about her. Every scrap of woodchip, every polystyrene ceiling tile, had gone for ever, replaced by smooth lining paper. And of course it was a huge improvement, the room was transformed, no one could argue with that, but . . .

The fact was that Betty, though she had spent days considering colour schemes, and taken to carrying scraps of curtain material and Dulux colour cards with her wherever she went, was now not quite sure whether her final choice was altogether a success. She had gone for cheerfulness, combining a bright clean yellow with several deep clear Mediterranean blues; It's A Breeze With Seaside Colours, the design magazine article had claimed, but . . .

Of course it was impossible to judge by one bald brilliant light bulb dangling from the middle of the ceiling. Anything would look garish under such conditions. And the carpet, the dark decent wool carpet on order from Lewis's, would change everything too, as would furniture, and the cosy velour curtains waiting in a zipped plastic bag in Betty's bedroom, but . . .

Supposing it didn't, after all, "work"? Betty, until her first glimpse of the finished room that afternoon, had not considered this possibility at all. She had had, she now realised, complete faith in her own taste and judgement. Supposing, after all, her taste and judgement had not really known quite what they were up against? She had followed the magazine's recommendations almost to the letter, and yet the end result did not, in some way she could not yet identify, have the bright fresh airiness of the article's accompanying photographs. It just looked, well, quite nice really, a yellow room with a blue paper border round the top; perfectly nice; you wouldn't have thought hours of careful consideration had gone into it, though, thought Betty. It wasn't going to bowl anyone over. It didn't say anything. It was just, well . . .

Ordinary, thought Betty, facing facts painfully. She had often imagined the Friends' first look at her refurbished office, their little involuntary cries of delight, the new respect in their eyes at her hidden artistic flair thus triumphantly revealed; but it seemed to her now that they would say how nice it looked, politely; that all she had in fact revealed were further depths of the personal ordinariness they all of them knew about already.

Still there was the fireplace to look forward to. She would telephone tomorrow morning and tell the men to go ahead. It was a plain pine surround she had chosen; possibly she would paint it white later on. And after that the carpet fitter. Such a shame about the concrete. Betty sighed.

"Could be flags underneath," the tall one with the flat cap had lately volunteered, but Betty had ignored

174

his use of the conditional and made herself feel quite ill for a moment, by picturing Miss Jakes overseeing an earlier generation of flat-capped dog-end sucking boors in the very act of pouring the hideous stuff from nasty crusted buckets.

"It must be removed," she had recklessly announced, and for a while was quite buoyed up by the idea, her old self again and full of energy as usual. De-Jakesing Cabotin! But the quotation for the work, when at last it arrived, was terrifying; and besides she kept imagining what extensive and of necessity painstakingly careful concrete-removal would sound like. And it would go on for weeks, and everything would be coated daily with gritty choking dust. Betty felt very tired when she thought of these things.

Conscientiously she tried once or twice to get herself going again, deliberately contemplating the lost fireplaces, the despoiled kitchen, the hideous gates, but somehow she was unable to work up much of a head of steam. Even re-playing the concrete-pouring scene failed to move her. Then she told herself that one must, after all, be realistic, and that her funds would simply not stretch to uncovering what might after all turn out to be (as the terrifying quotation had certainly stressed) irremediably damaged flagstones.

Nice piece of carpet, she had thought, and gone for a dark decent blue, but wouldn't this too turn out to be the ordinary boring choice? Flagstones would have had style; anything really old had style, you could count on it, it was a sort of protection; who would have thought a dark decent blue carpet could make you feel so exposed?

"Oh how nice," Audrey Hapgood would say, stepping lightly onto that carpet, and the thickest ankles in the world would not compensate Betty for the inner sensations this carelessly temperate phrase would evoke.

Betty left her office door ajar behind her and went moodily for a prowl. She climbed the stairs, caressing the banister's perfect swan-neck mahogany curve, and passed along the second-floor corridor. Various small sounds reached her from the residents, a gust of televised laughter, a murmur of Radio Four, a chink of teacups. They were lolling in armchairs, thought Betty, they were stuffing their slack old faces with bedtime snacks, they were scurrying about in slippers gleefully switching on electric blankets. Fantastic comforts lapped them round as they clucked and jabbered.

It was disgusting, thought Betty. Not one of them was worthy of this noble building. Not one of them approached it in the right spirit. Buildings such as this contain the soul of the nation. And no one understands it but me.

Betty took a tissue from the pocket of her cardigan and wiped her eyes. She reminded herself that she had done her best. And things would certainly look better once the fire was in and of course all the furniture, it was early days yet.

She went back to her own room, weighed down with this new and disturbing emotion. She had not disliked her residents en masse before. It felt dreadful but it was better than thinking about how boring the office looked. I have tried to do my duty to Cabotin, thought Betty piously, and the distortion of her feelings made it possible for her to believe this sincerely, without considering whether her duty in fact lay more with the inmates than with the stone walls.

She went to bed, but could not sleep, and in the morning, dozing at last, dreamt that she had not changed anything, that she had gone into her office and found it woodchip papered and false ceilinged and lit with neon and carpeted in vile clashing swirls, and none of it her fault, and awoken seized with joy and relief; for a moment, before she remembered.

What an absurd dream, Betty told herself. Quite ridiculous. And noticing within herself a slight disposition to the tremulous, she got up and thought about visiting the kitchen to oversee Rosemary, since it was Sunday. Rosemary was bound to need an eye kept on her, Rosemary was almost certainly doing something wasteful and duplicitous, thought Betty. She stalked off hopefully.

CHAPTER
TWENTY-FIVE

"Actually, Rosemary, I was wondering if you'd mind going to the Abbey some other day."

"Oh, well, I suppose, no, of course not, if —"

"The fact is, I'd rather take you somewhere else entirely."

"Oh? What, you mean — well, what do you mean, where then?"

"Little surprise for you."

"Ooh!" Rosemary's heart gave a great thump beneath her raincoat. Was he going to pop the question?

Oh, Gregory, but it's too soon, we hardly know one another!

We know all we need to know don't we, my darling?

"Ooh!"

"Jump in. It's only a few minutes," said Gregory, opening the car door for her. It was really too soon, he thought, as he slammed the door behind her, but what with one thing and another he felt he might as well risk it; leave it any later and he might have to disappear without even giving it a try, and that would never do, he thought cheerfully.

"So much for the heat wave," he remarked as they moved into the traffic.

"Well, it was lovely while it lasted," said Rosemary, and then blushed, for these were exactly the words she had imagined herself using to one or two women friends of hers, when Gregory had, in some perfectly gentlemanly way of course, let her know that it was all over, for generally Rosemary tried not to set her hopes too high. But supposing after all he was going to . . .

"How was work today? What did you give them, those lucky old ladies?"

Rosemary hesitated. She had not been altogether satisfied with lunch today. Of course she had known all along that given the numbers and the budget she should not have attempted roast chicken, but there had been one or two requests, and in anything to do with cooking Rosemary was always ready to oblige. But, really, what could you do with frozen battery-reared birds? By the time she had finished with them they had looked like roast chicken, and even faintly smelled as they should, but as to flavour . . .

"Not that anyone seemed to mind. And they only had a sliver to go on, it was practically all stuffing anyway, I mean I told her, you know, Betty Potts, I said to her, something's got to be done, I said to her, I don't know how much longer I can go on producing anything like a decent meal on that sort of money, I mean it's just not on, really."

"You know, it really doesn't sound as if she fully appreciates you, Rosemary, if you don't mind my saying so."

Rosemary snorted, to indicate how far Old Potty was from any appreciation whatsoever, and, as he had

179

expected, then behaved as if he had made this observation entirely off his own bat instead of listening to her saying as much at least half a dozen times: agreeing indignantly and listing further instances of Potty's lack of appreciation as if to back him up. Then she went into some long rigmarole about this Potts female turning up that morning and interfering in some way that Gregory simply could not bring himself to follow in any detail, despite his plans. Though it was clear enough, he felt, that the morning's turn of events was rather in his favour. Not to push, that was the trick of it. Let her get there by herself.

"Here we are," he said, pulling up.

"Where? Where are we?" Rosemary got out of the car. If it rains this hairdo's a ball of frizz, she reminded herself darkly. They were in one of the quiet Edwardian squares close to the sea front.

"Over there. Come on!" said Gregory. The wind caught at his coat, he had to pull his hat down hard. Breathlessly Rosemary took his proffered arm, and they ran in the sudden little squall of rain into one of the side streets that opened into the square.

"Here!"

"Oh." They were standing in front of an empty shop, a place Rosemary knew well, for long ago, when she was a child, it had been the baker's. Sometimes, when her father was in port, he had brought her here as a special treat on a Saturday evening. The whole street had smelt of baking bread in those days; as your place in the queue neared the door, so the smell would strengthen, calling deeply to your empty stomach and setting it growling with desire. And then at last into the shop, the door closing behind you in that luxury of scented warmth! She had just been able to see over the counter, where the whippet-thin sweating baker, using a thing like a long-handled shovel, would be hauling out the smoking trays of rolls, all sprung together in the oven.

Where now might she softly tear such a roll from its brother, with just that matt thick crust on top, and damp resilient flesh within? And surely that clean sweet earthy smell of new bread was so strong then that the tissue the rolls were wrapped in smelt delicious for weeks afterwards, when the bread was long gone; Rosemary had once kept a screwed-up ball of it in her desk at school, to sniff at privately in difficult moments.

"We used to take them to our neighbours," said Rosemary, having passed on some of this to Gregory as he unlocked the glass front door. Though this was not exactly true; Rosemary and her father had only taken bread to Annie Hogg, an old woman who lived in a tiny cottage at the edge of the woods. She'd hardly been a neighbour, thought Rosemary, remembering holding her father's hand as they left the pavement behind and struck out across a field or two towards the dark flaring shape of the trees.

Once they had been later than usual, and Annie had opened the door wearing only a long pink nightdress, and I can see her clear as day, thought Rosemary, it must have been candlelight so golden behind her, and her nightie all crumpled, and bare feet, as if she were a little girl, and what was dad up to really, it was a mystery why we were there, but then there were so many mysteries when I was a child, no one ever explained anything.

All housing estate now, the cottage, the dark woodland. Long gone. Like the baker's, she thought as she looked around. Not a trace of it to be seen. I can't see my dad here. If they'd left it as it was, if the old wooden counter was still here, perhaps I could have sort of seen him, remembered him, remembered something new.

"A travel agent," Gregory was saying, "and before that, ah, hardware, it says here. They obviously don't go back as far as you, Rosemary." He smiled. There was a pause. Then gently: "They sounded like very pleasant memories, you know."

This was an inspiration; she perked up straight away, he was relieved to see. Stay on the ball, he told himself, any little thing could push her either way.

"Oh they were," said Rosemary, with most of her usual bounce. "When are you going to tell me what we're doing here?" she demanded almost playfully. The travel agency had left a long Formica unit behind, its shelves strung with sagging elastic. The pale grey walls were covered in little rectangular stains, marking where Sellotape had once held posters; by the door someone had ripped too hard, and left a corner of paper still adhering. "You're not thinking of going into business, are you?"

"Well, as a matter of fact — I have had a little idea along those lines. I'm afraid you'll think I'm mad."

Gregory sighed, giving her his best rueful smile. "It is mad, I expect."

"Well, come on then!"

"All right. You asked for it, mind! It's — look, you're a cook. Aren't you. Frankly, you're the best cook I've ever come across, in a long career. No, wait! Just look at this little place, Rosemary. Small, I grant. Just big enough, I think. A few tables, not too close together. Very simple decor, cosy, inviting, you know the sort of thing. And your cooking, Rosemary — no, don't say anything yet, please — I'm thinking of dinners, and maybe Sunday lunches. A very select menu, not too much choice. Fresh local produce. Seasonal changes. None of your silly tasteless imports, none of your battery hens. Real food, real cooking, and believe me, real prices. That's my idea, Rosemary, for what it's worth. For you to think about. A business proposition. A partnership. I put in the money, you put in the expertise."

"You mean — give up my job?"

Gregory appeared to think. "Well, yes. I suppose it would mean that." He paused, and then, in the manner of one ruefully accepting an early defeat, said, "It means a lot to you, doesn't it, that job."

Rosemary sighed, too perplexed to speak. It was very hard for her to know what she was feeling. Foolish and disappointed; thrilled; hopeful anyway, since a business partnership was hardly a brush-off, after all, and might lead who knew where; overwhelmingly anxious, at the idea of it, well it was daft, a restaurant, the place was full of restaurants already —

Seizing on this last as the most presentable of her reactions Rosemary voiced it.

"Not one of them top-flight," said Gregory, without heat. "It's quality I'm thinking of, you see. Food like yours, well, people are going to come here from well out of town. Honestly, Rosemary, there are precious few really decent places in these parts, for people who really know what good cooking is. I agree with you, most people don't. But those who do are going to flock."

"Show me the back," said Rosemary flatly, and he opened a door behind the plastic counter the travel agent had left behind, and they went inside. It was not a large room, but, thought Rosemary, it would just about do. With all the best modern space-saving equipment. For a moment she pictured it, all gleaming steel, and the sort of plain professional-looking shiny saucepans chefs always used on television, saw herself with an egg whisk and eight gas jets all burning at once.

"I couldn't do it all alone."

"You'd have an assistant, of course. A good restaurant is at least partly good service."

"Waitresses!"

He laughed outright at her tone. "I hadn't thought about them much, but I'd say, off the top of my head, that we'd go for older women, part-timers, you know, women with children who need a bit of extra money, reliable, sensible. Professional. You see I don't think we should aim for what d'you call it, glamour. I think we

184

should go for dining at home. That sort of feeling, though of course most real home-cooking's something bunged in a microwave these days. You know, atmosphere anyway. An atmosphere of home."

"Oh, I don't know . . ."

"Of course you don't. Don't say anything yet. Just — think about it. That's all I ask. There's no hurry. It just suddenly occurred to me, when I saw this little place. That it might be fun. Hard work, of course. But rewarding. In every way."

"Thing is," said Rosemary pleadingly, "I sort of like knowing who I'm cooking for. I don't know if I'd really go in for cooking when I don't know who's going to eat it."

"Ah . . ." said Gregory, again as if acknowledging defeat. Oh blast, he was thinking, but natural talent as well as years of training allowed him to keep any trace of annoyance from showing in his face. "Well, you're an artist, Rosemary. I think that's an artist's attitude." He shrugged. "It was only a notion. Though I suppose you'd pretty soon get some regulars. Any good restaurant does. People who'd come in every week. People like me, I suppose! Who need a bit of home-life now and then. You'd have a circle."

Of admirers, Rosemary finished for him. People ringing up, begging to be squeezed in. Sending their compliments to the chef. Two sittings perhaps, seven-thirty and nine-thirty. Laundered tablecloths. Starched napkins, plainly folded. Candles in plain little glass lamps, very clean. Classical music, very softly, just to take the edge off any early evening silence.

"Rosemary's Dining Rooms," said Gregory, watching her face. Rosemary laughed girlishly.

"Oh but surely it should be your name, I'd just do the cooking —"

"No, if you do the cooking, it's your name people are going to want to know, believe me. And, to be honest, we'd get off to a better start in some ways if there was just a bit more money than I feel able to put in. Now I'm not short of a bob or two, Rosemary, but you know as well as I do, there's always that rainy day to provide for. I could do it all myself, and employ you; but on the whole I'd prefer it — if of course you were to agree — to be a proper partnership. I'm getting on a bit, I suppose. A few years back, and I wouldn't have hesitated. But now, it's the responsibility, perhaps. Can't quite face it all on my own. Just a bit more fragile than I was, d'you see what I mean, Rose? If you think we could possibly make a go of this mad idea of mine, I'd want us to share it all, the work, the hours, the risk. And the fun of course. Mustn't forget that."

All his small movements, a turn here to look out of the window at the light rain still falling, a small wry smile there, a sudden direct honest glance, a slightly bowed head, they were nothing short of masterly, thought Gregory. And the tone, the resignation and dignity! He was as moved and thrilled by his own performance as ever he had been on stage or studio; he had put his talent to passionate use and was satisfied. For a long pleasant moment all desire to fleece Rosemary left him, and he told himself that he could just disappear now, having brought off this absurd piece

186

of persuasion; that he had already won a great prize, that of achieving high art, merely by convincing her.

"Still. Let's leave it all at that, for now, shall we? I won't, how shall I put it, take it personally if you decide to turn me down."

"Oh, I —"

"No, no. Let's not talk about it any more for today. I say tea, hmm? D'you think that little place out towards Westbay might still be open? I could drop the key back in to the estate agents on the way. Yes? Jolly good. No no. After *you*."

CHAPTER
TWENTY-SIX

Alethea Troy lay very still. Every so often she dozed off, and woke with a sudden start, afraid for an instant that she had dreamt all the events of the last twenty-four hours. Once or twice she had to put up a hand to touch the bandage over her right eye, to make sure.

Betty Potts had woken her on the Sunday afternoon, had come straight into her flatlet and briskly shaken her, so that she had sat up gasping.

"Oh, what is it?"

Betty did not smile, or apologise for startling her, or say any of the soothing fluttery things that might have been expected of her. "The hospital rang. There's been a cancellation. They want you in by three. I'm going to take you there myself in the car. Is your bag packed?"

An anxious blur of journey, and the bursting noise of the hospital.

"Just going to pop you into bed . . ."

"Just going to check your blood pressure . . ."

"They'll help you sleep."

"They'll calm you down."

"Morning, Miss Troy, remember me? Just going to give you a little injection . . ."

A period of strange tranquillity, warm and hidden beneath layers of dark smooth cloth. Someone held her uninjured hand, and murmured to her now and then in a soft girlish voice, calling her Anthea, as people so often had throughout her life. She made no protest.

"He's started now. Did you feel anything?" While other distant voices conversed, just within earshot; Alethea strained to make out what they were saying.

"That's it. Keep it sloping backwards . . ."

"No, make them radial . . ."

"Short, deep bite. Good, good . . ."

It was all curiously familiar, thought Alethea, and spent some time puzzling over this before realising, with an inner smile, that she had been waiting for these tantalising introductory snippets to fade out so that the man from *Science Now* or *You and Yours* could come on and get the programme properly started.

Once she had suddenly thought of herself beneath the drapes, imagined herself lying with covered face like a corpse, enwrapped all but one living staring eye. The open eye, opened. Anatomised alive.

At this the Radio Four murmurings had abruptly stopped.

"You all right in there? Miss Troy? Anthea? Are you feeling something?"

"I am feeling *anxious*," announced Alethea after a pause, to a rather gratifying splutter of laughter from the three, or was it four, voices?

"Oh, well, anxious, I feel anxious, we all feel anxious. Are you feeling anxious, Peter? I thought you were. He's a terrible worrier, is Peter."

"I'm sorry," said Alethea, understanding now. "I moved, didn't I?"

"Just a bit, no harm done. Kept us on our toes, though, and that's the main thing. Nearly done now, actually."

"You're doing really well, Anthea," said the earnest girlish voice at Miss Troy's head. "Nearly finished."

"No, point the needle away. That's it. Very nice . . ."

Barely half an hour, they had told her afterwards, though it had not seemed so long. But it was all over. And they would take the bandage off tomorrow.

She must wait and see. Wait. And see.

The Duchess of York came in, smiling rather shyly, and Miss Troy, though not at first puzzled, realised slowly that she had been asleep again, panicked a little, and put up a hand once more, to touch the bandage, but it was still really there.

CHAPTER
TWENTY-SEVEN

Rosemary lay awake nearly all Sunday night, uncontrollably watching the younger slimmer mental image Rosemary, chef and restauranteur, being lavishly praised in the local press, featured in various glossy magazines, making television appearances, and attending Royal garden parties, sometimes accompanied by her friend and business partner and sometimes, particularly towards dawn, by her devoted husband. It was hard, under such circumstances, to have to face her undeniably older and fatter real-life self in the bathroom mirror next morning, so hard that for the next hour or so Rosemary was bitterly convinced that the scheme was mere idleness.

Monday was her day off, and she set herself to cleaning and tidying the bungalow as usual, but presently she could not help remembering how, when the money had started to roll in the night before, she and Gregory had bought one of those big houses on the outskirts out by the golf links, and had one of those swinging outdoor sofas in the garden at the back. Rosemary sniffed as she plied her vacuum cleaner up and down her front room.

This dump. Freezing cold in winter, an oven every summer. That job. Trying to feed thirty-five people on four cheap frozen chickens. What have I really got to lose? thought Rosemary, bashing the vacuum cleaner's little head against the skirting. Then she switched the machine off and left it standing while she went into her bedroom, took her three Building Society account books out of the top dresser drawer, and sat down on the edge of her bed, considering them.

Every extra penny she and George had earned had been saved in one of these three accounts, so that their old age would be comfortable, even luxurious. While her husband had been alive and well Rosemary had sometimes wondered aloud whether George was not getting rather carried away on the subject of saving.

More than once she had complained of his active parsimony to various friends and relations as well; but, though his death had paid off the mortgage, Rosemary had then carried on very much as before, living thriftily on her wages, paying in a pound or two herself from time to time, and adding in the interest, and while she had not exactly forgotten that gently burgeoning sum total, she had largely put it out of her mind.

It was George's money. He had worked for it, and too hard. He had stinted himself. In his final illness, too breathless to lie down, he had not let her buy him a new armchair, even though he sat so uncomfortably in the sagging old one. If he had lain dying, patiently wrapped in blankets, how could she spend his money on central heating when he was dead? It was the unfairness of such a proposition that had so affected

Rosemary. If George couldn't have it, then neither would she.

So the money stayed where it was, accumulating, and now and then Rosemary thought of it, a vague large reliable solidity, very much as George himself had once been.

But now! Now I must face facts, thought Rosemary, spreading each account book open on the counterpane. There was certainly enough here. She could match whatever Gregory put down and more. And she would not, she told herself, be spending the money, George's money, on herself. She would hardly be frittering it away. This was business. This, thought Rosemary, sitting up straight and catching sight of herself in the dressing table mirror, was an *investment*.

She pushed her hair back; the bedroom was her darkest room, always shaded by the front door porch, and in the dim light Rosemary's reflection was not so far short of the dreamy mental image, especially if she sat sideways.

Me and him in one of those padded outdoor sofas! Holding hands.

Rosemary put the three account books into her handbag, went to the telephone in the hall, and dialled his hotel room.

"Gregory?"

"Hello, there. Lovely morning. What can I do for you?"

Rosemary trembled all over. "That restaurant. You know, you said yesterday about . . ."

"Ah. That."

"Well, I . . ."

"Yes?" He was smiling, she could tell.

"Well, Gregory, you were serious, weren't you?"

"My dear Rose, I most certainly was!"

CHAPTER
TWENTY-EIGHT

"Anthea, how are you this morning?"

Alethea knew at once that she was the object of this question, but could not begin to answer it. She put up a hand to touch the bandage: still there.

"Be taking that down in a jiffy. Have you finished with this, now?"

"With what, sorry?"

"This, your breakfast, have you finished with it?"

"Oh, ah, yes, I think so," said Alethea, in confusion, understanding the question only with the sound-clue of a tray being removed. "In fact I hadn't realised — hello? Nurse?"

No one answered. Footsteps briskly retreated. Alethea leant forward, the better to peer about her with her one remaining eye. She could make out the bed next to her own, and a grey possibility of further beds beyond. Had she been here all the time? The room felt entirely unfamiliar, and large enough to disappear altogether at either end. Where was the loo? Alethea was suddenly in urgent need. Was she allowed to move, to get out of bed? Could you get up and walk with stitches in your eyeballs? Alethea had been told just before the operation whether she could or could not get up the next day but though she could remember this she could not remember what the nurse had actually said. Who, now, could she ask? Was anyone there?

"Hello?" she said feebly, into the void.

"Hi there," said a voice, throatily Australian and so close that Alethea jumped a little as she sat. "I'm Trudy, I'm looking after you this morning, how you doing?"

"Um . . ."

"Need a pee?"

"Well, I . . ."

"Here. Give us your arm. Nah, get yer legs down first. OK? Not swimmy? Good, right then, I've got yer, up you get, doing great! Just over here. There you go. I'll be outside. OK?"

In the lavatory Althea worked out positions by touch, adjusted herself cautiously, and sat down. She felt wretched, she noticed, aching everywhere as if she'd been mugged. From wanting to go so much and clamping herself up it took what felt like a very long time to let go enough to pee at all, and even then such a small exhausted amount dribbled out that she knew she'd need to come back almost straight away. But she felt too worn out to try any more just now.

After swiping at herself with toilet paper as best she could without leaning down — the thought of leaning down brought with it the notion of her eyeball bursting its stitches and emptying itself, a spew of thin jelly, at her feet — she held onto the toilet roll dispenser on the one hand and the wall bar on the other and hauled herself upright.

196

The walls seemed to shift as she opened the door. The nurse, whose name she had forgotten, had disappeared. A dark grey void enclosed her. For a moment Alethea stood anxiously holding onto the door handle; then abruptly, from one quickened heartbeat to the next, ceased to be Alethea at all.

Fear was beyond her now, a normal response when she was past all normality. The creature that had been Alethea Troy was aware only of an infinite enclosing height reaching up all around her, of herself only as something pinned and crammed alive, as if between walls of rock, deep buried in the earth. The being uttered unconscious animal whimpers.

"Sorry about that, couldn't get a chair. Had to nip next door. There. Brake's on. OK?"

The creature could not understand what the nurse wanted. She could not see the wheelchair, nor make out the friendly face. She stayed where she was, inert.

The nurse's voice changed. She yelled something, then after a little while there were two, three of her. They took Alethea by her arms and talked to her gently, they uncurled her fingers one by one from the door handle and caused her in some way to sit down. There was a pause, in which all sensations absented themselves. And then, gradually, Alethea could make out her own small green toilet bag sitting on a locker, and knew herself to be back at her own bedside, and that the mute and senseless terror that had so possessed her had vanished almost as suddenly as it had come.

"I'm most awfully sorry," she said. "I . . . I didn't know where I was, and I'm afraid I panicked, rather."

She heard herself with some surprise. *I'm afraid I panicked, rather!* How reasonable it sounded, already, when the horror was still so close that she had only to think back a little to remember that complete physical and spiritual despair! It was a glimpse of Hell, thought Miss Troy, as the nice Australian nurse wheeled her along yet another immensity of corridor.

"I've got one or two things to get ready. Wanna cup a tea?"

"Oh, yes please, very much."

A glimpse at Hell, a feel of it. That was why mad people killed themselves, thought Alethea, because they felt like that all the time. The loneliness! She suddenly remembered hearing an account on the radio by a man whose parachute had failed on a routine jump. He had pulled the tag for the emergency second parachute, and for a minute or two that had failed to open as well. He had had a minute or two to think and feel; and most of what he had felt, he had said, had been loneliness. You don't need a freefall, thought Alethea, sipping her tea from the spouted mug the nurse had brought her. You don't need any props at all: it is on feelings like that, remembered by survivors, that the great pervasive myths of Hell have grown.

"There, better?"

"Oh, yes. I'm sorry I was such a nuisance —"

"Nah, nah. Now then, doctor'll be along in a bit, I'm gonna take this down, now, this bandage, so you'll be all ready for him to have a good look at it, OK?"

"What, now?"

"Don't look so scared! Here . . ."

The nurse bent, and began pulling at the sticky stuff that held the eye pad on so firmly. "Nah remember, it may not be so great first thing, it's often a bit blurry for a few days, then it settles, OK? Anthea? You with me?"

"Yes. Yes."

"There. How's that?"

With difficulty Alethea opened her right eye. For a second the brightness seemed hard enough to blind her again, then she could open it properly. She looked: she saw. She was sitting in a room with walls of buttercup yellow, the nurse was in palest singing blue like a spring sky, she had auburn hair, she had freckles, she had a lovely velvety little face, she was entrancingly beautiful in every particular, as was everything else in that marvellous room, that box of colours, the maroon plastic on the wheelchair beneath her hand, her own blue flowered hospital nightie, the speckled Formica shelves of delightfully packaged items all bursting pinkly out of boxes, the sink with its tall silver gleaming tap dripping crystal, and the cracks in the tiled flooring, so engrossing, so unsuspected, greeny-blue tiles!

"Not bad, eh?"

Alethea wept.

"Lovely job," said the nurse, peering. "Very neat."

"Oh, thank you, thank you!"

"What did *I* do? I didn't do anything. I'll take you back to bed, bring you back when he shows, OK?"

"It's the colours, I can't believe how colourful everything looks!"

"Yeah, it's your colour perception that goes first, with cataract," said the nurse chattily. "And it's gradual, yeah? Creeps up on you so you don't notice. You can see to get about long after you can't make out colours. It's what most people talk about, you know."

"Is it?" said Alethea, hardly aware of speaking. She was smiling all the time, unconsciously. The ward had ends! Each bed had an occupant! Faces everywhere had an astonishing clarity, a perfection of fine detail, an unmatchable idiosyncrasy of texture and tone! A Holbein drawing, every one.

How could I have forgotten, she wondered, staring greedily about her. For now she could see it she could remember that once the world had always looked like this, and that she herself had thought nothing of it, had constantly inspected this riot of delineation and contrast and not even noticed herself doing it.

"Best not to read for a little while, OK? It's a bit of a strain, and you end up looking down a lot, so, best not for a day or two, yeah?"

Alethea nearly laughed. She thought how desperate she had been to read, and how little it mattered that she still could not. Not yet, anyway. Who would want to read, who would want anyone else's world when her own was so newly enchanting? I would be happy just staring at the wall, she thought, for the wall is such a beautiful colour, I could look at it all day. Perhaps I will.

It occurred to her then, that though today she had glimpsed Hell, she was also having a more extended view of the complete happiness of Heaven. What a busy day! She giggled.

Well, I will enjoy Heaven while it lasts, she thought, and sat back in her bed, her hands folded, to do so.

CHAPTER
TWENTY-NINE

The fireplace was in. It had only taken a morning. The two men from *Going Grate!* had arrived at eight-thirty, refused all offers of refreshment, closed the office door behind them and emerged at one-fifteen with the bill. Betty had kept right out of the way. Once or twice she remembered what they were up to in there but it was always with something very like a shudder. Certainly she felt no curiosity as to their methods. In fact once they had gone she found herself strangely reluctant to go in and view the final effect. More than reluctant, positively unwilling.

I'm not that interested, she told herself, as once more she walked straight past her office door on some errand or another. It was only an office, after all. It was just somebody's office, being redecorated, it was nothing to get all upset about. It didn't mean anything.

The trouble was that although Betty could tell herself these sensible things most of the time every so often she suddenly felt so shaky and overcome by the enormity of what she had done that she had to find somewhere to sit down.

Whatever made me do it, whatever made me choose yellow for the walls?

How could she have imagined such a shade would suit those high austere walls? With a blue paper border, so babyish, and obviously too high up, or maybe too far down. And the fireplace, suppose it was vulgar! Suppose Audrey Hapgood thought it was vulgar! No point pretending; if Audrey Hapgood thought it was vulgar it would *be* vulgar, and everyone would know that she, Betty, was a vulgar tasteless person, who didn't know what was what, who had absolutely no idea, poor thing, what a hoot!

That was what the Friends would think as they swept out all perfume and tittered off to their waiting BMW's. They wouldn't need to say it, they would just give one another little looks. They would all have a laugh later, but they wouldn't even bother to discuss it, thought Betty, by now in a positive lather of social self-depreciation. If only I'd put in an ordinary gas-fire, wouldn't that have been safer? Things that pretended to be other things, they were what poor stupid people wanted, people with taste and money always had the real thing or they didn't bother at all.

I shouldn't have done any of it, thought Betty. What had that old office to do with me? It was inherited. It wasn't my fault. All I have done is make different mistakes, mistakes with a price-tag and my name on them.

But it was remembering about furniture that most often made Betty need to find a seat. How could she go through with that now? Whatever she chose would be wrong. It would be pretentious or too heavy or turn out to be a funny colour that made everything else look even worse. She had imagined herself confidently striding into antique shops and picking out exactly what she wanted, but now she pictured smarmy antique dealers coming out from behind screens, and telling her lies she would have no way of checking up on, and selling her all the heavy pretentious funny-coloured stuff they'd been dying to get rid of for years, she would be helpless in their hands.

And Audrey bloody Hapgood would snort with laughter when she went in, she'd say, My dear Betty, where did you get this extraordinary, oh, Good Lord, Betty!

Could just keep the old stuff. Couldn't I?

Betty pictured this. Would it, in some way, detract from the overall vapid smartness she had (she now felt sure) so clearly created? If the furniture was to stay someone else's fault, wouldn't that make the whole room less clear in its statement of her Self? As it was her soul lay splayed on the boring new blue carpet like a butterfly under glass, waiting for the crushing heels of Audrey and the Friends.

If I don't replace the furniture I'll have a lot of money left over.

I could . . .

I could . . .

I could give it back to her, thought Betty at last, and as she did so noticed, though it was very small and far away like light at the other end of a tunnel, a feeling of relief and hope. The feeling was very localised, she thought, a definite sensation in her abdomen, a sort of loose pleasant surging about in there.

Suppose I gave it all back, somehow?

No. Impossible. Too late. And as she thought these things Betty felt her intestines tighten up and yet seem to turn over, all at once. Strange; as if emotion lay not in your heart or mind but in those twisting yards of wormy underwater tubing inside. They responded, when the mind could not. They must blush or blench, thought Betty, they must writhe and wriggle, and then we go and call all that squirming pride, or outrage, or devotion, all sorts of highfalutin things.

She covered her face with her hands and pressed her eyeballs. What time was it? Surely she had been sitting here in the empty kitchen for at least half an hour, and nothing done? Was it time to go and get Alethea Troy d.o.b. April 6 1897 from the hospital yet? She would have to phone them up to check. She could go into her office, and use the telephone there.

But with her hand on the doorknob she paused, and remembered that she would have to go up to her own room anyway, to pick up her car keys, and that she might as well telephone from there. It was only an office anyway. She would possibly move a little of the old furniture back in there tomorrow. If she had time.

205

CHAPTER
THIRTY

On Wednesday afternoon Rosemary left work a little early, caught a bus into the town centre, and called in turn at the offices of the three building societies, picking up at each a large bank draft made out to Gregory Banks, for it had been agreed between them that he was to handle all the financial side of their business to begin with. All Rosemary had to do was hand over her share of the capital, sign various documents, and, as Gregory put it, look out all her wooden spoons.

It was a damp rather chilly cold afternoon. The sea showed small white horses as Rosemary bowled along the prom sitting on the top deck at the front. They were meeting at the Grand, which of course was Gregory's hotel, he'd stayed in it, he'd told her, as a child, when there had been dancing every evening to a live band after dinner. It was owned by a chain now, and you had to make your own early morning tea, instead of someone bringing you a tray.

"But they still serve decent coffee," Gregory had said. "We'll start the ball rolling, then go out for a drive somewhere, shall we? Little celebration? Maybe even manage the Abbey this time, eh?"

206

Rosemary knew the Grand very well. As a teenager she had even been employed there, sometimes to bring people their early morning tea, a detail she had not cared to share with Gregory. The present manager was a local, too, and had been in the same class as Maureen at school. Rosemary remembered this as she crossed the large heavily carpeted hall to the reception desk. Maureen, who knew nothing of Gregory, whose opinion on the new venture had not been consulted. It's her father's money I'm spending, thought Rosemary uneasily. I should have asked her, by rights.

And wasn't it going on for six weeks now, since she had seen her daughter? Could it really be that long? No, longer! Much longer! She hasn't called me either, thought Rosemary, as her mood took a sudden sharp turn downwards. What if something's actually wrong? Suppose it wasn't just a child's carelessness? It wasn't as if Maureen really were that careless these days anyway. Or childish, she was nearly thirty, she was properly grown up; I've always heard from her every week or so before, thought Rosemary.

It's all because of Gregory, she told herself. I've thought of nothing but him. Well, I suppose that's hardly his fault. No. It's mine. I should have called her. All this time! I should have called her, whatever has been the matter with me, she might be ill, she might be in trouble, two months, three months!

All this went through Rosemary's head in a very nasty flash as she crossed the heavy floral carpet. I'll call her first, she thought, and instead of inquiring for Mr Banks she said to the pretty young receptionist,

"May I use your telephone, please?"

Inside the old-fashioned glazed wooden booth Rosemary found she had hardly any change, but went ahead anyway and dialled Maureen's work number.

"Hello, Ashby's Estate Agency, Beth speaking, how can I help you?"

"Um," said Rosemary, taken aback. "Can I speak to Maureen, please?"

A pause. "There's no one here by that name. Can I be of assistance?"

"No," said Rosemary flatly. "I want to speak to Maureen. Maureen Sholto."

"I'm sorry, there's no one here by that name."

"She's one of the directors!" cried Rosemary. "Don't you know who you work for?"

"I —"

"Get me the other one. It's what, it's Colin. Colin Thacker, or are you going to tell me he doesn't work there either?"

"There's no need to be offensive, madam."

"Who's being offensive, I'm not being offensive!" shouted Rosemary, "Is Colin there or not, because if he is I want to talk to him. Please."

"One moment," said the voice coldly. Stuck up bitch, thought Rosemary. There was a long pause, during which Rosemary was forced to put in her last fifty pence.

"Hello?"

"Colin?"

"Speaking."

"Er we have met, I'm Maureens' mother, is she not at work today?"

"Sorry?"

"Maureen, I'm trying to get hold of Maureen Sholto. Is she there?"

"I'm sorry, oh, unless you mean — d'you mean Molly? Molly Sholto used to work here."

"What?" Rosemary's mind went blank. Molly?

"We've never had a Maureen. Honest. Sorry."

"Wait, wait," said Rosemary, coming up with something at last. "What does she look like?"

"Who, Molly?"

"Tall? Dark curly hair? She's got a, oh a black leather jacket . . .?"

"Red Fiat, it's obviously the same person, well, sorry, she was always Molly here, and you're mum, hello, how are you?"

"Yes, is she off work or something, is she all right?"

"Well, I'm sorry I can't help you there. Oh, this is a bit awkward . . ."

"What d'you mean awkward, what is it?"

"No, don't get alarmed, please, only Molly, Maureen, whatever, she doesn't work here any more, we've er, parted company, her and me."

"Oh! Oh, but I thought — when?"

"Ooh, about a month ago now, well, it had been coming a long time."

"What, you bought her out, then?"

"Didn't have much choice as it happened." His tone altered, cooled. "I think this is something you need to discuss with your daughter, actually, Mrs Sholto, if you wouldn't mind."

"But what's she doing now?"

"As I say, I think you'd better ask her."

"But I —" Here the line was cut off; the money had run out.

Rosemary banged down the receiver, found a pound coin, and recklessly inserted it before dialling Maureen's number.

Molly indeed, she thought as it rang. How long had that been going on, then? At least as long as Ashby's and that was what, five, six years?

"Hello?"

"Who's this?" said Rosemary, indignant and afraid, for a man's voice had answered.

"Erm, is —"

"I want to speak to Maureen."

"Erm I sink you dial ze wrong numbair, sorry."

"No I haven't." Who was this! Bloody foreigner! "Is Maureen there? Or it might be Molly. Molly Sholto, is she there?"

"Moll-ee? Is Mollee Sholto?"

"I'm her mother," said Rosemary with emphasis, "who are you?"

"Um. I am, er, renting."

"What? No you're not!"

"I am sorry."

"How long for?"

"How long for, is six munts only —"

"No, no, I mean, when did you start?"

"Ah, I live here sree-four veeks, since she is coming to hospital."

"Hang on. Who's in hospital?"

"Oh. Forgive. I confuse. You are not ze muzzer?"

"D'you mean Maureen? D'you mean Maureen was in hospital? What for? What's wrong with her?"

"Moll-ee. Mollee was in hospital, is zis —"

"What for?"

"Ah, please, I don't zink I —"

"Which hospital?"

"Is right, is called You, See, Aitch?"

"Oh my God!" University College Hospital! "What's wrong with her?"

"I, air. I don' know. Sorry."

No job, no home, in hospital! What on earth was happening? Oh, Maureen! Punch-drunk, Rosemary gave a little moan, and began to cry.

"Oh please — ah, you call the hospital, yes? They tell you. I give the number. You wait, I give the number, yes?"

"I don't know," said Rosemary helplessly. She listened, sobbing quietly, to a series of clicks and thrubbing noises. Too busy! Too busy gallivanting to look after her own sick child! She was too ill to call me, thought Rosemary, and tears ran unchecked down her face and dripped onto the front of her raincoat.

"Hello?"

"Yes?"

"You ready, pen, pencil?"

"Oh, no, wait a minute, oh, God . . ." Rosemary flung the contents of her handbag onto the floor of the telephone booth, scrabbled through them, found the biro and folded flat the inside cover of her Glorious Devon diary. "Right!"

"Is 01 —"

The line went dead. The money, Rosemary's reckless pound, had run out as well.

Rosemary gave a small scream, gathered up the stuff on the floor together and squashed it back into her handbag, and ran across to the reception desk.

"Can you get me Gregory Banks, please! Room 19!"

"Oh, Mr Banks — excuse me, but are you ah Rosemary Sholto?"

Rosemary nodded breathlessly, wiping her wet face with several bits of pink tissue she had found in her raincoat pocket.

"Oh dear, are you all right?"

"Yes, yes," said Rosemary, and muttered something about some bad news, which had the unfortunate effect of making her eyes overflow again.

"Oh dear," said the receptionist again, uncertainly. She had not been in the job very long, and she didn't like the look of Rosemary, and she had heard the scream in the telephone booth.

"Um, Mr Banks asked us to pass this on to you. He said you were going to have some meeting here?"

She consulted the pigeon holes behind her. "Yes. Here." Gingerly, as one holding out a morsel to an unfamiliar dog, the receptionist proffered an envelope. Rosemary snatched it and ripped it asunder; the receptionist looked down to check the whereabouts of

212

the alarm button hidden in the heavy floral carpet by her feet.

"My dear Rose," read Rosemary,

"I'm so sorry to ruin what should have been such a special day, but I've had sad news. My brother has had a heart attack, and passed away. We were never the best of friends I'm afraid. But of course I must pay my respects. I expect to be away for three days at most. Don't, please, worry about the restaurant! Remember, they've accepted our offer. All we have to do is get the money to the solicitor before the end of next week. I put my lot in this morning, but there's bags of time. I wish I could have told you all this over the telephone, but no one seems to be answering at Cabotin. And I'm so sorry to have to disappear like this. We'll make up for it — shall we, when I get back?"

And he sent his best wishes, Gregory.

Rosemary allowed herself a bitter moment or two, to reflect that men were never ever there when you really needed them. Then she stuffed the letter and the bits of envelope into her gaping handbag, grimly thanked the receptionist, and left the Grand Hotel to make a rush for the taxi rank outside.

CHAPTER
THIRTY-ONE

Annie Cameron had had a letter from her son Michael.

"Over in December. On his own. I don't know what I'll say to him."

"It will be difficult."

Annie sighed. "And Naomi has gone back to her parents' end of the country, well, of course she would. And that's an aeroplane trip away. He's going to end up seeing his children about as often as he sees me."

Alethea, sitting beside the teashop's big front window, was covertly playing with her blindness. Close right eye: see grey shifting filmy shapes. See my fingers, just see them move. See blob of teacup, guess at handle.

But close left eye, open right: trumpet fanfare: see world. See that ferry on the horizon. See horizon. See sea. Oh, the glory!

"He married rather late," she said cheerfully, turning to face Annie across the table.

"He did. Thirty-five! We'd given up hope," said Annie. "There was always a different girlfriend; I was always calling them by the wrong name."

"Few have your luck," said Alethea, hoping to change the subject. "You met Edward at that school, didn't you? The Wentworth school?"

214

"Yes," said Annie. "I was twelve. He was fourteen."

"And?"

Smiling, Annie hesitated. She could remember every detail of the day she met Edward. She had told the story of it many times over the years. But she had never managed to shake off the feeling that in doing so she was somehow falsifying things. "Oh, love at first sight!" people usually marvelled, and sometimes they exclaimed *how romantic* or *how sweet*. And then Annie was embarrassed, even though what she had said had been perfectly true, and their reactions perfectly understandable.

"Do tell me," said Alethea.

And yet of course it was lovely to tell the story, to bring the past back so vividly for a little while.

"Well," she began, "We were queuing to go in after the dinner break. We were always lining up and marching about. Anyway there we were, waiting for the second flag, the signal, and I glanced over and I saw him join the end of the boy's queue. A new boy. It was his first day. I saw him and I felt a real shock, all over me. I didn't know what it was. I didn't think, Oh, I've fallen in love! or anything like that," said Annie emphatically (and far too loudly, thought Alethea affectionately) "I just felt this, like a *thump* inside me, at the sight of him. And while I'm looking at him, feeling this shock, he turns his face and sees me. He had a cap on, I can see him now. He looked at me, I looked at him. We didn't smile. I looked away, I was trembling like a leaf! And then the headmaster waved the flag and we had to go inside and that was that. And the next day, when we lined up! The state I was in!"

Annie laughed. "I couldn't remember what he looked like. I kept thinking, that boy, if only I could get a good look at him, then I'd be all right. I thought I just wanted a good long look at his face."

Alethea nodded, remembering. Yes, that was what it had felt like.

"And there he was at the end of the queue again, waiting for me. Smiled this time. That's when I knew what was up with me. That's all we did, you know, for weeks! Smiled at one another in the queues. Then he started to talk to me. Because he could, of course. There we were, all lined up in parallel rows, all drawn up waiting for the second flag to go back into school, and he could just waggle a few fingers at me, oh hardly moving, to say Hello there Annie, what a stinky dinner, eh, I'm starving, we've got Maths now, how about you? And if the coast was clear I'd sign back, Hello, Eddie, couldn't eat a mouthful either, History, it's my favourite. Of course we were soon in double trouble, boys and girls weren't allowed to be friends, and signing was against the rules as well."

"Really? I thought that was what you were there for."

"Oh dear me no. Signing means you can only talk to other people who can sign. Other deaf people, in other words. The implication being, what was the use of that? So the idea of the Wentworth Homes was that every deaf person learnt to speak. You were in real trouble if they caught you signing. I remember one wee lad with his hands tied together in front of him, day after day

216

they did that, because they kept catching him signing. It was, for your own good, sort of thing. That was why Edward was there in the first place, his parents had tried private teachers and some other school — his parents had money, in fact, owned textile factories. The Wentworth was a bit of a desperate measure for them. Because he just couldn't get it. Born deaf, you see, it's well nigh impossible. But he was in real trouble, caught signing and to a lassie! Got both hands knotted."

"What, you mean tied up?"

"Oh no, this was different, this was what, like a wee rope with knots in it, you'd hold out your hands, palm up, and the teacher'd swat you with it."

"Like a cat o' nine tails?"

"Yes, but not the metal bits in. The knots hurt a lot though, you'd get these big swollen welts on your hands. Couldn't hold a pen very well for a few days. They did both Edward's hands, for signing to me. And they put me in the blind side for a day, for signing back."

The sun came out and quick-silvered the sea. I will never get used to it, thought Alethea. Surely I will never be able to take it for granted again!

"Show me a sign," she said, turning back to Annie.

Annie picked up an imaginary apple, bit into it, and looked up questioningly.

"Well, an apple."

Annie peeled an invisible banana.

"Yes, but what about abstractions?"

Annie held out her right hand, with the thumb and little finger extended, and waggled it slightly. Her face, her faint shrug, also answered:

"Oh, perhaps!" said Alethea.

"Yes, you have to look at all of me, it's not just fingers. And look. This is 'I'm sure.'" Annie held out her left hand, palm up, and smacked the side of her right hand into it. "So, what's this?"

She held out her left palm again, this time with the right hand resting on it, and wavering a little from side to side.

"Well, obviously, not sure," said Alethea.

"This, then." Now Annie made a series of small gestures.

Alethea smiled and shook her head. "You were asking me something."

"Yes. Your name. I would say, What's your name? But I would sign, Your name — what? D'you see what I mean? It's not English. It's not anything. It's itself. It's Sign."

"But it's universal, isn't it?"

"Oh no, no. That's a hearing fallacy, I'm afraid, this cosy idea that there's a sort of deaf Esperanto. But really, why should Swedish deaf people have the same language as British ones? My Wentworth School had its own Sign. Local variations crop up everywhere."

"There are dialects, then."

"It's all different dialects. That's partly why it was forbidden."

"Not now, surely."

"Oh, no no. Gone too far the other way, now, I think, as these things will. Michael, my son, you know he teaches the deaf. Being something of an expert from an early age. He has some very odd ideas. The college he teaches at, they call hearing people TABS, have you ever come across that?"

Alethea shook her head.

"Temporarily Able-Bodied. Mean, eh? Like, *just you wait*."

"Well, I suppose they have a point," said Alethea, briefly winking her right eye, and temporarily disabling herself.

"No they don't. It's whistling in the dark. And mean-minded. Michael makes out it's not a disability at all. He'll say so, in so many words. You don't *need* hearing, he says. And I think, well, he's just never going to get over the fact that he has this ordinary gift and we, his mum and dad, we didn't."

"I suppose he is bound to feel guilty."

"Yes. When he was a baby, I remember, I sat him on his father's lap, facing him. And then I stood behind him where Edward could see me. And I crept up and then all of a sudden I clapped my hands together. I could feel it of course, I couldn't hear it. Edward couldn't hear it either. But the baby jumped, and turned his head to see. His father shed tears. Strange, isn't it, we were so happy. But really I think in his heart Michael wishes that he hadn't turned round."

Alethea thought of a poem she had written many years earlier. There are no happy endings, she remembered, only happy stages. In life we get to the happy ending and helplessly keep on going, sailing right past it as if we've forgotten to get off the bus. Annie and her Edward, what a perfect romance! The young lovers, the cruel authorities, the disapproving parents, the lengthy engagement patiently endured, the final triumphant wedding day, but not a happy ending at all, just a happy stage, long over now. That is what gives the lie to real romance.

A Temporarily Happy Ending, thought Alethea to herself. A THE. Like the healthy baby turning round. Since they are not lasting, how firmly one should celebrate these moments, if one has the luck to spot them as they arise!

"It's stopped raining," she said aloud. "Shall we have a little stroll along the front for a bit? Towards the bus stop. This is on me, by the way —" Alethea gave the bored waitress a little wave, and presently they made their way out of the teashop and into the chilly dampish unseasonable breeze.

The waitress watched them go. She was very young herself, and thus inclined to blame her late guests for having allowed themselves to get so very old; and there were so many of them about around here, too, she thought. Swarms of them. All those little watery red-rimmed eyes and thin legs ready to snap, all those sticks and glasses and hearing aids. It was sort of horrible really.

She clanged the door to behind them with relief, and nipped into the back to check her hair. Catch me getting like that, she thought complacently at her own rosy reflection. I'm going to die young.

CHAPTER
THIRTY-TWO

Betty had moved all the old office furniture back in, reconnected her equipment, and was in theory catching up on her paperwork, which during the past fortnight or so had made up a great deal of distance, drawn almost level with her in fact. But it was somehow rather hard to get going. A letter from her mother's elderly cousin had been sitting on top of the pile for two days now, not even opened, let alone answered. Betty felt languid, and inclined to wonder if she wasn't coming down with something.

Instead of making advances on the paperwork Betty rested her head on it and tried not to think about anything at all. So it was very strange that after several minutes of blankness the notion should suddenly jump into her head, all by itself:

I have spoiled the best thing I ever did.

Betty raised her head from the paperwork and stared unseeingly across the office at the new and still unused coal-effect gas fire.

It was the best thing I ever did. It was the best thing by miles. I don't know anyone else who's done anything even anywhere near as good. There's probably hardly anyone alive who has. None of those Friends, that's for sure. They'd have nothing to compare with it. My best thing.

She opened the bottom drawer of her desk and took out the envelope she had passed over to Valerie Elliott. The newspaper clipping was still inside. She drew it out and looked at it. There would have been pictures nowadays, she thought. Lots of them, not just the one blurred tiny one of me. It would have been on television, over and over again. And there'd be talk talk talk about what it all meant and whose fault it was and what it said about society. People would be frightened. That such horrors should exist!

Looking back on the last few weeks it now became strangely clear to Betty that all the time she had thought she was worrying about decorators and flagstones and coordinating curtain material she had really been thinking about something else; that décor had occupied only the surface of her mind, whilst deeper down she had been constantly replaying the events of that night in 1944, looking again and again at the details, the smells, the textures.

It's been like trying to read with the telly on. And I've only just realised I've been half-watching it all the time. No wonder it feels like something that happened yesterday! Every detail complete, familiar.

Herself on a bicycle, aged nearly twenty-four, Miss Betty Potts, Staff Nurse, with fat downy cheeks above a collar glossy with starch, slowly pedalling the blacked-out streets. Of course it hadn't been so bad by day, you could always ask, and people knew the uniform in those days. They respected it. But by night

222

she had often been afraid, and not only of air raids. No nights had been as dark as those for a hundred years.

Once she had passed down a road she thought she knew, and stopped at the end of it to check where she was with her torch shielded behind one gloved hand. The moon had come out as she stood there, and looking back she had realised that every house in the street was no house at all, only a façade, shattered in the darkness, not blacked-out but ruined.

It had shaken her. After that, she had never again tried to comfort herself with the notion that the entirely darkened houses she cycled past at night had normal life going on behind their curtained windows. You couldn't count on anyone being there at all.

She had remembered this on that special night, answering the emergency call yet again. Tiredness, thought Betty now, rising from her desk to pace the floor. All those interrupted nights. No. I was in a bit of a state anyway. On account of . . .

Betty stopped pacing, and thought hard, but it was no use. She had completely forgotten his name. Andy? Mike? There was his face, clearly enough. Not handsome, of course. Bony and blond, with long arms and his neck all Adam's apple. But tall. There he was in the pub, leaning against the wall with his hat on sideways, singing. And his accent, so pleasantly foreign, so classless. Nurse Potts herself, at nursing school, had been mocked by one of the teachers, for making raining rhyme with pining.

"Rining, Nurse Potts, what ken you mean?" the stuck-up gink had smirked, and the whole set had

223

tittered as well, as though any of them had anything to be stuck-up about.

No, he'd sounded like a Yank. She could remember kissing him in the street outside. She remembered the shock of his hand, his arm, the sudden burrowing lunge right up her skirt, as if he was trying to snatch back something he'd somehow lost up there. Was this what girls who had boyfriends had to put up with?

She had been more than shocked, she had been highly alarmed, for her mother, whilst chary with all other sorts of information and advice, had come across very clearly when it came to Men.

Mrs Potts had closed the door and lowered her voice in order to impart this information.

"Men," she said, in a low fierce whisper, "Men can't stop theirselves. Once they get past a Certain Point. They can't stop. It's not their fault. They have to go on. Because they *Can't Stop*."

Betty's mother, a person of ferocious working class respectability, never lied. And the vehemence of her whisper gave her words an over-powering force. Betty quaked with horror, a horror spiced all the same with a deep and shameful excitement. Men! Unable. To. Stop. Like *animals*.

So that was it, that was why Men ruled the world! That was the great grownup secret children must be protected from! It did not occur to Betty for an instant that her mother might simply be misinformed; or might be basing her opinions, poor thing, on a very particular personal experience. No, Betty had spent her teens and early youth shying away in fascinated horror from even

224

the most unlikely-looking of these helpless and ungovernable rapists, shooting suspicious glances at the greengrocer, the boy who delivered the paper, sizing up the milkman, keeping well out of sight of any of her brother's friends. Though simultaneously she longed for friendly admiring masculine contact. For a boyfriend. But who was likely to accept such a challenge? Besides she was fat and bespectacled; painfully aware that no one would look at her unless she was openly encouraging.

Suppose one of them felt so encouraged that he *Couldn't Stop!*

It was a puzzle Betty had no way of solving.

Billy? Timmy? The only man who had ever asked me to marry him, thought Betty now, concealing from herself with the ease of long practice the fact that it had not immediately been difficult to refuse his offer, arising as it incontrovertibly had from a condition of almost total intoxication. But after she had broken in outraged excitement from his embrace — for clearly being tight as a tick might well hasten a man toward that Certain Point — and rushed back to the dismal safety of the Nurses' Home, she had lain awake all night wondering whether to change her mind and accept him after all.

Next day she had enjoyably confided her dilemma to a friend. Could she be happy in Canada, if her fiancé were to survive the Invasion? Was it just a Wartime Romance? It had certainly been unlucky that the same friend had been with her when she had met her admirer by chance in the street that afternoon, and he had clearly had only the vaguest notion of who she was. Though he had still, she recollected bitterly, been amiably drunk.

And that was, of course, the day. I was upset. Of course I was. Was that why I behaved the way I did?

Betty sank down at her desk again, remembering. The street had been down by the Docks. Twilight darkened into blackout as she cycled slowly between shoulder high heaps of rubble and then down two completely undamaged streets, past singing and a muffled shouting from a pub on the corner. Then a long winding alley between warehouses, another right turn at the end, and could this be it? Here? She had consulted the little chart she had drawn for herself from the big map in the office, her torch well shielded by her woollen-gloved hand.

She remembered the warning notice, a demolition order tied to a lamppost. Briefly she had shone her light over it, noting the marks made by stone-throwing. She was at the entrance to a tall crescent terraced street beside the river. A quick cast of the torch showed her that nearly every pane in every immense sash window was shattered. Surely all the houses were empty, nearly derelict, ready for oblivion?

She had dismounted what with all that broken glass and pushed the bicycle carefully along the gentle curve of the cobbled street, until she reached the last house, number fourteen at the end of the crescent row. Fourteen still had a gatepost, or rather part of one. The number had been roughly painted on it in whitewash. There was no gate. No railings, of course, to lean the bike on. Nubs of those, long gone. Like the gates of Cabotin, thought Betty now, sighing, resting her head on her paperwork once more.

No door knocker either. For a minute or two Nurse Potts had stood nonplussed at the top of the stone steps up to the front door, a small hefty figure in belted gabardine raincoat and hard black lace-up shoes.

It's four, no, five stories high. They'll never hear me if they're at the top.

She rapped hard at the door for several seconds before noticing the bell-pull beside the door. Was it still connected?

She heard a very distant shrill jangling as she pulled it. She waited, shivering a little. You got so cold cycling. Was there anyone in at all? Perhaps the address was wrong, misheard, misunderstood; such things often happened when whole streets might after all disappear altogether from one day to the next. She flexed her numb toes inside the heavy shoes, and at last heard faint approaching sounds from inside the house. Presently the door shifted a little in its frame, as bolts were undrawn top and bottom. A key turned, and slowly the door was opened an inch or two.

"Hello, it's the nurse," called Nurse Potts, starting cheerfully enough and then instantly trailing off as the stink hit her; a great breath of mingled decay, like an exhalation from the grave. Crikey, what a pong! Though the sickeningly sweet smell of putrefaction was hardly unfamiliar, for a nurse, in those days.

"Who is it?" The voice came from behind the door, a man's voice, low and hoarse.

"It's the nurse," she said again, speaking into the palm of her hand, trying to breathe through her mouth. It was dreadful but not, of course, unprecedented. Nurse Potts had got used very quickly to the surprising contents of other people's houses, the herds of bugs looking down as if with benign cross-species interest from the ceiling or clattering noisily for cover across the floorboards, the leisurely stroll of the well-fed bed-bug, full and encrusted saucepans standing in for chamber pots and left in full view, whole blocks of flats with no running water, some of them spotless even so, and some of them reaching levels of filth you could smell on the sleeve of your coat when you left, Well, some people obviously *liked* living like pigs.

She could not see the man in the doorway. There was no light behind him.

"Mr Carradine?"

"You are too late, I fear," said the man. The voice, though hoarse, was educated, well-spoken.

"What d'you mean?"

"It's all over, that's all. We don't need you in the least. You can go." It was the sort of voice directed often enough at Nurse Potts thus far in the course of her working life; reedy with unconscious scorn, it was the voice of the Edwardian gentleman dismissing a servant, careless, lordly, male.

Nurse Potts saw red. It was barely hours since the Canadian soldier had publicly forgotten her. All her life arose before her furious gaze, years of being called Fatty or Potty, of being sneered at or ignored, and of being frightened, so frightened, of Men! And you were

228

supposed to respect them as well, and look up to them, when all the time they couldn't Stop Themselves! And look at this one, stinking, filthy! Still thinks he's giving me orders!

She switched her torch back on, and shone it right at the man's face, at the white stubble, at the scabbed creases at the corners of his mouth, his neckful of grimy tendons, the blackened vest showing beneath the collarless shirt.

"I've come to see your wife, not you!" Sneering at me, from all that filth! "Get out of my way at *once*, please!" And ferocious with anger she had actually reached out and bashed hard at the door, taking him so by surprise that he had simply staggered back behind it. Nurse Potts swung her heavy bag up to her chest and held it there like a shield, her torch aloft in the other hand, lighting the scrawny stubbled face.

"Right. Where is she? Have you got a light?"

"No. No light."

"You must have something."

"No. You don't need to come in. You can go. What can you do, in the dark? Come back tomorrow."

"I've got a torch," said Nurse Potts, ignoring him. "Where is your wife?"

"In her grave."

"Oh. Your daughter, then."

"Miss Carradine." He spoke the first word with such venom that Nurse Potts, who usually had no time for unmarried mothers herself, thought Lumme, poor kid!

"Just show me where she is, please."

The man shot a furtive look up the stairs, before turning back to her. "I told you," he said, and again his voice, so refined, so clearly lording it, made Nurse Potts, whom he had summoned to this freezing stinkhole, feel almost ill with fury, "you're too late. She's gone, she went yesterday. It so happens. To my sister's. She couldn't stay here, it's condemned, you know. No place for her."

"Who called me, then? I'm not here by chance."

"I'm afraid I really don't know, neighbours, perhaps, interfering."

"You haven't got any neighbours," cried Nurse Potts impatiently. She had seen enough, she thought. Dirty lying little beast's told me clear as day there's someone upstairs. Anger made her, she would decide afterwards, think rather as she imagined a man would: she discounted Mr Carradine as a threat simply on account of his size.

"She's not up there!"

Because I was a big girl in those days, thought Betty, remembering with satisfaction how she had simply turned the torch onto the staircase above her and left him standing down there in the hall on his own, turning just long enough to say, in ferocious unashamed Cockney, "You lay a finger on me, you dirty tyke, and I'll have the coppers round here doing you over before you can blink, you got that?" Shut him up straight away. Bit of firm handling, that's all it took.

The staircase was bare, the treads worn into curves of antiquity. The walls were set about with strange hanging shapes made by dangling wallpaper, and

230

studded here and there with bulbous crumbling growths on the plaster. The banister was smooth and damp to the touch.

"Miss Carradine! Where are you please, it's the nurse, Miss Carradine!"

Panting a little but not in the least frightened, Nurse Potts stamped angrily up to the first floor. There were three doors, all ajar.

"Hello?" The first an immense drawing room, thought Betty, looking back at it from a perspective of forty years. Three beautiful arched windows, floor to ceiling. What a magnificent room it must once have been! With views, no doubt, over some long-vanished graceful square of private garden.

Nurse Potts had barely noticed the windows. What on earth was that, hanging from the mantelpiece? Creeping inside, she could make out a long string dangling in front of the empty fireplace, and tied about with — she went closer, peering, her shoes gritting on the bare floorboards — with all sorts of small things: a shrivelled carrot, a bakelite doll's leg with bare pointed toes, a corkscrew, a bit of broken china, some twisted rags, and what looked like lots of sweet papers. Like a sort of very nasty Christmas decoration, thought Nurse Potts, backing out. The other rooms were completely empty.

"Miss Carradine?"

Was that dirty little sneak following her, creeping up the stairs behind her? Nurse Potts paused, listening, but heard not a creak. What was he up to down there?

Had he in fact been telling the truth? Surely there was no one up here in this freezing dump. She reached the second landing. There was nothing in any of the four rooms on this floor. Up another floor. Nothing here either. Not a stick.

Probably didn't have a daughter at all. Still, since I'm here, might as well check them all. The way he'd looked up and all. Every step creaked now as she climbed.

Then she reached the top landing; then, for the first time, she was really afraid.

"Oh, yuk!"

Lots of things dangling here, a forest of them. Things on strings fastened in some way to the landing ceiling, and hanging down so low that she would have to stoop to go beneath them. Nurse Potts began to tremble. The smell here was different, and she could see that amongst the sweet papers and bits of broken china there were also bones, big ones, beef bones by the look of them, and not picked clean. One or two strings held large pieces of gristly meat, raw, touched here and there with a greenish fleck of mould; various stinks of death came from them.

Nurse Potts crept closer, but before she had time to really think out what she most feared about those lumps of flesh she realised that they were bits of mutton, the cheap gruesome innards her own mother sometimes boiled up for the dog, lights, they were called, the lungs and bronchus. There, coiled round the string like a snake, a shrivelled papery windpipe, held in place with a scrap of blood-stained yellow ribbon!

232

Two rooms here, their closed doors barely visible behind the horrible danglers.

Nurse Betty stood very still, her heart pounding in her chest.

Once when she was a very little girl, Betty's big brother Wilfred, then aged eight, had in the course of an innocent boyish game involving matches accidentally set his little sister's counterpane on fire. Luckily Betty had not been in the bed at the time; Wilfred had deputed her to toddle downstairs to put Ma in the picture, and the infant Betty had been so shocked and frightened by their mother's violent response to the news that, though she had trailed back upstairs after her and stood uncertainly outside the bedroom, from which issued now even more terrifying crackling and roaring noises, along with furious shrieks and yells of command, that she could not risk a single peek through the half-open door. When Wilfred and their mother at length emerged, soot-blackened and shaky, from the ruined bedroom, she was conscious of an immediate and tremendous sense of outraged loss. They had fought the flames, and won, and she had not been part of the battle! She had stood afraid on the landing, and missed the glorious sight of her own bed consumed in flame!

Standing now on the landing of a very different house, Nurse Potts remembered this absurd childish sensation. She thought also of her brother Wilfred, who had died at Cherbourg in 1940. So show a bit of gumption, she told herself. Like a soldier should. Because if you don't you'll always be wondering.

Thus, despite her thumping heart, she crouched right down so that nothing would touch her, crept forward, and opened the first door. It was empty but for a wooden table, thick with dust, dead centre; and in the middle of the table, heels together, almost akimbo, and lightly draped with dusty cobwebs, stood a pair of women's shoes.

For months afterwards, recounting the tale, Nurse Potts would have to stop there for a moment, unable to get past those well-worn soft leather pumps; they popped up in her dreams for years afterwards, which was perhaps strange in that as she backed out of that room, breathing heavily and keeping her head well down to avoid the stinking dangling strings, her torch fell on the threshold of the second door, and showed her a little damp purplish puddle of what could only have been fresh blood.

The telephone rang. For a moment Nurse Potts, frozen with fright on an attic floor of a bombed-out street in 1944, made no move; then Betty quickly rubbed her face with her hands and picked up the receiver.

"Hello."

"Hello. Is that you, Betty?"

Betty gasped, and tore the telephone from her ear. Her! Calling now! Her voice! She heard the telephone buzzing, and slowly brought it close again.

". . . could see you," Valerie Elliott was saying. Was it really her? Perhaps it was just a mistake, from thinking about all that so hard.

"Who is this please?"

"It's me, Valerie. Don't hang up, please."

Betty breathed.

"Betty? Are you there?"

"Yes."

"Please, don't worry about anything. Everything's all right, honestly. I was just wondering if I could come and see you."

"What for?"

"Just to talk. A chat."

"No. I don't think that would be a very good idea at all."

"I would really like to see you."

Betty, to her baffled surprise, felt her eyes fill with tears. She could not speak, for fear of sobbing.

"I thought I'd come tomorrow afternoon, about three. Would that be all right? I won't stay long. There's something I think I ought to tell you. All right?"

Betty made a small sound, which could have been agreement.

"Good," said Valerie Elliott. "Three tomorrow then, goodbye now!"

For the first time in many years, Betty uttered the name that had fallen out of her mouth at the sight of those well-worn ladies' shoes, that Nurse Potts had spoken aloud as a prayer.

"Oh, Jesus!"

CHAPTER
THIRTY-THREE

Rosemary ran all the way along the platform, jumped onto the train at the last minute, sank breathless into her seat, and began at once to torture herself so painfully that several times she was forced to groan aloud. Luckily the carriage was nearly empty most of the way.

Why hadn't she asked for a forwarding address? Whoever was in Maureen's flat would need to forward the mail. Why, if there was a forwarding address, had whoever it was, some Frog or Dago, not simply given it to her, instead of messing about looking up the hospital telephone number? Maureen must still be in hospital; in which case why had she, Rosemary, not simply gone home, dialled directory enquiries, and called UCH first? Because you just didn't think, Rosemary told herself, venomously, at intervals. Because that man, that Frog! he said three weeks, and I sort of thought, well, she can't still be in hospital, not after three weeks — but of *course* she could be, of course she could, oh, it must be something really serious, oh, why didn't you tell me, Maureen! But perhaps he hadn't really known what he was saying in the first place, he was only a foreigner, whereas that Colin Thacker . . .

I never liked him, thought Rosemary fiercely. He was sly. He hadn't mentioned hospitals though. Perhaps it was all a mistake. All this Molly business. Perhaps they'd all been talking about someone else somehow, and Maureen, robust and healthy as usual, would open her own front door, astonished and probably none too pleased. Rosemary found herself constantly imagining this comforting scene, Maureen realistically rather fed up and asking her in a little grudgingly, herself all of a flutter, well it was such a relief! and explaining everything nineteen to the dozen and then they'd obviously have a bit of supper together and perhaps even laugh about it all, what a fuss, mum, honestly, trust you! and she would have to spend the night there, on the sofa probably, would Maureen have any spare sheets, she was so impractical!

And then Rosemary would suddenly remember the long long silence, and the hospital, and the small concern of extra sheets or no toothbrush would be snapped off with a jerk, so that she jumped in her seat.

Suppose she was in trouble with the police! No. Not Maureen, not my Maureen. But why else would she have so suddenly abandoned her job, and let her flat? That sly Colin Thacker. He knew something all right. He'd got rid of her somehow. That was it!

Suppose she'd been attacked! Horribly injured! Picked up unconscious on the streets, no handbag, no one would know who she was, to let her mother know!

But then the lodger had known. He'd spoken to her in hospital. Hadn't he?

Or had he?

After nearly three hours of this sort of thing it was a tremendous relief to get off the train and pound down the stairs to the Tube station. The right train, luckily, came almost immediately and in the anxiety of getting off at the correct stop and then on again somewhere else Rosemary had a few more moments of blessed respite. She had not been to Maureen's flat often enough to feel sure of the way, either, once she was outside on the pavement. Why did Tube stations have so many entrances? Come out of the wrong one and you were lost straight away.

Turn you round and you're lost, said her husband's voice in Rosemary's mind, heavily teasing, as he had often said it in life. Oh George! Help me, thought Rosemary, quickly getting frantic again. Is it this street, or that one?

I'll have to ask someone, thought Rosemary in fear. She looked about her for someone who looked nice, a woman, someone who could tell her which shops to look out for, not too much of that first left second right sort of thing, that was so hard to keep straight, and as she thought this Rosemary remembered going past a new Tesco's, with Maureen, that day last year when they'd tried the Harrods sale. Peering ahead she could just make out a promising sign. Wasn't that Tesco's?

She hurried on, and made sure. Yes. This street then, and then on until you reached a hedge someone had trimmed into a shape that looked quite a lot like an elephant, if you were feeling generous, when you turned sharp left. Ignoring her feet, that ached so dreadfully in her good shoes that she'd put on for Gregory, she

238

almost ran through the darkening street, threading her way through the crowd, who all seemed to be coming the other way, and after a good ten minutes, when she was beginning to give up hope, saw the just about elephant-shaped hedge.

Her heart thumping now with running and anxiety Rosemary hobbled up the last street, Maureen's own, up the right path — overgrown, a bit scruffy? hard to be sure in the dark — and rang the bell.

Oh please!

After an agonising two minute wait, a light came on above the door, and a chain rattled across. The door opened a few inches.

"Hello?"

"It's me, it's Maureen's mother!" said Rosemary tremulously.

"She is not here," said the foreign voice. The door closed and the chain rattled again.

"Come in please."

Smelt different: those cigarettes Frogs all smoked. Looked pretty well the same. Rosemary stood stiffly in the little hallway. The foreigner was about twenty, and very slender. He had shoulder length wavy brown hair, blue eyes, and a tender girlish smile. "Hello," he said again, anxiously. Rosemary regarded him briefly and decided that he was clearly nothing to do with anything, and almost certainly no use at all. She wanted to swat him from sight, push him fiercely out of her way, trample him underfoot if need be.

"Can I use the phone, please?" she said, brushing past him into the front room. Where was Maureen's lovely red sofa? And the end tables had gone as well, the phone was sitting on the floor. Different rug in front of the fireplace.

"Hello? University College Hospital please . . . thank you . . . yes. Goodbye." Rosemary glanced up at the foreigner, who was hanging about in the doorway.

"Ah, I make tea, yes?"

"Not for me, thank you. What ward is she on?"

He made a distress-face, and was still apologising and waving his hands about while Rosemary, ignoring him, dialled the switchboard.

"Hello? I'm trying to find — someone, who I think is in the hospital, only I don't know which ward or anything."

"Name?"

Rosemary hesitated. "Um, Molly Sholto."

"Just a moment please."

There was a long pause, then another voice: "Hello, can I help you?"

Rosemary explained again, and after another long pause was put through to a ward; it was the wrong ward, however, a male medical, and the Staff Nurse, trying to connect Rosemary with the corresponding female ward, inadvertently cut her off altogether, so that she had to start all over again.

This time she asked for the number of the female medical ward, and dialled it directly, but it was engaged, and went on giving the engaged signal for four whole minutes. During this interval Rosemary dialled the ward so often, immediately hanging up and re-dialling, that when she finally got the ringing tone she automatically hung up again, realising what she had done instantly and giving such a sudden sharp angry bark aloud that the foreigner, who was keeping out of Rosemary's way in the kitchen, gave a little jump of fright, and wished with all his heart that he had never thought of leaving home.

Dialling again instantly Rosemary got through at once to the female medical ward.

"Hello, is Molly Sholto there, please, this is her mother."

"Just a moment please."

Pause.

Another voice, very brisk. "Hello, Staff Nurse, can I help you?"

"I'm Molly Sholto's mother, is she there please?"

"Um, one moment please."

Another pause.

"I'm sorry, we don't have anyone here by that name, could you have got the wrong ward? This is a medical ward."

For a moment Rosemary was unable to reply. She made a small choking noise, and the Staff nurse said more gently, "It's your daughter, is it, you're looking for?"

Rosemary managed to agree that it was.

"What's she in for, that's the first thing."

Rosemary sobbed aloud for several seconds. "I don't know!"

"Now there. Tell me the name again, and birth date, I'll look it up on the central computer. All right? You'll have to hang on. I won't have forgotten you, I'll get back to you as soon as I can, all right?" There was another very long pause.

During this one the foreigner tiptoed in with a mug of tea and stood for a moment hesitating on the threshold. He was terribly bothered by Rosemary, by her emotion and size and baleful glances. Besides she was paying him so little attention. It was as if he was hardly there at all, a sensation he had, it so happened, become painfully familiar with already, these lonely last few weeks. Bad enough to feel wretchedly invisible here in this empty flat all alone; how much worse to find one's invisibility confirmed by the behaviour of others! He put the mug down about a foot from her hand, and was slightly reassured to see her reach out and take it, though in fact Rosemary drank the whole mugful without even noticing what she was doing.

"Hello?"

"Yes?"

"Molly Sholto, aged thirty-one, was admitted under the care of Mr Vincent, but she was discharged three days ago, all right? She's gone home."

"Three days ago. What, Sunday?"

"Yes. All right?"

"What was she in for?"

"Um, I'm sorry, I think this is something you should ask her. Actually. I mean, she's not a patient, I can't really . . ."

"All right, all right. Erm. Does it say where she went to, I mean is it —" and Rosemary repeated Maureen's own home address, where she herself was presently sitting on the alien rug beside this gormless Frog, who stirred uncomfortably as she glared across at him.

"Yes, that's the one," said the Staff Nurse.

"Thanks," said Rosemary, hanging up abruptly, (so that the Staff Nurse felt rather miffed for a while, and inclined to take things out on her juniors) and rising painfully to her swollen feet. "Right, you. Where is she?"

The foreigner's eyes bulged. "Please?"

"She must have left a forwarding address. Where has she moved to?"

"She is in hospital."

"No she isn't. Not any more."

"Then, I don't know."

"Where d'you send her letters to?"

"I keep."

"What, all this time?"

"I visit, I take in."

"You visited her! You mean you knew what bloody ward she was on!"

"No, no, how to go there, her friend take me, I know how to go there only."

"What friend?" Of course; Maureen must be staying with a friend. Still needing a bit of looking after. And hadn't asked her mother! "What friend?"

"Er, er . . . Harry? Is Harry?"

"*I* don't know," said Rosemary a little bitterly. Could Maureen be staying with a man? But she's just got out of hospital, thought Rosemary in confusion. Perhaps this Harry would know where she was though.

"Can I get hold of him? Have you got his number?"

He fiddled about with some papers in a heap beside the telephone, and presently held out a small white card, rather thumbed. A business card. Harry Tailor Associates, read Rosemary. Two addresses, two telephone numbers. Home and business? Which was which?

She dialled both numbers, but no one answered. Rosemary let both ring and ring, just in case someone at the other end was trying to ignore the noise or still considering getting out of the bath. But no one answered. On his way home? Out for the evening? What to do now? Go to the nearest?

"Right. I'm going round there then," said Rosemary. Her feet pulsed in the shoes, filled every single part of them, but she was glad of the pain, and trod down hard on it. "Goodbye."

The lodger followed her along the hall, bobbing anxiously, since years of training made it imperative for him to open the front door for her, but she got there first, yanked it open, slammed it behind her in the foreigner's face, and instantly forgot all about him.

The lodger, however, was far too upset by Rosemary to put her out of his mind, and had to take himself off to the local pub and drink several pints of beer in order to do so. Thus he was out when his girlfriend telephoned, out all evening, confirming her worst fears, so that she spent a sleepless night sobbing and all the following day pale and sniffing; this so depressed and irritated her father, the judge, at lunchtime that he sentenced a woman shoplifter to two months in prison, which was to cause quite an outcry, as the woman had three small children, one of whom had very bad asthma, and often needed his mother in the night.

CHAPTER
THIRTY-FOUR

Sometimes Betty thought about not being there. What could be simpler? Just be out, when she came. Pop out.

Betty? Oh, I think she's just popped out, sorry, no, I've no idea I'm afraid, would you like to leave a message?

But then she'd ring back; and every time the telephone rang I'd be afraid to answer it, in case it was her. She knows where I am, thought Betty, with a stifling sense of entrapment, she can just come round anytime and catch me.

But she wouldn't want to, would she, why should she? She's the one with something to hide, for heaven's sake! Let her come, get it over with, be ready for her, thought Betty. The trouble was that she could not imagine what Valerie Elliott could possibly want to say to her. More gentle reproaches? Or something with a little more bite?

Perhaps she would be accompanied by a policeman. Or be wearing what American policemen on television always called a *wire*. Would Valerie Elliott be wired? If so, would it be possible to talk to her without once giving away anything that could be used in court? And if it were possible, would it not then be completely impossible to sound anything other than half-cracked with the tension and effort required?

It was all right for blackmailers on films, thought Betty resentfully, the fact was they were always played by actors and actresses. So they could *act*. Faced with a wired victim, they could act nonchalant ignorance easy as you like. They always were nonchalant too, and heartless, in films.

It was always the victim of blackmail you were meant to sympathize with, Betty saw. Why was that? They'd always done something wrong, or no one would have been able to blackmail them in the first place; but it was always their anguish that you were shown, not that of their blackmailers, who were risking so much, taking on so much, exerting force and will and courage.

You never got to see the blackmailer's frightful anxiety, you never saw them trying to nerve themselves up for the ordeal of that first encounter, or lying awake at night wondering if they had got away with it. It's like: if you're bad enough to blackmail someone you must be inhumanly bad, completely bad without any doubts or remorse or guilt or terror. Much worse than being a murderer, say, in that case. Murderers often had a terrible time with remorse, in films.

It's because of the money, thought Betty. Isn't it? If a blackmailer didn't ask for money, but for something else, some wrong to be righted, perhaps, or some duty or responsibility properly undertaken instead of being neglected, would that still be blackmail? Indeed not; from that angle it was a device familiar from innumerable stories, the baddie forced out of some wrong-doing because the goodie was somehow at the end in the know, and able to lean on him.

I wish I'd just asked her there and then, on the phone. "Tell me now," I should have said. "You got something to say, you say it now." I just didn't think. Still can't, I'm so tired!

Betty decided to go to bed early. She had a long hot bath, a milky drink, took a hot water bottle to bed with her, and peacefully fell asleep straight away. Waking up in the dark she was at first convinced that she had slept a long time, but presently discovered that it was only one thirty, and that she was wide awake. Soon she remembered that later today Valerie Elliott would be coming to see her, and with something particular to say, and her heart began to jump in her chest as if she had been running instead of lying quietly in her bed.

She got up and put on her dressing gown and wandered the corridors for a while, half-hoping someone needed attention, as was fairly often the case at night. Perhaps someone would pull the alarm in one of the bathrooms, mistaking it for the light switch, happened all the time; even that would do. But Cabotin Court was silent, except for the creaking of the floorboards beneath her own feet, and not even recalling their lost seventeenth century oakedness could take Betty's mind off the coming interview.

She went into her office, and sat down in one of the two small blue-covered armchairs she had placed on either side of the new gas fire. Now, surely, would be a good time to turn the thing on, to luxuriate in instant cosiness; but even as she reached out a hand to the dial

248

Betty found that she somehow did not care to try it. She folded her arms and sat rocking, wondering if what she felt was fear, and if so, why she felt it.

After all look how brave she had thoughtlessly been, all those years ago! Nothing kept me awake at night then, thought Betty, but my patients. Far more a vocation than a job, in those days. Look how I climbed those black stairs all alone, with just a torch and my bag in my hand! Not that I'd thought I was being brave, at the time. It didn't occur to me that any bravery was involved. Of course I didn't know what I would find there. The blood on the threshold, that was when I knew.

"Oh, Jesus!"

Dark purple in the torchlight, a large flattened tumulus of clot. She had put out a finger, touched its particular jellied resilience. She recognised it, immediately had no doubt that it was placental. She turned the torch upwards, to find what she already knew would be there, and yet when she found it uttered a little groan of fright and dismay: her hand shook at the sight of the fresh glistening human afterbirth entwined round that lengthy knotted string, amongst the mouldy bits of lights and stained curls of ribbon. She remembered the doll's leg on the string in the first room downstairs, the little broken leg, and got round the blood somehow, crawling carefully, keeping her head down, and pushed open the very last door.

"Hello?" Her voice still familiar, still her own, she felt much better for hearing it. She turned the torch around the room, and there, with a gasp of indrawn breath she saw a dead body on an iron bedstead beside the boarded window.

There was nothing else in the room. The body, a woman, lay on its back, naked but for a sheet. Nurse Potts, after a moment's utter stillness, approached. Her mouth was too dry for speech.

She set down the torch to beam upwards at the ceiling, put out a hand, and touched the narrow wrist. It was icy, but held tight there was a steady pulse. Almost immediately the woman's eyes opened. Her dead-white face glistened. Her lips were grey, split here and there, the splits showing black with blood. She whispered:

"Who are you?"

"I'm the nurse," said Nurse Potts. She dropped the wrist, and held the hand. For a moment the fingers closed on her own.

"Help me," she whispered, and then she was gone.

Nurse Potts pulled the sheet down, and laid her head on the dead girl's chest, between her tiny buds of bosom. There: not gone, not yet: the same fast galloping rhythm. But what to do? Miles from anywhere, in the dark, with the madman downstairs, Oh and how mad, how very mad he was! How long would it take to get help, and who was she to send for it if she was not to go herself? Because I can't leave her here, can I? I'm not going to anyway, if I have to flaming well carry her!

Pulling the sheet right back she looked for blood loss, but found very little. Lying on newspaper, Christ alive! Emaciated. No wonder she was so cold, too, just a sheet. Dirty legs, no: bruised legs. Great greyish bruises all down them. Uttering unconscious little groans of distress Nurse Potts measured pulse and blood pressure, and gently touched the abdomen, feeling for the fundus, rather soft, needed a little pressure. There. That was better. And where —

She gave a sudden gasp, and looked round, grabbing and turning the torch although she knew the room was empty. She thought again of the broken doll's little leg on the string downstairs, and put a hand on the girl's thin shoulder, and shook her, urgently.

"Where's the baby? Come on. Wake up. Where's your baby?"

A sigh. The split lips parted.

"Wake up!" She made a cruel fist, and rubbed the knuckles hard against the bony sternum. That worked.

"Where's the baby, did he take it?"

The eyes focussed. The girl sat straight up in the bed, she bent in the middle and drew breath. "Is he here?" She made a movement towards Nurse Potts, scrabbling with her hands against the starched bibbed apron, as if she would hide in her arms. "Don't let him —"

Her voice was interrupted by a sound Nurse Potts was to describe many times over the years. It was a noise (so she would one day put it) like someone emptying a bucket of water onto a floor, a heavy gushing pouring noise. It was the sound of the girl's blood overflowing onto the floorboards, the sound of exsanguination.

For a moment Nurse Potts, who had in her sketchy wartime training heard of post-partum haemorrhage but never yet seen one, or of course heard one, did not believe her own ears. Just for a moment, while the girl fell back unconscious again on the mattress; then she flung away all the sheet, bent back the bony legs frog-fashion, hesitated again for half a second, which way round? which hand where? before she pushed her whole right fist into the vagina, pushing upwards, the other hand hard against the great soft gushing uterus within.

"Oh help me, God," groaned Nurse Potts as she did this, as she knelt beside the cold waxen figure still so hot within. "Oh, don't die don't die, please, don't die." Beneath her hand the womb hardened, just a little.

Ergometrine, of course, but how could she risk letting go? Slowly, carefully so as not to move her hands, she shifted her position until she could reach her bag with one foot. Hooking it against the upper of her left shoe she brought it by degrees to within grasping distance. Wait again, but how long for?

She counted out a minute, then withdrew the bloodied fist, very slowly. Several huge clots slithered free with her fingers. How much blood could you lose, and live? Lots, in childbirth. Pints and pints, all extra runny, thin special pregnancy blood, don't give up yet.

She felt perfectly calm by now, sure of what she was doing. With steady hands she opened the bag, withdrew everything she needed, made up the injection, and gave it. Wait three minutes, wait five. A hand now on the abdomen: yes. There. Perfect. The womb like a little stone in there. Part the frog legs, pull free a few more immense slitherers. But no more. Pulse? Yes. Thready.

252

But safe to leave for a minute or two, enough to get round to that pub on that corner, not that far away. Except . . .

She pulled at some of the newspaper beneath the poor skinny bottom, rolling up most of the clots, leaving her on the thin bare stained mattress but fairly dry. She took off her coat, only the cuffs were really wet, and then her cardigan, and laid them over the girl, stopping for a moment to brush the hair back from the forehead, tenderly, with a sort of love, because she had needed so much help, and because she, Nurse Potts, had been able so completely to give it.

"I'm going to call an ambulance," she said, in case any consciousness lurked behind those closed marble lids. "I'll be as quick as I can, I promise, and I'll be back straight away."

The eyes opened once more. She was trying to speak. Nurse Potts bent her head close, put her ear to the patient's lips, which moved, just a little, heavy with effort.

"I . . . heard . . . him."

"Who? Your father, him?"

The lids closed as if in assent. Fingers touched Nurse Potts's bare arm.

"He . . ."

"What? What?"

The lips were stickily strung together. The tip of a thick white tongue tried to moisten them. Nurse Potts could hear the tongue moving in the dry stickiness.

"What?"

"He was . . . outside."

"Outside? What, you mean, outside here?" She glanced over at the door, where the danglers still swung a little from her own entrance.

The fingers grasped, just a little. The eyes strained.

"Outside — you mean, in the garden?"

"He was . . . digging."

CHAPTER
THIRTY-FIVE

It was nearly seven o' clock when Rosemary arrived at the second address on Harry Tailor's business card. The first had been another estate agent's, shut and in darkness, in one of a long narrow curved roadful of shops, all closed now, on a pedestrian precinct.

A gang of youths, talking very loudly, one of them singing, had turned a corner as she stood there, and at the sight of them Rosemary had got straight back into the taxi she had just climbed out of, and told the man the next address to try. But now she could risk no further taxi fares. Already she did not have enough money to stay the night, not anywhere she would feel safe in anyway.

She put off thinking about this, and hobbled across the pavement, trying to see street numbers. It was another shopping street, but far less threatening, with passing couples here and there, dallying in at the brightly lit windows full of smart swanky dresses or nice bits of furniture, it was altogether a better class of street than the first one; and here was number seventeen, this was it, with its big curved window all coated from the inside with Windowlene, big white swirls, and nothing else to see at all.

Moving towards the kerb Rosemary looked up at the second storey windows, but these too were in darkness.

Now what?

Suddenly the pain in her feet was absolutely unendurable. She crept into the dark shop doorway and sat down, actually sat down on the cold triangle of mosaic in front of the door, and eased off both her shoes. The toes, released, throbbed damply in her fingers. Both her heels were bleeding; the stockings were stuck to weeping wounds. Gingerly she pulled them free, and began to cry a little, out of helplessness.

She thought back over the afternoon, all the daft thoughtless things she had done, racing off to London without trying any phone calls first, chasing all over the place without planning anything, and all on her own, and now here she was, worn out, hopeless, practically broke and hardly able to walk another step and still no nearer finding Maureen than when she'd first started. Useless, that's what she was. No wonder Maureen hadn't bothered to ask for her help. Useless, and too busy messing about with boyfriends, and at her age!

Rosemary, at this final piercing thought, put her face in her hands and for a minute or two cried aloud for wretchedness, only hiccupping and trying to control herself when she became aware of a passer-by stopping quite close by, hesitating, as if unsure what to do, and who could blame them, it wasn't every day you saw a respectable raincoated middle-aged woman with no shoes on crying in a doorway. Someone, some interfering Good Samaritan, was going to ask her if she was all right, thought Rosemary, panicking, but as she pressed her fingers harder over her eyes, willing whoever it was to mind her own business and leave her alone, a voice spoke beside her, tentatively:

"Mum?"

Rosemary quivered all over. She turned, saw, and scrambled to her feet, feet of joy, healed at once.

"Maureen!" She flung her arms around her daughter's neck. "Oh, Maureen, where've you been, I've been worried sick, are you all right, what happened, oh Maureen!"

Maureen didn't sound fed up, not a bit of it. Pleased, really. Surprised. Voice a bit croaky:

"What are you doing here!"

"Looking for you!"

"Let me open the door, just a minute." She took a bunch of keys from her handbag, and opened it while Rosemary, barely stopping to draw breath, told her everything that had happened to her that afternoon, though not in the right order, or in any order at all, still talking as she followed her daughter up the steep flight of stairs at the back of the empty shop, an emptiness which reminded her of the little place just off the seafront that would one day be Rosemary's Dining Rooms, and so she started to tell Maureen about this as well, which, when she got to about halfway through, meant mentioning Gregory, which she did easy as anything, though this in turn meant going back to the bench on the prom where she had first met him, by which time Maureen had put her shopping down and put a lamp on here and there in a very nice sitting room with her own lovely red sofa in it, and Rosemary could look at her properly in the light; and then she stopped dead, appalled.

"Oh my God!" said Rosemary, and her eyes filled again. "What have they done to you?"

And she ran to embrace her child again, for in the light Maureen was really scarcely recognisable, her face so thin and white, great dark circles under her eyes, so scrawny the bones in her forehead showed, it was some flaming diet, thought Rosemary wild with shock, remembering all the rejected pies and dumplings and cheese puddings she and Maureen had once fought so bitterly over, and here was Maureen doing what her mother had most feared so long ago and slimming herself through the narrow doors of Death itself.

"Oh Maureen!" She held her child in a closer embrace than she had tried for years; for a second; then jerked back in horror, her fingers digging into Maureen's shoulders.

"Are you . . .?" Frightful terrors filled Rosemary's mind. The stick-like body she had held was all hard and swollen in the middle. Rosemary's aunt had felt like that, just before she died of cancer of the liver.

"Yes," said Molly anxiously, who had no idea what her mother was thinking, and supposed her to have recoiled in shock merely at the suspicion of the truth. God, she'd known her mother would make a bit of a fuss, but it was hardly the end of the world, not nowadays. "Yes," she said again firmly to her mother's blubbering white face, "I'm going to have a baby."

"Y'what?"

258

Rosemary's instant crazed expression of joyful wonder was so comical, and her evident happiness at the news such a relief, that Molly had to laugh. Rosemary laughed as well, a little wildly.

"A baby! Oh Maureen! And you're all right, really? You were in hospital!"

"Complication. I had this, it's when you get morning sickness only it doesn't stop. I kept thinking it'd go away but it didn't. They kept telling me it'd go away as well. But it didn't. So I sort of starved a bit. And I had to go to hospital, they had to give me a drip, you know, because I couldn't even drink water, I was bringing that up as well at the finish, I was getting dehydrated, so they had to treat it."

"Is the, is the baby all right?" The baby! Oh Maureen!

"Apparently. Odd, isn't it. He's doing fine."

"He?"

"Or she. Due sometime in December." They smiled at one another.

"Can you eat now, are you still being sick?"

"Not so much. Well, quite a bit. But nothing like as bad as before, I have to keep eating little and often. And of course I had to leave work early, well, that was why I ended up not telling you anything, I didn't plan it like that, I'm sorry. But we're setting up our own business."

"Who are, is it this Harry?"

"Yes, this Harry. You know I'd been thinking of setting up on my own for years now, and when I met Harry it just made sense to go into partnership, except the baby wasn't meant to happen just yet. Let's have a cup of tea, shall we? Actually, I think I'd better lie down for a bit, sorry mum, d'you mind, it's just that I'm beginning to feel a bit . . ."

"No, no no, don't you say any more. You go and lie down, I'll bring you your tea, don't you worry, I'll find everything, I'll put this away. Have you had anything to eat, something light, shall I poach you an egg, on toast, on a tray, would that be nice?"

It seemed to Molly that a poached egg on toast would be perfect, would stop any creeping hyperemesis dead in its tracks.

"Ooh mum," she said greedily. "Yes please."

CHAPTER
THIRTY-SIX

Now that she could see again Alethea was very busy. Her desk seemed to have dozens, perhaps even hundreds of bits of poetry in it, on various slips of paper thrust in anyhow. Since most of her verse related to mood or a specific event sifting through the pile was as engrossing and time consuming as coming across a forgotten diary.

Besides the handwriting was startling evidence of unwitting decline: the lines sloping into one another like a child's, the strangely variable size, huge or spikily microscopic and sometimes both on the same page. One page held just half a poem, just the beginning of every line, which was a real puzzle until she laid the offending paper down slightly to one side of another, and realised that in her gathering gloom she must have done so when writing the poem out, and written across both; presumably the other half was on another slip of paper somewhere else in the pile.

Some of the verse pleased her, more did not; however, there was enough she liked to make her consider another slim volume, and, when she wrote to her god-daughter Fredericka to thank her for the flowers, boldly ask her also for the names of one or two literary agents who might consider taking her on.

Apart from the desk, the whole flatlet rather needed attention, thought Alethea, though this of course was far less enticing. The agency cleaning lady had vacuumed and dusted in her perfunctory way, but had not, it seemed, noticed the cobwebs swinging so lightly in every corner. Nor was it her job to wash up private tea things; Alethea had done that, of course, and every cup seemed to have a ring in it, and every plate a smear of egg. Her clothes, too, which had been perfectly all right before her operation, were now all of them clearly the worse for a dinner or two; or three, some of them.

With some faint suspicion about her own motives she mentioned all this to Annie Cameron after lunch. Sure enough Annie immediately volunteered to help out, arriving with rubber gloves and scouring pads and several different plastic bottles of cleaning fluid. As if she thought I wouldn't have any of that stuff myself, thought Alethea, but as this was very nearly the case she could hardly feel aggrieved about it.

"I have always hated housework," she said, "and on the whole I don't mind advertising the fact. But I see now that I can't really do that any more. Not if I still want to look TAB."

"What was that? Oh, that. You mean you're going to keep it spick and span from now on?" Annie, feeling rather daring in her rubber gloves, risked a tease: "I thought you had a lens implant, not a personality change."

262

Alethea laughed. "Once I cooked Charles a duck, some special occasion, I forget what. Anyway we didn't finish it, I put the dish in the oven. And I forgot about it. And months later Charles said to me, What's this, what's this thing in here? Opening the oven. And I looked and it was the remains of the duck, black charcoal, absolutely mummified, it had been in there baked over and over again for months, it had somehow got stuck to the grill-thing at the top. I'd taken the dish out, you see, and left the duck in there, stuck to the ceiling . . ." Alethea stopped, giggling helplessly.

Annie joined in, half politely. Charles? Who was this one? She wanted a map, she thought, some kind of chart, to get Alethea's life straightened out.

"Was um, was this in America?"

Alethea stopped laughing. She picked up another cup and dabbed at it with her tea towel. "Oh, no. No, this was in London. Just before the War. I came back from the States."

"Because of the earthquake?"

"No, not really. Partly. It brought me to my senses, perhaps."

Having an affair with Meredith Pope, thought Annie. Wearing a towel in the dining room.

"I was just running away, when I left Wayward Brothers," she said. "It was because of Sally."

The pretty one in the photograph, thought Annie. There was a pause. Annie went on washing up, and appeared to be giving a chunky piece of Hornsea pottery her fullest attention as she spoke:

"You were friends."

"That would be the screenplay," said Alethea sadly. "Did I ever tell you how we used to construct our screenplays? It was such fun." Her tone brightened.

"There'd be four or five of us all sitting round smoking like chimneys, we'd have a very vague plotline and several stars in view, that had to be got in somehow. We were churning them out these films, couldn't get them done fast enough. Anyway, suppose it was a costume drama, we went in for highwaymen a good deal when we weren't at sea with Nelson, someone would say, 'well, it so happens that our hero — oh, say, Sir Richard — well, his dearest friend George is in frightful financial trouble, debt of honour, and Richard's in a stage coach going, where's he going?' And someone else," (here Miss Troy's hands, held palms facing to her own left, indicated another speaker; perfectly clear Sign, thought Annie) "would say, '— on his way to Plymouth' and someone else would say, '— to join his ship' '— to the West Indies, it so happens that he's inherited huge plantations out there' '— from his father, everybody happy? On his way to Plymouth, stopped by highway man, ohmygod it's George!' — 'and it so happens that Richard's uncle the hanging judge is actually in the carriage at the time!' '— and it so happens that the wicked uncle's driver's got a pistol, Hold hard there, young gentleman if you please!' "

Alethea put down the wooden spoon she was aiming, and laughed. "All shouting at once sometimes, and someone trying madly to scribble it all down. The real difficulty wasn't in making up stories, I'm sure any

264

group of people would be able to come up with enough to keep things rolling along happily for an hour or so. The real art lay in translating "it so happens" into plot. It's perfectly easy to say, you see, in your smoke-filled room. But in a film it's a jump. It's a bit without an explanation. Unless you put up storyboards. But that holds up the action, you have to leave them in place long enough for the slowest readers in the audience to work their way through them while everyone else gets restless. How did I get on to this? Oh yes. Sally."

"Was she writing scripts, too?"

"No, she had my old job, in continuity. And I thought we were friends. We went to parties together. I used to lend her jewellery. She was far more careful with it than I was."

And found more pearls than Ronald Colman, laughing, crawling under a sofa, There's one, there's another, look, Alethea, under there, look!

Annie said nothing. It was clear that talking about Sally was still painful, even now, when Alethea was generally in such tearing spirits.

"One day at a viewing she fainted. Well, it always was so hot and smoky in there, I didn't give it a thought. And she was off work next day. That happened too, we were always going to parties and having far too much to drink. Then we heard she was in hospital, appendicitis. I took her some flowers after the operation. I sat on the bed chatting, no doubt loudly. I think I was rather full of myself in those days. She was wearing a pink silk bed jacket, I remember coveting it. She looked like a little girl. She seemed absolutely fine. She was twenty-one. She died the next day."

"Oh dear," said Annie.

"Yes. Oh dear. Went to the funeral, of course. The press turned up, there were so many well known faces, Wayward Bros Bid Farewell. Her parents, she was their only child. Their faces, stunned. And Maggie, Stylist to the Stars, crying her eyes out, I remember thinking, what a soft heart she has, poor old Mags. And I still didn't know, I didn't guess for one minute."

"What, then?"

"That she'd had an abortion. That was why she died. It all came out, afterwards. And when I looked back I thought I could see that she'd been nothing like her usual self, for weeks. But I hadn't troubled to ask her anything."

"She didn't want you to ask. She must have made that clear to you, in ways you didn't quite register."

"It's kind of you to say that. I've thought of that too. But really it won't wash. I was supposed to be her friend. And I was clearly not the sort of person she could go to in any trouble. She'd gone to Maggie, who had told her who to go to, Maggie helping her out. She knew I would be no help. And she would have been right. What could I have done, except let her know that I thought she'd been a fool? No doubt she knew that already. I could only think, What sort of person am I, that my dearest friend, for that was what I thought she was, hadn't told me that she had passed that, that barrier, as it was in those days. I was so bewildered; I felt all my sophistication, holding down this marvellous job, knowing what was what, saying sharp things to sharp people, well, it was all such a piece of pretence; I was a virgin, and not at all a wise one. And I couldn't stand my job anymore. It was an absurdity, constructing silly stories for other silly virgins. And I told myself, it's not writing, it's not *my* writing. Not my own. It so happens this, it so happens that. I decided I needed a fresh start. Or, I ran away. Depends on the storyboard."

"But you went to America . . ."

"Such a mistake. It was all a mistake."

"But it sounded so exciting; you've seen the world; you've done things, don't you feel that?"

"Danced with Clark Gable, you mean?" Alethea smiled. "It only sounds romantic."

"That's all it needs to do."

"Not to me. Which matters most, what something was, or what it looked like?"

"Well, you could say: more people saw what it looked like than know what it felt like, couldn't you?"

"So, the majority view must prevail?"

"Not exactly. Just that you shouldn't discount it. Just because he trod on your toes."

"He did not tread on my toes! I should like to stress that he was what I believe is known as a lovely little mover."

They laughed. And it was true, thought Alethea, for a moment allowing her younger self to look up shyly into those large beautiful humorous eyes, that at his touch her virginal insides had melted with innocent pleasure; as she laid her hand on his sleeve she had been almost overwhelmingly aware of the shirt beneath the immaculate dinner jacket, of the arm beneath the shirt, the warm skin; it was indeed romance, she realised.

Romance is desire with its clothes on, innocent faithless desire, that doesn't really want to see the naked skin beneath the shirt; the graceful male fold and fall of the shirt will always be enough in itself for real romance, the spectator sport of women.

Not much to do with the real thing, either. An adjunct. An appetiser, perhaps, to the food of love. Alethea sighed, and looked up.

"Shall we have a cup of tea now? In some of these absolutely spotless cups?"

"Bib-bib?"

It's when she's thinking about something else, thought Alethea. Or just tired, probably. I don't think she even knows she's saying it, so one can hardly ask what it's meant to be.

She picked up a teacup and held it suggestively, in makeshift Sign.

"Yes, please," said Annie.

CHAPTER
THIRTY-SEVEN

Today Valerie Elliott looked a little less well-groomed; she had not bothered to have her hair done this time, thought Betty, but perhaps last time's had just been a coincidence anyway, you had to get your hair done some time, after all.

"Hello, Betty. Gosh what a difference! It looks really nice. Is that one of those gas fires? I like the armchairs. Can we sit in them, d'you think, please? I feel sort of squashed over there. Isn't it nice, is this what you spent the money on?"

Betty, who had been feeling pretty stiff anyway, went stiffer. She felt like a rock in an armchair, a rock full of lava boiling within. How dare she bring that up, was Betty's outraged thought. It was, what was it? It was *rude*, it was in the most appalling taste.

"If you must know," she said, trying for chilly dignity, "yes, it was."

Valerie Elliott grinned, she looked like someone holding in a laugh. And she looked young, thought Betty, almost girlish in her loose trousers and her floppy dark hair. Though of course if you looked closer you could see the lines all right, and you could see the bulge of the skin where it was beginning to soften over the jaw line.

"Why did you come here?"

"Why didn't you tell me what you wanted the money for?"

"It was none of your business."

"Yes it was. Of course it was. If you'd told me, I'd've given it to you."

"You gave it to me anyway. Is that what you came to say?"

"No. Not at all. Can you put the fire on?"

"Why?"

"I just want to see it, that's all. See if it's a good one, some of them you can see it's all pretend. Is it one of those?"

Betty made no reply. She could hardly, she felt, admit that she had not yet been able to bring herself to light the beastly thing at all. She leant forward and inexpertly twisted the dial, but when she let go the pilot light went out.

"You have to count to twenty, or something," said Valerie Elliott. "We had one at home. Look, like this." She reached forward in turn, twisted the dial, counted aloud, and then gave the thing another half turn. There was a tiny pause, and then the fire gave a little thump, a gassy hiccup, and burst into life.

"It's all blue," exclaimed Betty bitterly.

"No, don't worry, it'll settle down in a minute. They always look a bit funny at first. Look, it's starting to go yellow already. See? D'you mind if I smoke?"

"Yes," said Betty shortly.

270

"Oh, all right then. There. It's one of the good ones, I think. You can hardly tell, can you. You ought to paint that gas pipe though, you know, matt black, so it doesn't show. Don't you think?"

Betty briefly closed her eyes. "What was it you wanted to tell me?" she said at last.

Valerie Elliott was still gazing into the fire; as if it was real. "D'you ever think about that night?" she said.

"No."

"Bet you do. Bet you have. Lately, I mean." There was a pause. "I have, anyway," Valerie went on after it. "I mean there was a time when I thought about it a lot, then I suppose it did fade, for a while, but since I saw you again, I don't think I've thought of anything else. Not really."

"What are you getting at?"

"Well, I suppose I just wanted to ask you one or two things. You see there have always been things about it that I didn't understand. I'd got used to not knowing, you see, I never thought I'd ever be able to find out. I've tried to put it all out of my mind, because you have to, don't you, and I had other things to do, you know, other children. But then you came along, you! And of course it was a shock, I won't deny it, I didn't know what to do, I didn't know what I was feeling, it was like being a child again, the sort of child I was, horrible . . . Anyway once I'd thought it over I realised that I just had to come here and talk to you, and ask you some things, so that I'd really know at last what happened, because all this time I never have. Not completely. You don't mind, do you? Talking about it? I've been telling myself that you wouldn't, I've been telling myself, Well, if it was me — if I were you, I mean — then it would have been the most wonderful thing I'd ever done, you see. I mean, perhaps you wouldn't agree, I don't know, there could be dozens of other things you did that you're just as proud of, but if it were me —"

"No," said Betty, suddenly interrupting. "It was the best thing." She too looked into her false glittering flames. "I have thought of it. Since I — saw you."

"What, though? What have you thought?"

Betty hesitated. "I can't tell you," she said at last.

"Who else can you tell? There is no one else in the world who wants so much to know!" Her voice shook. No laughter there now: she'd been nervous, thought Betty. Nervous and being all bright. Telling me to paint the gas pipe! She felt a curiously painful little pang of sympathy.

"I . . ."

"What? Tell me!" Imploring.

"I thought how brave I had been."

Valerie Elliott clapped her hands. "Yes! Weren't you! I can hardly believe how brave you were! Why didn't you get a medal or something?"

Betty shrugged, smirking. "There was a War on," she said.

"There is one thing."

"What?"

"My father. He sent for you. Didn't he?"

"I don't know. I think so. I don't see how anyone else could have."

"Why did he let you in?"

"He didn't want to," said Betty, leaning forward. "He opened the door and we had a bit of an argument on the doorstep."

"You weren't at all — afraid of him?"

"No, not a bit of it. Why should I be?"

"I don't know. I was."

"I just pushed the door open," said Betty. "Knocked him flying. I've never told anyone else that. It seemed unprofessional. Is that funny?" she ended, because Valerie Elliott was suddenly lying back in her chair, snorting into her hands.

"I'm sorry," she gasped eventually. "I'm glad you knocked him flying," she said, wiping her face. "No. I'm glad about everything you did. I was so lucky. Suppose you'd just said to him on the doorstep, Oh a mistake was it, oh dear, well, so long then. You could have, couldn't you. Easily. You could easily have been that sort of person."

"It was the way he talked to me," said Betty. "As if I were dirt."

"Yes. He was good at that. Tell me what happened. Did I tell you I'd heard him digging? Sometimes I think I dreamt that. And why didn't he try to stop you? Or did he?"

Betty sat back too, considering. She wanted to choose her words properly. She had told the story many times when it was new, and enjoyed telling it; but this was different. Recounting it to Valerie Elliott herself, she felt dimly, was rather like telling it to the recording angel: definitive.

"I didn't know, then," she said. "When you said digging, I didn't, you know, catch on. Of course I didn't. Well I was pretty sure he must be mad, but I didn't know how mad. I didn't know people could *be* that mad. Anyway my first concern was you." Valerie Elliot's face, then, glowing! Well, it was true. But if you actually said it aloud to the patient, the person, concerned, it sounded like a declaration of love: my first concern was you. Strange: it felt a bit like one too.

"I had to leave you, and that meant leaving you with him. You'd already made it clear that you were scared stiff of him."

"Had I? How?"

"Don't you remember? I asked you if he'd taken the baby, and that's when you sat up and started, well, bleeding. You know you nearly bled to death. I thought you might die still. But I had to leave you."

"Of course you did. But what did you say to him?"

"I didn't say anything." Betty blushed. "I locked him in the cellar."

"No!"

"I came down the stairs, I saw him waiting at the bottom. I was in a bit of a state quite frankly. I'd never nearly lost a patient before. And I was all on my own, you know, and it was so dark, and of course there were all those things on strings, horrible nasty things . . ."

"Offerings," said Valerie.

"Offerings?"

"To the gods."

"What did you think of all that, then?"

"Me? I thought he was mad."

"Why'd you stay then?"

"That's another story. Go on, please."

"Where was I, oh yes, he was waiting. I shone my torch in his eyes, I remember thinking, God help me if the batteries run flat, it was lucky they were new ones just that night."

"Did he say anything?"

"Oh yes. He said something all right. He said, 'Get out of my house, you fat bitch.' That's what he said. And he makes to come at me, up the stairs. And I see he's got a shovel, he's coming at me swinging it back, see, he's going to clout me round the head with it."

"Oh no!"

"Oh yes, I thought. Well, I was a big girl, see? I let him come a bit closer and then I just, well, I kicked him. Right in the stomach, and he just dropped the shovel and fell over, only down two steps mind, and he's lying there all dazed."

Ha! Superior lordly Can't-Stop-Himself! Stopped *you* all right, didn't I!

"And I grab him! By his shirt! And I pull him round the foot of the stairs, and there's a door, and I reckon it's the cellar, and I unlock it, see a few stairs, and I sort of push him at them, and then I roll him out of the way so I can lock the door again!"

Betty had not spoken with such eager vehemence for years; and never to such a desperately appreciative audience.

"Oh Betty!" breathed Valerie, her hands clasped, her eyes shining. Perhaps Betty's soul, that starved and etiolated possibility, here stretched itself inside her, and raised its cramped extremities to the glow; at any rate she felt a wonderfully pleasant stir within, at once stimulating and relaxing.

"Then what, Betty?"

Betty thought. "I reckoned I'd just have a quick look round, before I shot off to that pub I'd passed on the corner."

"The Fox and Hounds."

"Was it? Oh yes. I remember the landlord. He was at the trial."

"You went into the kitchen."

"Yes. I had a quick look round. It was a shock, you know that? Because it was so tidy. It was a really nice kitchen. Lots of copper pans on shelves all polished, one of those big scrubbed tables, and a clock ticking, you felt everything must be all right, seeing a kitchen like that, it brought me up short for a second, it was as if I'd imagined everything else. It was warm, too, there was a fire going. In a, oh —"

"What?"

"In a range. I'd forgotten that. A little black *range*, with a fire, funny . . ."

"Why?"

"Nothing. Not important. Anyway. I looked all round, you know, drawers and cupboards and so on. I thought he'd made off with it, you know, the, the . . ."

"Baby."

"Yes. I had this idea he'd dumped it on a doorstep, because that had happened actually, a week or so before, to a friend of mine, another midwife who had her own house, she'd come down in the morning and

276

there was this basket with a baby girl inside, see? Oh, and one of the things he'd said to me on the doorstep was that you'd already gone to your aunt's, the place being condemned and that. So I had this aunt in the back of my mind as well."

"Why did you go in the garden?"

"Ah. Well I wasn't going to. As far as I was concerned, I'd had a quick look round, hadn't found the baby, and it was time to go and get and an ambulance, and the police, I was going to call them as well, because, well, he's told me all this stuff about aunts and that but he was nutty as a fruitcake and I wanted, you know, big blokes with boots and truncheons and so on, I didn't want to come back on my own, not if I could help it. But I just happened to look out of the kitchen door into the garden. And I remembered the shovel. It seemed such an odd thing for him to try and hit me with. And you had said about him digging. And I picked up the oil lamp that was on the kitchen table, and I went and picked the spade up from the bottom of the stairs, had a good look at it."

"Like a detective!"

"Yeah. All that damp earth on it. You know, fresh. And I thought, So, he *has* been digging. That's a funny thing to do, this time of night. And then I thought, Oh I know what he's done."

"What? What?"

"I thought, it was a stillbirth. Born dead, and this he's gone and buried it in the back garden. Like a dog. And I thought, Right, I'm off, I'm getting the coppers here ack dum."

"Why didn't you though?"

Betty shook her head. "I think because of those dangly things on strings. There were bits of a doll in one. And outside, you know, the room where you were: he'd tied in the afterbirth. It had dripped."

Valerie just nodded. "So you went out into the garden."

"Yes. I put the lamp back on the kitchen table and I went outside. God, it was dark. Those blackout nights. I had my torch though. I don't know what I thought I was looking for. I thought, this is ridiculous, well, you know how big the garden was, right down to the river, I could hear it, lapping, I could hear water. Then I thought, he won't have gone far. Where would I have put it? Somewhere easy. Not under grass. Somewhere where the earth was already turned. So I went on along the path, I could see trees at the bottom, where the river was. And there's the kitchen garden, herbs, I trod on something that smelt nice, rosemary, across the path, and then past all these cabbages and Brussels sprouts and so on. Currant bushes. And raspberry canes. And this little patch of turned earth."

There was a silence.

"And it just came to me. That he'd buried it alive."

Valerie was crying now. But then, so was Betty. She wiped her eyes but they just kept overflowing, though she could go on speaking, and did:

"I moved some of the soil aside, with my shoe. Then a bit more. And I'm thinking, Oh no, oh no, oh no. Then I got down on my hands and knees, I tried balancing the torch but it kept falling over and pointing

278

the wrong way, so I says, the hell with that, and I start digging with my hands. Like a dog! I can't see what I'm doing. And I was crying, I was crying out loud like a kid, shouting I was, Oh no, oh no, oh no! I could hear myself doing it, as if it was someone else, I was all panicky. And I can't see anything and this bloody hole's getting deeper and deeper; and then, honest, it was like Heaven helping me, the moon came out, just a bit. And there was just enough light to see . . ." Betty sobbed for a moment or two, helplessly, "to see the baby, ah, ah —"

Valerie knelt on the floor, and put her arms round Betty, and rocked her to and fro.

"You saw his face?"

Betty sniffed, considering. "He had covered it. He'd wrapped it in a cloth. A tea towel, I'd pushed it aside, digging. I was all right then. D'you know what I mean? I was all right then. I sort of hauled; I got both my arms in and hauled. It was like another birth. Like a difficult birth. And I had it in my arms. I didn't stop. I didn't think at all. I ran, I left the torch! I ran back up the path into the kitchen. And I put the baby on the table, on the oilcloth, and I'm wiping his face, with my fingers, I'm covered in mud! I wipe his little face. He's blue — white, limp. He was dead. And see once, I'd been at this bad delivery. When I was training. Three days labour, the baby comes out dead I'd thought, but the midwife, she says to me, It's worth a try after all that, and she blows into the baby's face, she put her mouth over its nose and mouth and she blew, and after a couple of goes the baby pinks up and yells and there's your daughter. I didn't think, How long? How long's he been buried? I don't know why. You know I've often thought that if I'd ever stopped to think about what I was doing and why I'd never have done it. I just sort of thought, What have I got to lose? And I pulled the baby's head back a bit, and I opened his mouth, there was a bit of earth in it, I pulled that out, hooked it with my finger, and then I put my mouth on him and I blew."

"Like Elishah."

"Dunno about him. It was like this midwife I told you about. Then I remembered about his heart and I put my fingers on his chest and pushed down a bit. Honestly. I didn't know what I was doing. I just kept on breathing into him and stopping now and then and having a little go at his heart, and then, there was this —"

"Yes!"

"This bubbling sound, like inside him, I thought, there's earth inside him, shifting, that's all I'm doing, but it happened again, and then I saw his chest move, his little ribs like a chicken's, they all moved up and down again, I could see, oh, the tendons round his throat sucking in, he was trying to breathe, and I turned him, onto his side, and he gave this crowing noise, choking and straining. And he sneezed. Mud came out! and then he was alive. Terrible breathing it was, too sick to cry. Still blue, he still looked dead. And I pulled my apron off and I unbuttoned my dress and I yanked my vest up and I stuffed him inside, he was cold as ice, it was like ice on me, I got him right under my vest, on my skin, cold as ice. And I felt, I felt . . ."

"Triumphant. Glorious."

"I felt happy. I felt worthwhile. I was justified. You were right. It was my best ever thing. And I spoilt it. I'd thought it hardly mattered any more, being so long ago. It all seemed to have worn off long ago, that feeling. I thought I'd get something I wanted for once. I didn't know I didn't really want it. I hate this room. I hate everything I've done in it. I wish I'd never started. And I wish I'd left you alone. Could I give you the money back? I've only spent half of it. I don't know if I'd feel better if I did but I might. The rest'd have to be in stages though, like a sort of mortgage, would that be all right?"

"I don't know." Valerie Elliott rubbed her face all over with her hands. "I mean, you can give back the bit you haven't spent it you like. But you could just forget about the rest. I can do without it. Really. I'd just as soon you had it. You have to understand what I owe you. I owe you everything. Suppose you hadn't come along and done all that you did. I might have lived. But my son wouldn't have. I would have had to live knowing that my father had buried my baby alive, and that I had laid in my bed and let him die. How do you think I could have coped with that? What could I have done with myself after that? As it was my father was, *thank God*, put in prison and I was safe from him, and so was my son. I went to live with my aunt for a while — she was real enough, she lived in Westmoreland — and then I got a job as a housekeeper when Joseph was

281

old enough to go to school, and it was through that family that I met my husband. And he was a really good man, loving and kind and a good father to all our children, and all of my life I owe to you. When I said earlier that if you had just asked me for the money I would have given it to you, that was the truth. Can't we pretend that you just asked me for it, and that I gave it to you? Because I did, in a way. Actually."

"What do you mean?"

"Well, you see, I really don't care who knows what my father did. He's long dead, I'm a different person. My husband knew anyway, and he's dead, and so are his parents. What does it signify now? I don't care who knows. I wanted to do what ever you wanted me to, though. I thought, you seemed to want to feel you had some power over me. So I sort of pretended that you had. I talked it over with Joseph."

"Joseph? You mean . . ."

"Oh yes, he knew already. I told him when he was in his teens. I thought he ought to know, though not too soon, not when he was little, I was always worried that someone would tell him before I did, when he was too small to be anything other than horrified. I waited as long as I could and then we told him together, my husband and I. He'd always known he had a different father, of course. But I had to tell him about what his grandfather had tried to do. In case anyone else did."

"So. So I didn't really blackmail you at all. Did I?"

"No, I suppose you didn't really. Does that make a difference?"

"I don't know."

"Some of the money was his. I borrowed it. You could give that back if you like. Not that he really needs it, he's got so much, he earns so much, he's a barrister, he won't miss it."

"Did he know what it was for?"

"What, the money? Yes. I told him." Valerie half-laughed. "He didn't know what to think! Stuck for words. Not like him. I suppose in the end he was disappointed, really."

"Disappointed?"

"Yes. In you. I'm sorry. You were so special to us. That was partly why I wanted to come here to talk to you. I thought it must be against your nature to do what you did, I mean the blackmail-thing. And it was, wasn't it."

Betty thought, or tried to, but like this Joseph, a barrister for heaven's sake, a grown man with a bow tie probably and a loud braying voice and one of those silly intimidating wigs, like this same Joseph, whose fragile naked body she had once pulled from the soil with her bare hands, she did not know what to think.

"And I thought it would be making you miserable, that you'd made this use of such a special thing. I don't want you to be miserable. I don't mind about the money. I forgive you. It doesn't matter."

Betty shook her head. "Can't be undone," she said at last.

"Oh dear. Can't it? I don't think you need to take such a tragic view. I don't. Look. I'll tell you something else. This is something Joseph doesn't know. I'm going to tell you, though, to show you that I trust you. And to really put myself in your power again. Then you can cheer yourself up by not blackmailing me about it, d'you see?" Valerie gave a sort of laugh, or a noisy smile.

"Well, I —"

"It's this," said Valerie, holding up a hand for silence. "This is what Joseph doesn't know. Or anyone else, except for my husband, and he's dead. Everyone assumed at the trial, didn't they, that my father tried to kill my baby because I wasn't married, that burying a baby alive was a sort of mad-person version of making me have it adopted or throwing me out into the storm or whatever other beastly cruel trick people used to get up to when some poor girl got into trouble. That's how it seemed to me, from what my aunt told me. But no one suspected and no one ever knew that the reason my father tried to kill Joseph was because he was his own child. His and mine. Joseph is my father's child. He doesn't know that. But you do. I don't want him to know about it. Not even when I'm dead. What's that?"

"What?" said Betty, in bewilderment, until she too noticed the small red flashing light bulb high on the wall by the door, and pulled herself together. She felt damp all over, she noticed, and worn out as if she had run or swum miles, and yet somehow rather buoyant all the same: light on her feet. "It usually means someone has pulled the wrong switch," she said, getting up to check the console. "My deputy's on duty, she ought to . . ." She trailed off; it had occurred to her that she had not seen Rosemary Sholto all morning. Where had she been at coffee time, when she usually tried to sidle

284

into the office with her loaded tray? Where had she been at lunch, when fat Susan had dropped an entire tinful of sponge pudding onto the kitchen floor? Nowhere, that was the answer. Not at Cabotin Court, at any rate. And the alarm was still flashing.

"I'll have to go."

"Me too."

"It's been, it's been —" Betty stopped. She didn't know what it had been. Hardly what you'd call a pleasure.

"We'll meet up again some time," said Valerie, which sounded a little chilly, perhaps not intentionally so. Betty lingered, but the alarm went on flashing, and still no Rosemary came bolting or huffing into view.

"I'll leave you to it," said Valerie, and she went away, just too soon for Betty to remember Friendship, and ask whether Valerie would still — no. Perhaps better not.

God, what an afternoon! Betty, so tired, so careful still not to look too hard at what felt like the peace inside her, in case it turned out not to exist at all, like a rainbow's end, trudged wearily up the stairs and along the corridor to the bathroom shared by Mrs Dobbs and Miss Troy. Which of them had mistaken the alarm for the light switch? Mrs Dobbs, probably, she was the daftest, poor old thing. Betty assumed her reassuring face, and went to make sure.

CHAPTER
THIRTY-EIGHT

Mrs Dobbs had been roused from her lengthy afternoon nap by the gathering storm within her. For a while, when she awoke, she was forced to emit a series of tremendous noises, expressive, moody, and occasionally shape-specific: a bored lazy whine there, a swift round explosive bark here; a string of bubbles; a sudden immensity, a fart as big as a loofah.

Mrs Dobbs sat up with some difficulty, failed to catch her book as it slid from her stomach to the floor, and by degrees got up and prepared to visit the bathroom. But it was locked; Miss Troy had got there first. This of course happened fairly regularly. Mrs Dobbs shuffled back to bed, and sat down to wait. Time passed.

She picked her book up again, and spent some of it trying to find her place, which was difficult as she had fallen asleep rather slowly, and gone on reading, it seemed, partly in her sleep, so that odd paragraphs were strangely familiar in the middle of a sub-plot she could remember nothing about, and Diana kept mentioning someone called Barry in ways that implied she was going out with him, so what had happened to Craig?

Presently inner discomfort ruled out even this interesting question. Mrs Dobbs became a little vexed. It was not like Miss Troy to be inconsiderate; bath times were strictly adhered to, so that one had warning; expenses properly shared. Was there some mistake?

Mrs Dobbs got up again, and went to the bathroom door. Should she knock? She did not like to, it seemed an invasion. But the toilet downstairs was such a very long way away. Mrs Dobbs was not at all fast on her feet. There was a definite chance that an attempt at the downstairs toilet might end in disaster. She knocked.

No answer. Had Miss Troy somehow left without making a sound, then, despite the hefty bolt? She tried the handle again. But the door would not open. It at last occurred to Mrs Dobbs that something might be wrong.

"Oh dear," said Mrs Dobbs. She went back to bed and tried to pretend that the thought had not occurred to her after all, but this did not work, and after a minute or so she abandoned the attempt. She got up again and walked about touching things, the bedside table, the back of the armchair, the kitchenette counter. Finally, seeing nothing else for it, she opened her door, turned left, and knocked on Miss Troy's, which had been left on the catch. No answer. She knocked again, and called, a trembly whisper.

"Miss Troy?" No answer. She pushed at the door. Miss Troy's flatlet. Rather untidy! Papers everywhere. "Miss Troy?" Mrs Dobbs went right inside, and here, standing beside the bathroom, she could see Miss Troy's shoes, curiously upturned beside the bath.

Strange. Mrs Dobbs ventured a little further, and realised at last that the shoes had Miss Troy in them, that she was lying there full length, and clearly not at all well.

"Oh dear!" cried Mrs Dobbs aloud, but almost straight away she remembered what she must do. Raise the alarm! She looked about her, saw the cord, reached out her trembling hand, and pulled the light switch, leaving herself in almost total darkness.

"Oh dear!"

CHAPTER
THIRTY-NINE

"But I don't understand what your mother was doing. Was she mad, or what? She didn't know a thing about him!"

"I know, I know," said Molly. She hoped he would stop talking and eat faster. She had already finished, and had her eye on the sweet trolley. Now that she had stopped being sick she had begun being so hungry that these days she never left the house without thrusting several bananas into her handbag, in case she was caught out snack-free at a difficult moment.

"She's bloody lucky. She could have lost the lot."

"Yes; if it was made out to Gregory Banks then really it was his. Or his creditors'. The Grand Hotel, for instance. But leaving it in a telephone booth, for Pete's sake. Five thousand quid! I didn't know you had a moneyed background."

"Adds to my charm," said Molly.

"Couldn't do that," said Harry. He smiled into her eyes. She had to look away, even now; she felt as if she were in a lift when he looked at her like that, in a lift and going down too fast.

"When am I going to meet her anyway. This gaolbird mother of yours."

"Don't say that. They only wanted to talk to her, it was obvious she wasn't involved in anything else. She didn't do anything, except trust this awful man."

"No sign of him then."

"Well, he's obviously practised at doing bunks. The receptionist saw him apparently, leaving the hotel that morning, with some other bloke. She said he looked anxious. But the doorman said he looked fine, said Good Morning cheery as you like. Take your pick."

"Funny time for him to disappear, though, wasn't it? I mean, from his point of view. I mean, he only had to hang on another day or two and he'd've had all your mum's money. He'd've got the lot, wouldn't he?"

"Oh, I should've been around more. Looked out for her."

"From your hospital bed, yes? Come on." He laid down his knife and fork. "When are you going to tell her about me. Hmm?"

Molly made a face.

"It's got to be done, Moll. The longer you leave it, the worse it's going to be. You know, like you've kept the terrible truth from her on purpose."

"Don't talk like that. And don't look at me like that, either. I couldn't face it. Not all at once like that. She had enough to be going on with. And now all this business with that horrible man . . . She just assumed things; well she would, wouldn't she. Anybody would. *Tailor*. How's she supposed to know it's some vile imperialist imposition? I mean, Patel would be a bit more of a giveaway, wouldn't it, even my mother might have twigged something there. How's *your* mum now, anyway?"

"Oh, calming down. I told you it'd be all right. It's handy having Ravi of course. Means she can't really go on about *me* too much. Or you: you're educated, a good business woman, not married to somebody else. Or dyed blonde. All these things in your favour. She's bound to come round."

"Eventually."

"The baby'll fix it."

"If we get married."

"We'll get married. What's the hurry? Name the date, I don't care. I mean, you know I'll marry you any day you want me to. All right?"

"Right."

"Fancy a pud?"

"Christ, I thought you'd never ask."

Harry, or Hari as his mother insists on spelling it, smiles across at his darling. Harry, thinks Molly. "Something else we've got in common."

"What?"

"Do I look like a Maureen to you?"

CHAPTER
FORTY

Annie held Alethea's hand, and talked to her. She had read that stroke victims, despite appearances, were sometimes conscious in some inner and inexpressible way; that of all the senses hearing was the last one to be lost. Though that will not apply to me, she had thought more than once, taking up her position by the bed.

"Hello, Alethea. It's me again. You can't get away from me, I know. But I've got something to tell you though, this morning! We're all agog at Cabotin, we don't know what to do with ourselves, because yesterday afternoon, about four, the police arrived! Two in uniform, and another one in mufti. I saw the car, I thought, had there been a break-in, something like that. I was looking out of the window, I saw the car arrive. About ten minutes later, would you believe it, out they come again, with Rosemary Sholto! And she gets into the car with them, and off they go! What d'you think of that?"

Alethea made no response. Her hand lay in Annie's without a twitch.

"Kate Derry says they arrested her, but no one really knows. She didn't have handcuffs on or anything. She looked frightened. I saw her face as she got into the car.

And she hasn't been back since, and Miss Potts was in a terrible tizzy because she was having some sort of party, apparently, a sort of office-warming, and Rosemary was supposed to be doing all the cakes. There, that's something isn't it! Alethea. Are you there?"

A hand touched Annie's shoulder, so that she jumped, and turned to find a nurse beside her. The nurse said something, her face at the wrong angle, and too quickly.

"Bib-bib?"

Again the nurse spoke.

"Oh, sorry, am I in the way?" Annie rose, and stood back while the nurse drew the curtains round the bed. After a moment she drew them back again, but now Alethea was facing the other way.

"OK?" the nurse mouthed at Annie. She hurried away. Annie walked round the end of the bed. There was nowhere to sit, on this side. She took her friend's hand again. It felt like a glove. Had the operation caused the stroke? Kate Derry said so.

"But you wouldn't have wanted to live, blinded, would you? All that waiting. I thought you'd have longer, I saw you jump out of bed so happy when you saw your friend. But I don't see how that can happen now. I must have been wrong. I suppose I am sometimes. How would I know? And I had such a horrible one yesterday. When they were taking Rosemary away. I was watching her getting into the car, and I flashed on a man, and there was something terrible about it, the way he was standing, I don't know why. He was standing in front of some sort of door or gate, I was seeing him from the back standing there, and I felt straight away he was lost, he was so lost and alone, and the voice says to me, *the gates will never open*, and it was so frightening, Alethea, I wanted to tell you about it, I would've, if you could have listened. When are you going to come back, Alethea? Was it right, to get to be my dear friend, and then go away? Come back. Please, Alethea. I miss you so much."

This time, facing the door, Annie saw the nurse come in, and turned away to wipe her eyes while the nurse went over to the empty bed beside Alethea's and began folding it down, ready for some new occupant. She was speaking as she did this, but Annie did not try to understand her. Presently the nurse stopped fiddling about at the empty bed and came closer, saying something. A question, from her eyebrows and the tilt of her head.

"Bib-bib?"

"Oh, never mind," said the nurse, briskly departing. Annie saw that she had bored and irritated the nurse, but quickly forgot about her. She noticed a plastic chair before the washbasin, and went over to check. Yes: light enough. Still it took some effort to coax it round to the right side of Alethea's bed. She was more than ready to sit down. She took Alethea's hand again, and wondered briefly why her own mother had suddenly come to mind. Something in the set of the nurse's shoulders, perhaps. Her mother had been so angry so long. And so determined that nothing was wrong all those years.

"Once," Annie told Alethea, "she came rushing out of the kitchen and hit me round the head. What's that for, I says, I'm crying, she hit me really hard and all of a sudden, she says, I'll teach you to ignore me! And she says, I told you to set the table, I told you twice! I didn't hear you mammy, I says, I didn't hear you. And she shouts, Don't you give me that you little liar, and she hits me again. She was always hitting me. She'd say something, I'd say, Beg your pardon? and she'd hit me."

Still holding Alethea's empty glove of a hand, Annie laughed the strange laugh so common amongst adults when they are remembering parental cruelty.

Beg your pardon, beg your pardon, begyourpardon: the words she had used most often to her mother, that year in which all sound began to fade away. They are the only words Annie, so luckily losing her hearing at eight and not at six or seven, ever really forgot how to say. Did she forget them because saying them made her mother hit her, or was it that her mother hit her for forgetting them, for talking already in garble? It is many years since she knew she still uttered them aloud.

Bib-bib?

I'll have to go soon, thought Annie at Alethea. I'll be back tomorrow though. With more on Rosemary, maybe. I wonder if that young girl will come to see you, the one I flashed on that time? It'll be a sad thing for her if you can't see her, Alethea. Sad for you too, you were really going to be pleased. So. You come back, now. Come back. Come on now, Alethea. Come on. Please.

CHAPTER
FORTY-ONE

"Apparently she'd trusted this man with a considerable amount of money, that's how they connected her with him. It seems he had some very large debts. Anyway they've found no trace of him, they think he was using an assumed name, probably one of several."

"Poor Rosemary," said Valerie.

"She's had a lucky escape," said Betty, careful not to say anything too downright. Who was she, after all, to cast aspersions on Rosemary in the presence of Valerie Elliott? Besides, she had already most enjoyably cast as many as she liked with the Friends the day before. How they had gaped and exclaimed and sympathised; Betty had not enjoyed herself so much for years. And there would certainly be no prospect of Rosemary trying to gatecrash any future meetings, not for years, probably. If ever. Five thousand pounds, carelessly discarded in a telephone booth!

"If the manager of the Grand hadn't been at school with Maureen I dread to think what might have happened," said Betty. "He could have put in a claim apparently, but chose not to, because, if you can believe it, Maureen used to help him with his Maths. That's what Rosemary told me anyway."

"I don't see why it shouldn't be true," said Valerie. "So. This is them?" They were standing by the gates of Cabotin Court, the Jakes-gates.

"Yes. What d'you think?"

There was a pause.

"Well . . . they're obviously not original. And they're not really tall enough. But. They have to be left open most of the time anyway, don't they?"

"I would close them at night. If they were, you know, proper ones."

"What, and get up really early every morning to open them again? I can't really see it as important. I'm sorry, I know you do."

"Let's go in, shall we, I'm freezing, would you like some coffee?"

They walked back round the building to the back entrance, careful over the frosty flags.

"And how are your plans coming on," asked Betty. "Have you heard from the council?"

"Yes; it's all going ahead."

"Oh, that is good news!"

"Oh, there's still a few hurdles to be got through yet. But I think I'll manage, eventually. And there's such a need, you see. There's always more disturbed children around than there are places to put them, let alone try to help them."

"Children? D'you mean boys as well?"

"Oh yes. I've told them eight. I can take up to eight, I mean I've worked in places where there were more, but I think that you then lose out on any possible family-type of atmosphere. Children who have no idea what a loving family can feel like need to be given a glimpse of it if you possibly can."

"Here we are. That's better. I'll put the fire on, shall I? Do sit down."

"Thank you. It does look nice in here."

"Oh, I'm er, glad you like it."

"Sorry, I forgot, Betty, I really didn't mean . . ."

"No no. Please. Let's um, have our coffee, shall we? There."

"Lovely."

Betty sat down, sipped her coffee, and said: "You must have the money back. There's simply no two ways about it. There's nothing here that needs doing, I mean as much as your hostel needs it. You'll need, what, decorating, and plumbing, all sorts of things, I mean eight rooms, that's re-building, practically."

"Yes. It's your money, though. There was no real compulsion, remember. I chose to give it to you. I wanted to."

"But you can make better use of it really."

"God has been so good to me," said Valerie, but Betty was used to this sort of thing from her by now and hardly raised an eyebrow. Privately she thought He could have got a move on a bit earlier, as far as Valerie was concerned. Nor was she very keen on the God's-Instrument view of her own part in Valerie's salvation.

"Think of it, Betty, why else were you able to climb up those terrible stairs to me? God Himself was with you, guiding you. Didn't you tell me yourself you did things that night you can't account for? Why did you go into the garden? Why did you do any of it? You were guided!"

"I was nuts."

"You were an angel, I thought. I thought it for years."

"Until you came here."

"It was a mistake. That's all."

"Whose? I mean, I've got away with it, haven't I. You've let me get away with it."

Valerie had looked away then. She was right, thought Betty now, staring into her coffee cup. I have not got away with it. Cabotin Court has got a redecorated office. That's all. And I ruined myself to get it. She can forgive me all she likes; but I can't. I don't know who I am any more. I used to think I was all right. Someone who's made the best of a not-very-good deal. Decent enough. But now I don't know. And I'll never be sure again. It was brave, to blackmail her. But not as brave as walking up the stairs to save her. It was a different sort of bravery. And I couldn't tell the difference, when it mattered. It was like a test, and I failed it, and I'll never imagine I can pass a test again; I have no confidence in my own goodness, and that is a very strange feeling. I can't get used to it. And I don't think it will ever go away.

"You'll take the money back, then?"

"Of course, if you're sure you really want me to."

There was a pause. Valerie looked up. "How's your new old lady getting on? Settling in, is she?"

CHAPTER
FORTY-TWO

Far away, in the general hospital now, Alethea Troy, deep in the second month of her coma, becomes aware at last that there is someone in the room. She heard the door open. She knows somehow that it is someone important. With an effort she opens her eyes, and for a moment cannot believe them.

"Maisie! Oh Maisie, can it be you?"

"Hello my ducks! Hello!"

Alethea sits up, she jumps lightly out of bed and in an instant is in dear Maisie's arms.

"Oh, Maisie! I thought I'd never see you again!"

"Oh, I always loved you so," says Maisie, "you know that."

"And I loved you," says Alethea joyfully. What is Maisie doing here? And why is she still a blooming girl, after all these years? How strange it is! How wonderful!

But these questions do not worry her for long.

Sometimes on sunny days Rosemary takes her grandchild out along the prom in her pushchair. At first, when she met up with friends or acquaintances who had not yet seen Jasmin she would say, "Isn't she lovely! Shows what a touch of the tar brush can do!" to punish them anyway, just in case they were thinking it; but that stage didn't last very long. Rosemary has stopped bothering. She loves Jasmin, who is indeed a very pretty child, with a good appetite too for the wholesome rice puddings and custards with which Rosemary so often regales her, whenever she comes to stay.

She seldom thinks about Gregory Banks. Sometimes, when she sits on that very bench where they had their first encounter, she remembers caring about him, but already she has difficulty remembering what he looked like. True, she was miserable at first, grieving for the man she had thought he was; but that was largely swallowed up in the knowledge, reaching her at intervals from the police, that of all the women who had encountered Gregory (or Timothy, Leslie, Anthony or Gerry) on park benches, in art galleries, in wine bars and in golf clubs, she had come out of things pretty well. And there had been poor Maureen to think of, and the extra shock of Harry, and then the baby, so utterly delicious and perfect in every way.

Jasmin crows in her pushchair, and waves a little fluttering pinwheel at the sea. Far out, deep in the water, shifted by dredging and by the storms of many years, lie the railings, saucepans, and bedsteads which so overwhelmed the town council in 1941. Here, too, beneath a moving frond of weed, encrusted here and there with barnacles, lie the great gates of Cabotin, gold-tipped, engraved, enamelled. And upon them, caught there, snagged by the handcuffs that still, for the moment, hold his hands together in front of him, lies the body of a man. It is Gregory, posed there in the dark water as if waiting; but the gates will never open.

If there were another test like that, would I realise, would I know? Would I pass it? wonders Betty in the small hours. She still sleeps badly. She cannot respect herself.

"Take it to God," Valerie has suggested more than once, but Betty feels that she and God will never be on speaking terms. What can she do? How unhappy she is, all the time! A low-level unhappiness, to let her know how contented she once had been.

What had passed through his mind as he was tipped so ruthlessly into the water?

Well Christ if I'd known he was going to kill me — well I'd have paid him wouldn't I? I mean, I didn't know. What's the *point*, he won't get his blasted money now, will he?

Why didn't he tell me he was going to *kill* me?

One morning Betty's post contains a letter in a hand she knows. But why? She knows it, but does not realise why. Yet all the same her heart beats fast at the sight. With trembling hands she opens it.

Dear Warden, she reads.

I take the liberty of writing to you directly, in my request for application to the sanctuary of Cabotin Court. Many years ago I had the honour to be, I

302

hope, of some service to that delightful place. I have only happy memories of my stay there. I imagine there is quite a waiting list! But I hope my own name may find a place at the end of it. Life has been a little difficult for me lately and I have come to hope that one day I shall be at home again under the care of the Warden of Cabotin. Please send me the relevant application forms. I enclose a stamped addressed envelope, and look forward to hearing from you.

Betty's eyes glint. The test has come upon her, and it is a hard one. How can she bear it? How can she refuse? It is enough to make her wonder about the existence of Valerie's God after all. If He's there, He certainly seems to have a sense of humour.

The letter, in its strangely familiar if slightly wobbly hand, is signed,

> *Yours faithfully,*
> *Flora Jakes.*

The fish and the little crabs are busy with Gregory now, nibbling at his moorings. One day, perhaps, he will be free of the great closed gates in front him, and will rise and fall with the tide. Meanwhile the ferries pass above him, to and fro. The waves grow choppy, and still again. The days and nights progress.

Goodnight Nobody

Jennifer Weiner

Who said life in the suburbs was sleepy?

Kate Klein loved her life in New York, but when she was robbed at gunpoint on the streets of Manhattan her husband decided it was time to get out of the city.

Cue a move to the upmarket suburbia of Upchurch, Connecticut, where the immaculate supermums routinely snub her and her husband is hardly ever home. Kate's life revolves around looking after her children and trying to keep up with the other mothers, at least until the mysterious death of Kitty Cavanaugh, the neighbourhood Queen Bee.

Kate is drawn deep into the dead woman's double life when she launches her own investigation with the help of her best friend Janie, and former flame, Evan McKenna.

ISBN 0-7531-7636-X (hb)
ISBN 0-7531-7637-8 (pb)

Unfeeling

Ian Holding

Davey is in the attic when the militia comes. At 16, he's almost the man his father wants him to be, and almost the child he was. Locked in shock, he is barely aware that beneath him his parents have been murdered and his family's farm, Edenfields, "reclaimed".

The neighbouring farmers — his parents's closest friends — take him in and try to care for him, try to bring him back into their community of normality: the club, the church, after a few weeks, his boarding school. They look to cope. But Davey is on a different path. One night he escapes from his school and embarks on a harrowing, terrifying journey across Africa, home to Edenfields, looking for redemption.

ISBN 0-7531-7596-7 (hb)
ISBN 0-7531-7597-5 (pb)